The Magic Between Us

TAMMY FALKNER

sourcebooks
casablanca

Published by Sourcebooks Casablanca, an imprint of Sourcebooks, Inc.
P. O. Box 4410, Naperville, Illinois 60567-4410
(630) 961-3900
Fax: (630) 961-2168
www.sourcebooks.com

Printed and bound in the United States of America
VP 10 9 8 7 6 5 4 3 2 1

Prologue

CECELIA LEANED BACK AGAINST A TREE AND WAITED. He would arrive soon. He'd grown later and later each night for the past sennight, but he would come to meet her. She was certain of it.

His bulk settled beside her and the heat of his body chased away the chill of the cold, dark evening. "You came," she said. She wrapped her arm through his and leaned into his shoulder.

"Yes," he replied, but he didn't look her in the eye. "I'm here."

"Is something wrong?" Cecelia unwound her arm from inside his. He didn't stop her.

He ran a frustrated hand through his unbound hair. He never wore a queue when he was in the land of the fae. Instead, he let his hair fall softly around his face and often tucked it behind his ears. "No. Nothing's wrong."

Cecelia stretched her legs out in front of her and waited for him to do what he normally did. She waited for him to lie back with his head upon her thigh and look up at her as though she was the most important thing in his world. But he didn't. He just sat there beside her, his hands clenched in front of him.

She laid a hand upon his arm. "Talk to me, Marcus," she urged. They'd been best friends for as long as she could remember. And he'd never been this reserved. He'd never avoided her gaze. He'd never shut her out.

"I received word from my father today." His shoulders slumped as he turned to face her. "He wants me to succeed him."

Cecelia laughed. That was impossible. "But doesn't he know you have responsibilities here?" She laughed again. Because it was quite a laughable topic. The very thought of Marcus leaving the land of the fae was ridiculous. "You told him no, right?"

He reached out to touch the side of her face, his hand shaking as he let his thumb trace her lower lip. "I'm going."

She pulled back, gripping his wrist to push his hand down. "What?"

"I'm going to their land. I don't have a choice."

Cecelia's heart pounded in her chest like a team of runaway horses. "I don't understand."

"My parents want me to be there. There's a lot I don't know about being a viscount and my father's holdings. I need to learn."

"But what about his oldest son? Isn't his name Allen?"

"I'm the oldest son. Allen is a year younger than I am."

"But he's been groomed to become a viscount."

"But I'm the oldest son. We're all going to be

introduced to the *ton* as their children. They're going to claim us."

Marcus had always wanted a family. His grandmother and grandfather had raised them all, but he'd spoken often of how he wanted a mother and a father. Now he had them, apparently.

"So, you'll go there and take care of your duties and then you can come back." Hope bloomed within her, but only for a moment.

He took a deep breath and closed his eyes, wincing as he said, "I'll be expected to marry outside the fae, to produce an heir and a spare, as they say."

Cecelia gasped. "They said that?"

He shook his head and the viselike grip of fear on her heart eased a bit. "They didn't say that. I said that. I need to dedicate myself to their way of life. I need to learn how their world works. I'll need to marry a human."

She bit back a gasp. "No, Marcus…" she began.

But he just shook his head and held his hands out as though in surrender.

"You're giving up the life of the fae?" He wouldn't do such a thing. It was too much a part of his being.

"Probably not entirely. Sophie and Claire still go on missions. But they're not the eldest son. I'm simply afraid it's going to take too much of my time. I have a lot to learn." He reached for her face again, but she caught his hand and shoved it aside.

She looked into his brown eyes. He wasn't avoiding her gaze right now. But he was done. She could tell. He'd made his decision. He hadn't asked her to go with him. He hadn't asked her to marry him. He hadn't asked her to wait for him. He hadn't asked for anything. And that was because he didn't want anything. Not from her.

"I wish you the best, Marcus," she said, her voice no more than a whisper to her own ears.

"Cece," he breathed. He reached for her again. His head lowered toward hers.

"No," she said. She turned her head at the last minute and his lips grazed her cheek.

"Cece," he pleaded, his mouth still pressed to her cheek. Hot, moist breath rushed against her skin. "Please don't be angry."

She wasn't angry. She was furious. And hurt. Damn it all, she'd dreamed of a life with him. But it wasn't going to happen. And she refused to beg. "I'm happy for you," she said. "I know you've wanted to connect with your parents for a long time. I hope life in their world is everything you're hoping for."

"Cece," he breathed. His voice cracked. "Please don't hate me."

She couldn't possibly hate him. Not when she loved him as much as she did. She got to her feet and walked away.

"You have to try to see things from my point of view, Cece," he called to her retreating back.

"I highly doubt I could shove my head that far up my own arse, Marcus," she called back.

He groaned and flung himself on the ground. She kept walking.

One

Six months later…

MARCUS THORNE PULLED HIS HAT FROM HIS HEAD AS HE stepped across the threshold. Before him were the elite of society, the lords and ladies of the realm. The very people he'd detested his whole life, but now was expected to live and interact with. He was supposed to become one of *them*. Good heavens, he was dicked in the nob.

Wilkins, his sister's butler, took his hat and his coat, and opened his mouth to announce him. But Marcus held a finger to his lips and shook his head. He didn't want the butler to herald his arrival. He didn't want these people to even know he was here. Wilkins glared at him for a moment and inclined his head. The man was nothing if not proper.

"Are my parents here?" Marcus asked.

"Lord and Lady Ramsdale are involved in a waltz," Wilkins informed him.

"And my sisters and their husbands?"

"Lord Phineas and Lady Claire are in the nursery, I believe, checking on the twins."

Marcus chuckled beneath his breath. Claire was infatuated with her children and insisted on taking them everywhere with her and Finn. "And Robinsworth and Sophie?"

"Meandering about the room," Wilkins said.

Marcus's sister, Sophie, had stepped into the life of a duchess as though she'd been born to it, instead of being born with wings and magic dust. Marcus ambled into the room and pushed to the edge of the throng, heading toward Robinsworth's study. He was almost certain the man had some brandy secreted in a cabinet that would ease some of Marcus's anxiety.

Marcus wasn't at all comfortable in these gatherings. But he would someday step into the role of a viscount, and he supposed he had much to learn to be able to do so. His parents hadn't even known of his existence until two years ago, when he was five-and-twenty.

Good God, he needed a drink.

He continued on toward Robinsworth's study, stopping briefly to bow at people with whom he couldn't avoid making eye contact. There were whispers behind his back; he could hear them all. But he chose to pay them no mind. Perhaps if they were whispering about him, they would cease their relentless whispering about his sisters and their chosen husbands. It was the price he was willing to pay. He might even choose the most scandalous woman in the room and ask her to dance.

Marcus stepped into the study and shoved the door closed. He leaned heavily against it and took a deep breath. These things rattled him more than he wanted to let on.

"It's about time you arrived," boomed a voice from the other side of the room.

Marcus searched the shadows of the dark room. But then the chair behind Robinsworth's desk kicked back and he saw Ronald, the family's garden gnome, resting there in the chair. Although he was no more than two feet tall, he was a sight for sore eyes with his purple waistcoat, green breeches, and pink cravat. He was familiar. And Marcus dearly needed familiar.

"What are you doing in here?" Marcus asked as he crossed to the cabinet and retrieved a crystal decanter. Though he was secretly happy to see the little man, he didn't want to appear overly friendly. Ronald did live to tease him, after all. Marcus splashed a generous amount of the amber liquid into a glass and drank it in one swallow. Then he put the decanter away and turned to face Ronald. Marcus adjusted his waistcoat and wiped some invisible lint from his sleeve.

"I was waiting for you," the garden gnome said.

"Why?"

The little man pulled a scroll from his inner pocket and held it out to Marcus. "You have a mission."

A mission? Marcus hadn't had a mission in months. He took the scroll and tucked it into his pocket.

"Don't you want to read it?" The gnome's red eyebrows drew together sharply.

"I think my attendance at the soiree is mandatory. Father sent a reminder of it. Three times." Marcus heaved a sigh. "The mission will have to wait."

The gnome's voice grew weary. "How are things with your parents?" he asked.

"Things are fine with the parents," Marcus said.

His younger brother, Allen, was the problem of the moment. His brother had been groomed from birth to become a viscount, and now Marcus had stepped into his place. If given the choice, Marcus would have let his brother precede him, even though Marcus was the oldest male. But, apparently, it wasn't a choice. He would have to step into his father's shoes at some point. And in doing so, he would stomp all over Allen. "Allen isn't too keen on me, however."

"He'll come about." The gnome tapped the desk with one neat fingernail as his eyes narrowed. That look never boded well. But then his face softened, as if the thought had left his head as quickly as it had entered.

A flutter in Marcus's coat pocket drew his attention. The soft shiver in his pocket always made him think of a trapped bird. He jerked the chain that was connected to the compass his grandparents had given to him on his twelfth birthday and pulled it out. He flipped it open. "Northwest," he said aloud.

"That's what I needed to know." Ronald got up and stretched widely.

"You're returning to the land of the fae tonight?" How he longed to go with the gnome.

"I am now that you have pointed me toward a portal." Toward home. The compass always pointed toward home. The land of the fae. Marcus was the only one who had such a device, and no one was at all certain how it worked. But the compass always pointed him and others like him toward home.

He longed so deeply to go home. The rolling hills and the peaceful streams. The bare feet and the house he'd grown up in. Ladies with wings and faerie dust.

Ladies who knew him. Ladies who didn't expect him to be something he wasn't. One lady in particular.

Ronald shoved open the shutters and began to climb over the windowsill.

"Will I see you again soon?"

The little man shrugged. "I know not the future." Then he winked and threw himself from the window. Marcus bit back a smile. Then he steeled himself and went back to the ballroom, which didn't call to him the way home did. In fact, it did the opposite.

Marcus heard his name called from across the room and turned to find his mother, Lady Ramsdale, walking toward him with her arms outstretched. "I'm so glad you're here," she said, smiling broadly enough that he felt somewhat guilty for hating these affairs so much.

"As am I," he lied, the sentiment falling from his tongue more easily than it used to. This was to be his lot in life. He might as well accept it. "Did I miss the big announcement?" he asked.

She beamed at him as she shook her head. "No, you're just in time. I think everyone is in place."

"Are you certain this is going to work?" he murmured out the side of his mouth.

"I'm not certain at all," she replied. "But there are enough fae here, I think…"

Marcus looked about the room. There were fae mixed with the peers for the sole purpose of this night, to solidify this announcement in the eyes of the *ton*.

Marcus's parents planned to welcome their three fae children into the fold publicly. The only problem was that the *ton* had no idea they even had these three children. So, it would take a bit of creative maneuvering to convince society that the Ramsdales had known of Marcus, Claire, and Sophia's existence all along.

The quartet's song slowed and then stopped, and the musicians put away their instruments. A slow rumble of voices rolled across the room. But then Lord Ramsdale, Marcus's father, clinked a utensil against the side of a glass. Every head in the room turned toward him.

"If I may have your attention, please," he said with a smile. "We'll go back to the merriment in a moment, but I wanted to say a few words, if possible."

The crowd whispered loudly to one another and strained to hear him as he pulled Marcus's mother to stand beside him. He beckoned the duke and Sophie, and then Lord Phineas and Claire, who had found their way back from the nursery. Then he called Marcus and Allen forward as well.

"You're all aware of the new additions to our family. Our daughter Sophia married the Duke of Robinsworth and they recently had a son of their own, and we have claimed Lady Anne, Robinsworth's first daughter, as our own grandchild. She tolerates us, most days." Laughter rumbled through the crowd. "And then Claire met and married the duke's younger brother, Lord Phineas, and they gave us not one, but two new grandchildren. Lord Phineas always was an overachiever."

Lord Phineas raised a glass and grinned.

His father stopped to clear his throat. "As you're aware, Marcus, Claire, and Sophia spent much of their time in the country with Lady Ramsdale's parents when they were younger, and we're delighted to have them in Town with us this season."

That wasn't exactly true. But that was the point of the gathering, wasn't it? They were to plant memories in the minds of the *ton*, making them think the Ramsdale children had been the darlings of Society all along, rather than never having been heard of. By the end of the ball, everyone would leave with knowledge of the three, believing the three of them had always existed.

"My younger daughters, Rose and Hannah, are not quite old enough to join us, but my sons, Marcus and Allen, are here, and I hope you'll all welcome Marcus, Claire, and Sophia with as much enthusiasm as you would my wife and I." He stopped and spoke very clearly and slowly. "You all knew of my six children since the days of their births. You knew of all six of them."

Marcus looked around as magic dust began to swirl in the air. It lived and breathed, as did the supplanted memories. The fae held the magic aloft, and even his sisters and his mother and grandmother helped to stir the dust. Their power made the air in the room shake, and Marcus reached out a hand to a nearby table to steady himself.

Everyone in the room, aside from the fae, was frozen in place as the dust fell. It shimmered like diamonds in the air, and Marcus's gut clenched as he realized that this act sealed his fate. He couldn't go back home. Now the *ton* knew who he was. In fact, they would probably be telling stories of him as a small lad, all figments of their own imaginations, of course, before the night was over. He hadn't grown up in this world, but now everyone would think he had.

His father repeated, his voice rising in volume,

"You all knew of my six children since the days of their births. You have memories of them as children, as adolescents, and as adults. You welcome them with open arms." His father's words could do nothing without the fae and their magic dust. But he spoke them clearly, and when the dust settled at their feet, the people in the room all woke, and they raised their glasses in a toast. "To my children, their health, and their happiness," his father said.

Everyone drank, including Marcus. This was his world now. There would be no going back home after this. He was well and truly trapped. Trapped being a viscount. Trapped being a gentleman. Trapped being a man in need of a wife. Trapped without her. Trapped without the woman he loved.

The compass in his pocket fluttered. Marcus tugged the chain to pull it from his pocket as the orchestra set back up and music began to flow around the room again. He glanced down at the dial. It pointed across the room. Marcus followed the direction of the arrow, and it landed on *her*. It landed on the one woman he thought he'd never see again. He picked it up and shook it beside his ear. Perhaps it was broken. His compass was supposed to point the way home. But it pointed to her. What the devil was going on?

❦

The hair on the back of Cecelia Hewitt's neck stood up, and a shiver crept up her spine. He was there. And he was looking at her; she was certain of it.

Cecelia frantically searched the room, looking for his long, dark hair, which was probably pulled back in a queue to hide the tips of his ears. She reached up to adjust a pin over her ear for the same purpose. Living in the human world was difficult. One couldn't let the humans see one's magic, and that included one's fae ears. Aside from her wings, which she could bring about or make disappear at will, her ears were the only evidence of her heritage. She looked as human as everyone else. But she wasn't. Not even close. Because she had magic inside her. Magic she couldn't do away with if she tried.

The mission tonight had gone well, Cecelia thought. She hadn't wanted to be here at all, but Marcus's grandmother had bid her attendance, and she couldn't turn the widow down. She'd come by way of the wind the night before. She'd spent the night at Ramsdale House and was doomed to stay until the next moonful when she could ride the wind back to the land of the fae.

"Thank you, dear," Marcus's grandmother said, laying her hand upon Cecelia's arm. "I know you hadn't planned to come to this world, but I appreciate that you did. We needed all the magic we could gather."

"My magic is at your disposal until the next moonful," Cecelia replied. She didn't have anything else to do. She might as well stay busy. Marcus's grandmother patted her arm again and left her standing there.

Another shiver traveled up Cecelia's spine. He was nearby. She hadn't seen Marcus in more than six months. Not since that night when he'd told her he was done with her.

Now she hated him. He could go burn in hell and

she wouldn't care. Six months. It had been six months since she'd seen him. And he hadn't sent one letter. Not a single correspondence. He hadn't reached out to her at all. And then she'd been asked to come and contribute her magic to his success. She'd done it. But she wasn't happy about it. Not at all. She was, however, happy to have a brief respite from home.

"Miss Hewitt," a voice said near her shoulder. She turned and flinched when she saw the familiar dark eyes and dark hair, and the breadth of his shoulders. It wasn't Marcus, although he looked enough like him that they must certainly be brothers. He bowed in front of her, and she dropped into a quick curtsy. "Please excuse me for the impropriety of this, since we haven't been properly introduced, but I'm in need of a dance partner." He picked up the dance card that dangled from her arm and saw all the empty spaces. "May I take my pick?" he asked with a grin.

She opened her mouth to speak, but a hand to her shoulder took her attention. "Sorry, Allen, but the lady is already spoken for," Marcus said. Marcus took her hand and laid it upon his arm.

"Hello, Marcus," she croaked out as she pulled her hand back from his arm.

He looked down at her hand, as though confused. "Hello, Miss Hewitt," he replied. "I hope you have been well."

Miss Hewitt? She should have called him Mr. Thorne. They weren't in her world anymore. "Mr. Thorne," she corrected. Her tongue was unwieldy and suddenly felt two sizes too big for her mouth.

"I see you've met my brother," he said.

So this was Allen, the brother that Marcus had displaced. "We just met, yes." She forced herself to smile at Marcus's brother. Perhaps a bit too brightly. But she didn't care. "We were just about to dance," she said, reaching for Allen's arm, arching her brows at him.

"I thought you were spoken for," Allen whispered to her as he let her tug him onto the dance floor.

"Not by him," she replied.

He chuckled. "I believe you're the first person to choose me over him in months," he said, his face dulled by... pain? Perhaps. She couldn't be sure. He tilted his head and looked at her, his gaze searching her face. "You're one of them, aren't you?" he asked quietly as he led her into a waltz.

"One of what?" she replied.

He sighed heavily. "Where are you from, Miss Hewitt?"

"I'm certain you've never heard of it."

His eyes narrowed and he heaved a sigh. "Just as I thought. You are one of them."

A grin tugged at her lips. "Is it that obvious?" she asked.

"No, not at all. Only if you know what to look for."

"And you know what to look for?"

"I was just looking for a pretty lady to dance with." He jostled her in his arms. "I found one." He looked down at her as they circled the floor. "And thank you for letting me draw you away from Marcus. Something tells me he's ready to knock my head off my shoulders for it." He nodded toward the edge of the dance floor where Marcus stood with his arms folded over his chest.

"Mr. Thorne," she began.

He interrupted. "Call me Allen, please." When she
didn't reply, he said, "Pretty please?"

"Allen," she corrected, clearing her throat a little.
"It's lovely to meet you."

"Not as lovely as it is to meet you," he said, his grin
making her feel warm all over. "If I may be so bold
as to ask, what's your relationship with my brother?"

"We don't have one," she said, blinking back the
tears that pricked at the backs of her lashes.

"That bad, is it?" He pulled his chin closer to his
chest and looked down at her. "You're the one he left
behind, aren't you?" His voice was quiet. And yet it
raked across her heart like broken glass.

She didn't reply. Did she need to?

"When will you return home?" he asked.

"The next moonful."

He quirked a brow. "That long? That gives us
almost a month to remind him of how much he
loves you."

Cecelia tripped over her own foot. Allen caught
her and drew her closer to him. "I don't know what
you mean."

"Never you mind, Miss Hewitt. Just that little
fumble has him ready to leap to your aid."

"You're mistaken, Mr. Thorne," she said. But if
Marcus's scowl deepened any further, he would be marred
for life. Did this really affect him? He'd left her, after all.

"I assume you're not here hunting a husband?"
he asked.

"I'm just here to lend my magic to the cause."

"Yes, the install–Marcus–in–his–place cause. Thank
you so much for doing that."

His last comment was bland enough to make her laugh.

"Your laughter is lovely, Miss Hewitt," he said, his voice soft. "Marcus doesn't know what he's missing."

"Thank you," she said. Was he being kind? Or was he entirely self-serving?

"Would you like to take a ride with me in the park tomorrow?" he asked as the music slowed to a stop.

"I suppose I could," she said. Is that what they did here?

"I suppose you should, my dear," he said with a laugh, glancing at Marcus, who still scowled at the edge of the dance floor. "Let's allow Marcus to be the one displaced for a day or two, shall we?"

"Yes," she blurted. "My answer is yes."

"There's a smart lass," he breathed. Then he bowed to her and returned her to the edge of the room.

Did she just make a deal with the devil? She supposed she would find out.

Two

"She's lovely, isn't she?" Claire said from beside Marcus's shoulder. Marcus didn't take his eyes off Cecelia, except for a moment when he looked down at his sister. Her eyes twinkled with merriment.

"Shut it, Claire," he growled. Cecelia was beautiful. Tall and willowy, with hair as black as night and eyes as blue as the sky.

Claire looked up at him, her head cocked to the side like an inquisitive puppy. "What's the matter, Marcus? Is something wrong?"

"Claire," he warned. God, his sister knew how to get his blood boiling. She always had. Sophie was the sweet sister. Claire was the nuisance. He pitied Lord Phineas, because he would have to put up with her sharp tongue for the rest of his life. Marcus, on the other hand, did not have to.

"They make a lovely couple, don't you think?" she asked. The corner of her mouth tilted up, but then she composed herself.

Allen held Cecelia much too close to his person for Marcus's comfort. And she looked up at Allen and smiled. That was his smile, damn it all. It was not meant for another man. "Lovely," he replied, as soon as he realized she'd asked for his opinion.

"If they decided to marry, I wonder if we could bring her father from the land of the fae to this world so he could give her away."

The idea of Mr. and Mrs. Hewitt coming to the other world to sanction a marriage between Cecelia and Allen was enough to make his heart leap. But that could never happen. Marcus wouldn't allow it. Marcus grabbed a glass of champagne from a passing footman and tossed it back in one big swallow. Then he scowled down at Claire. "You are not amusing."

"I don't intend to amuse you, Marcus. I intend to help you." She patted his arm.

"I don't need any help." He took another glass from a waiter and drank it quickly.

"If you didn't need help, then the woman you love wouldn't be in the arms of another man, you idiot," she snapped. "You need help. Lots of help."

"Did you ever stop to think that I might not want your help?"

She shrugged. "All the time. I just don't care." She smiled widely at him. What a pain in the arse.

"Mind your own matters, Claire," he warned.

"Or what?" She made an O with her lips and then pressed a finger to them. "Or you'll be angry at me? Frankly, Marcus, I don't give a damn if you're angry at me. Because you're about to let the love of your life walk right into the arms of another man. You're practically shoving her at him."

"She's not the love of my life," he grumbled.

She said one word. "Liar."

"Stop it, Claire." He was ready to beg for her to desist at this point. It hurt too damn much to talk about it.

"Did you receive news of a mission today?" she asked.

He patted his coat pocket and nodded. "Do you know what it's about?"

"The Earl of Mayden has been spotted."

Marcus's heart stopped. The Earl of Mayden had nearly killed Claire the year before. "Where?"

"In France. Apparently, when I shoved him into the painting, I put him right in front of Sainte-Chappelle." She shrugged at what must have been his perplexed look. "What of it? I liked painting the windows." She waved a hand in dismissal. "He was penniless and more than a bit mad, but he has made do. We're to take a trip to Paris to ask around and see if anyone knows his whereabouts."

"You have time for a trip to Paris?" She had twins, for goodness' sake. And a husband she hated to leave.

"It'll only take a few hours. We can walk through the painting I shoved him through months ago. Then we can come back the same day."

Sometimes Marcus forgot that his sister could walk into paintings. If the painting was of a real place, she and anyone who touched her person could walk into the painted area and actually be in the physical location.

"Will it just be the two of us?" he asked.

"Three." She pointed a finger toward the dance floor.

"Absolutely not," he barked. He had no desire to be in such close quarters with a woman he couldn't have.

"I do not assign the missions, Marcus," she reminded him. "The Trusted Few do."

"They need to unassign this one."

"I highly doubt that will happen." She looked quite pleased with herself. "She's the only one of us who speaks French. We'll need her."

Marcus already needed her, though not for the same reason as Claire.

⁂

Cecelia closed the door to her chambers and sagged heavily against it. She wasn't made for this way of life. Her feet protested the fit of the crazy other-world slippers that had pinched her toes all night. And her head positively ached with all the pins her maid had stuck in her hair to hold it in place. She began to tug her gloves from the tips of her fingers and crossed the floor.

A rap at the window jerked her from her misery. She sighed heavily as she opened the window and threw open the shutters. Milly climbed over the sill and landed on her short legs with a thump. "What are you doing here?" Cecelia asked.

Milly put her hands on her tiny hips. "What am I *doing* here? What am I doing *here*?" She shook her head and climbed onto the bed. She crossed her short little legs and rested her chin on her palms and gazed at Cecelia. "How was it?" she blurted out.

Cecelia shrugged. "Fine."

"I have been with your family for centuries," the garden gnome began.

"I know, I know." Cecelia held up a hand to stop Milly's diatribe. She knew it was coming. She mocked

Milly's tiny voice. "I've been with your family for centuries. I've brought you missions, followed you on disasters, and taken care of you when you needed help."

Milly sniffed. "The least you could do is tell me what happened."

Cecelia scoffed. "As though you weren't watching from the bushes outside the ballroom window."

"I couldn't hear anything from out there," the gnome admitted with a grin.

Her merriment was contagious. A grin tugged at the corners of Cecelia's lips, too. Then she heaved a sigh. "He acted like I was an old acquaintance."

Milly had been with her family since long before Cecelia's birth. Every fae family had a garden gnome who was assigned to the household. They ran errands, helped with missions, and carried missives to and from the land of the fae. So Milly knew all about Cecelia's relationship with Marcus. Or her former relationship.

"I met Marcus's brother," Cecelia finally said. The gnome wasn't going to go away. Not until she got some details. "He asked me to dance."

"And what did Marcus think of this?"

"I think he positively hated it," Cecelia said, finally feeling a buoyancy of spirit. "He hated every second of it. And he hated it even more when Allen asked me to take a drive with him in the park tomorrow." It was terrible to be happy about making the man jealous. But she *had* made him jealous. Hadn't she?

Milly waggled a finger at her. "Don't cause problems between the two of them. You won't like what will happen if you do." She drew in a deep breath. "He obviously cares about his family."

"What he feels for his family is obligation."

"And you don't like that, I suppose?"

"They are not his family. His family is in the land of the fae. His family was supposed to include me." Her voice cracked on the last comment, and she forced herself to steel her spine. She flopped down on the bed. "What am I going to do, Milly?" she asked. "I'm stuck here all by myself until the next moonful."

"It's better than being at home with your father, isn't it?" Milly asked.

It was. It so was.

Milly reached over and pushed Cecelia's hair back from her forehead. "You're going to go for a ride in the park with a handsome man."

"He is handsome, isn't he?" she asked.

"Sinfully," Milly affirmed. "He reminds me very much of Marcus."

Cecelia growled. "You had to go and ruin it for me, didn't you?" She threw a pillow at Milly's head, and the gnome scampered across the bed and over to the window. She threw open the sash and waved at Cecelia. "Have a good time on your ride in the park," she said. But then she stopped. She pulled a rolled-up piece of parchment from her décolletage. At the disgusted shake of Cecelia's head, Milly shrugged and said, "I like to keep my hands free."

"What is this?" Cecelia took the parchment and began to open it.

"A plan to thwart your revenge against Marcus, I believe," Milly said. But then she sobered. "It's a mission."

"But... but..." Claire sputtered. "I'm on holiday."

Milly shook her forefinger at Cecelia. "You're in the land of the other world until the moonful. You're not on holiday."

Cecelia harrumphed. "What's the mission?"

The gnome glared at her.

"I know you read it." Claire tossed the parchment onto the bed. "Tell me what it says." Milly couldn't keep herself from reading the missives she carried back and forth.

"You're to go on a mission tomorrow." She shook a finger at Claire. "No rides in the park with the younger Thorne."

"What kind of mission?"

"Do you remember last year when Claire threw some earl into one of her paintings?"

Cecelia vaguely remembered it. The man had been missing ever since. She nodded.

"It's imperative that he be found. He's a danger to everyone."

"Who's my mission partner? Claire?"

"Yes…" Milly said the word slowly.

Cecelia watched Milly closely, narrowing her eyes at the gnome in warning. "What do you know that I don't?"

"Nothing," Milly clipped out. She held her hands up as though in surrender. "Not a thing, I swear." She probably had her toes crossed. Garden gnomes could do mad things with their toes.

Cecelia shrugged. She didn't mind spending the day with Claire. "This mission will be dangerous?"

Milly nodded. "Very."

"I'm surprised they're not sending a man with us."

"They are."

Cecelia's head spun to look at the gnome. "Who?" she asked.

Milly ignored her and kicked at the floor with the toe of her wooden slipper. "You haven't heard word that Ronald is about, have you?" she asked without looking up at Cecelia. Her voice was quiet. For some reason, she didn't want Cecelia to know that the answer to her question mattered.

"If the Thornes are about, Ronald is about, I guarantee. Why? Did you need him for something?"

Milly scoffed, looking down at her fingernails as though they held the secrets of the fae. "I don't need him for anything," she said, her tone flippant.

Either Milly had more than a passing interest in Ronald or she wanted to distract Cecelia from her questions. Cecelia narrowed her eyes at the gnome. "Tell me who the man is who's going on the mission with us."

But Milly threw herself out the window. Cecelia supposed she would find out who it was tomorrow.

Three

CECELIA FILLED A PLATE FOR HERSELF AT THE SIDEBOARD in the big breakfast room and sat down at the big empty table. She lifted a fork full of boiled eggs to her mouth and had just taken a bite when Allen breezed into the room. "Good morning, Miss Hewitt," he said with a quick nod of his head.

His hair was damp and he smelled like the soap his valet had used to shave him. "Good morning," she chirped after she forced herself to swallow.

"I trust you slept well?" he asked as he began to fill a plate for himself.

She hadn't slept well. Not at all. But she smiled and said, "Quite well, thank you."

"It must be a bit off-putting to be so far from home," he said.

She shrugged. "It's nothing I'm not used to." She looked around the room. "Although my normal lodgings in this world don't typically involve breakfast with the family. I'm usually with the children. Or the servants."

As a faerie, she was often installed with the servants

to give herself the most access possible to the children or the others she was there to help. Her accommodations were adequate, but nothing nearly as nice as Ramsdale House. "Do you live here as well?" she asked.

His brow furrowed. Had she just made a mistake? "I do not live here, actually. I share bachelor's lodgings with Marcus in town." He leaned close as though he wanted to impart a secret. "There's only so long one can stand living with one's parents and younger siblings."

"Marcus doesn't live here, either?" she asked. She wanted to smack herself in the forehead with the heel of her hand when she realized what she'd just revealed. "Not that it matters," she went on to ramble.

He chuckled and covered her hand with his. He opened his mouth to speak, his eyes dancing with playfulness. But just as he did, Marcus walked into the room. Cecelia jerked her hand from beneath Allen's, and her face became hotter than the fire in the grate. Marcus stopped and arched a brow at them. He tugged his jacket closer to his body and said flippantly, "Don't let me interrupt. I merely wanted to break my fast."

"Interrupt what?" Cecelia asked.

He motioned toward them. "That," he stopped to grit his teeth, "hand-holding thing you were doing."

"We weren't holding hands," Cecelia corrected.

Allen covered his mouth with his hand and pretended to cough. He murmured, "Pardon me," when she shot him a look. He looked over his shoulder at Marcus finally. "Yes, brother dear, there was no hand holding." He chuckled out loud. "It was simply a hand cover. Entirely my fault. She looked as though she needed covering."

Marcus's gaze rose quickly to meet his brother's. His brow furrowed. "Beg your pardon?" Marcus growled.

"Her hand, that is," Allen stumbled on. He was enjoying this. She was sure of it. "Her hand needed covering. Not her, per se. Just her hand." He looked down at her hand, which was now clutched into a tight fist in her lap. "Such lovely hands they are," he said absently. He looked back at Marcus again. "But I'm sure you're already aware of how lovely Cecelia is."

"Lovely," Marcus grunted, as he came to the table and sat down across from them. He took a bite of toast. "So, just what was it about her that made you think her hands needed covering, Allen? You were overcome by the sheer beauty of them?" He took another bite. "Because I could see it if her hands were cold. Or if she was injured and you needed to squeeze her hand to stop the flow of blood." He leaned over and looked at Cecelia's hands. "But they don't appear to be injured."

"Stop it, Marcus," Cecelia warned as she tossed her napkin into her plate. "You're being ridiculous."

His brows rose so far she feared they would blend with his hairline. "Me? Ridiculous? Because I want to understand why he was holding your hand?"

"Marcus," she warned.

Allen got to his feet. "Oh, I can clear this up for you, Marcus," Allen said. He crossed to stand behind Marcus and put his hands on his shoulders. "I was holding her hand because she's bloody beautiful." He shook Marcus roughly in his grip.

"Bloody beautiful," he breathed. He stopped shaking Marcus, who appeared stiff as a board, and winked at Cecelia, grinned broadly so only she could see it, and then stole a piece of bacon off Marcus's plate and shoved it in his mouth. Then he quit the room.

It took all of Marcus's self-control not to jump from his chair and throttle his younger brother. How dare he? When Marcus walked into the room, he felt like he'd been kicked in the stomach by a mule. The sight of her hand beneath Allen's as she looked up into his brother's eyes was like a kick to the gut. And to his lungs, because he suddenly found it hard to take a deep breath.

It had taken all of his composure not to toss Allen from the room and kick his arse all the way out the front door. But, if he did that, he'd only have to deal with his father's, his mother's, and his four sisters' wrath.

"You are an idiot, Marcus Thorne," Cecelia said, jerking him from his misery. Then she shoved her napkin to the side and picked up a half-eaten piece of toast. She threw it at his head. "How dare you do that?" She picked up a berry and threw that at him, too. A handful of them, apparently, because one hit above his eye. And yet more hit his shirt.

"Cece," he began, covering his head with his hands as he ducked the flying food. "Would you stop it?"

"No, I won't stop it." This time, she turned to the sideboard, and a slack-jawed servant made a move to place lids on all the dishes there. She pointed a finger at him and he blanched. The poor man had no idea what he was up against. But he held firm and kept his hands on top of the silver domes.

"Damn it all, Cece," Marcus said as he jumped from his chair, hoping to save the poor servant from her wrath when she ran out of things to throw. He took her by the shoulders and spun her around. "Stop it," he warned quietly as he pulled her closer to him. He wrapped his arms around her and held her tightly. If he held her arms, she couldn't throw more food, could she? Definitely not.

"Don't ever do that again," she warned. But she stilled in his arms and her angry little breaths tickled his freshly shaven chin. The feel of her in his arms shot straight to his groin, and he turned to the side to keep from showing her how very much he wanted to hold her in his arms forever. Preferably when they were in a bed.

"Don't do what?" he taunted. He motioned toward the servant, nodding him toward the door. The man quietly left the room and pulled the door shut behind him. "Don't stop my brother from touching the woman I love?" He set her infinitesimally back from him. "You think I'm going to just sit back and watch my brother try to win your heart?"

"All he did was touch my hand," she murmured against his shirt. Her eyes were wet when she raised her gaze to meet his, and he felt that punch to his gut again, only this time, his heart clenched as well. "And don't tell me you love me."

She shoved his chest until he let her go. She turned to stare out the window. "I find I can't quite live without telling you, you ninny. So, if you don't want to hear it, you had better stay far, far away from me."

"Don't promise me things I can't have, Marcus," she said, her voice heavy, as if she needed to swallow. She didn't turn back to face him.

"I have given it a lot of thought, Cecelia, ever since that night I left the land of the fae." He cleared his throat. But there was a lump there that wouldn't go away. "I shouldn't have ended things. Because I'm not certain I can live without you, damn it all."

She spun quickly to face him. Instead of the sincere relief he expected to see, her cheeks were flushed and she was apparently livid, if the crease between her brows was an indication. "You see me with another man and you suddenly can't live without me? Is that it, Marcus? You're jealous?"

She stormed past him and walked around the other end of the table where he couldn't grab her as she walked past. She tilted her nose up in the air and said, "You're going to have to stay jealous, Marcus. Because I don't want a man who threw me over to become a viscount. I want one who will choose me over all things. And he very well may be a member of this world." She stuck a finger out at him, and it was as though she waved a sword at him.

"I, unlike you, would like to have someone who loves me and wants to hold me and have children with me. I want someone who will share a home with me, whether it be here or there, and someone who will cherish me and *choose me over all things*." She pressed a hand to her chest. "And that person isn't you. So, don't interject yourself into my life, Marcus.

You manage yours. And I'll manage mine. And never the two shall meet."

With that, she stomped out the door, slamming it loudly behind her.

Marcus flopped into his chair and buried his face in his hands. But then the door opened again. Marcus's heart leaped at the thought that Cecelia had come back. But his mother stepped into the room instead. "Goodness, you've gotten yourself into a bit of trouble, haven't you?" she asked. She began to whistle a tune beneath her breath.

"Why are you so happy?" Marcus grunted.

She shrugged and smiled even more broadly. "No particular reason." She retrieved a piece of toast and bit a corner off it. She pointed to the spot above his eye. "You have a bit of blueberry here." He lifted a napkin to swipe at the area. "Matter of fact, you might want to go and change clothes. You're a frightful mess."

"Yes, Mother," he groused.

"I do like that girl," she said, her voice chipper.

So did he. That was the problem.

Four

CECELIA STORMED DOWN THE CORRIDOR TOWARD THE stairwell, intent upon flinging herself down on her bed and having a full-out temper fit, provided that she could ever find her blasted room. Ramsdale House was a maze of corridors, and Cecelia quickly found herself lost. She turned corner after corner and went down corridor after corridor, until she finally heard voices from a nearby chamber. With a house this big, there had to be some servants about, didn't there? It was only logical.

She walked toward the voices and stopped when she got to the sunny morning room and stood in the doorway. She cleared her throat gently to get their attention. Lady Ramsdale looked up. "Cecelia," she said as she got to her feet. "I thought you were in your chambers."

"I would be if I could find them, I assure you," Cecelia said, fluttering her hand nervously in front of her.

"But you stormed out of the breakfast room a little more than an hour ago." Lady Ramsdale's brow arched delicately. "Have you been lost for that long?"

"Unfortunately, yes," Cecelia admitted. "And I'm very sorry that you saw me storming about at all. It wasn't my intention to upheave your household."

Lady Ramsdale bustled her two younger daughters quickly from the room. Then she motioned for Cecelia to have a seat. "Life's not worth living without a little upheaval, dear," she said. She regarded Cecelia with warm eyes. "Do you want to talk about what's bothering you?"

Not at all. She couldn't possibly discuss the fact that the lady's own son had taken her heart and squashed it like a bug under his shoe. "Nothing is bothering me," she said, forcing herself to smile. "Thank you for letting me stay until the moonful," she added.

"Thank you for lending us some of your magic. I know it's not easy for you being here."

"Life does go on, doesn't it?" Cecelia said with a heavy sigh.

"Does it?" Lady Ramsdale asked. "Does it go on? Really?"

Cecelia stuttered. "I'm certain I don't know what you mean, Lady Ramsdale."

Marcus's mother waved a breezy hand in the air. "Oh, posh. You're in love with one of my sons, and the other is using you shamelessly to needle him." She took a sip of her tea and offered Cecelia a cup. She waved it away. "Not very sporting of Allen to pick you as a way to get back at his brother. But it might be what Marcus needs to do the right thing."

"The right thing?" Cecelia reached for a cup of tea after all, because she suddenly couldn't swallow the lump in her throat.

"My son is an idiot if he thinks he can follow society rather than his heart. I think he's regretting his decision. And he regrets it even more every time you step away from him."

"Marcus has no regrets. Sometimes I think he wishes he'd been born human rather than half fae." She murmured the last.

"Marcus is chasing a dream he's had since he was a small lad. Since he was taken from us, he never knew what it was like to have parents, and he's dead set on pleasing his human father." She set her teacup down. "What he doesn't realize is that his father doesn't care if he takes over his title. He just wants him to be happy."

"He's happy now, from what I understand," Cecelia said quietly.

Lady Ramsdale laughed loudly. "Happy? That young man is miserable without you."

Cecelia set her own cup down. "Did you call me here because you needed my magic? Or so that you could toss the two of us back together?"

Lady Ramsdale tilted her head from side to side as though weighing the value of her response. "A little of both, perhaps."

"I wish you hadn't," Cecelia said clearly. "I wish you'd just left me be. It was just starting to get easier without him." Things weren't getting any easier with her father. But that was neither here nor there.

"Oh, you poor darling," Lady Ramsdale cooed. "I would never have sent for you with the intention of making you miserable."

"Yet, you have," Cecelia said as she got to her feet.

Lady Ramsdale stood up just as quickly. "What can I do to make it better?"

"I don't think you understand, Lady Ramsdale." She heaved a sigh and pinched her eyes closed tightly.

"Help me understand," Lady Ramsdale pleaded.

"All I've ever wanted to be was Marcus's wife. That was our plan. We've talked about it since we were young. We would go hunting for frogs when we were young, and we talked about how we would teach our children to do the same. And when we got a little older, we talked about how we would go on missions together, even into our old age. And we planned our future. We used to sit out under the stars and talk about it all. He'd put his head in my lap and everything felt right. Until he decided that he didn't want the life we'd planned."

"I had no idea Marcus had made such a muddle of things," Lady Ramsdale said, scratching her head.

"Our dreams were gone. And he had new ones. But I didn't. I had nothing. So forgive me if I'm a little bitter about the whole situation."

"No need to forgive you, dear," she said quietly.

"I just wanted you to know. He threw me away. And it has taken me over six months to pull myself back up to stand on my feet. And just when I thought I could, you summoned me here. So, I came. But don't expect me to act as though things are all fine and good between us, because they're not. He doesn't love me anymore. And I am too angry to love him."

Lady Ramsdale wrung her hands.

"And if you'll point me toward my chambers, I'll go and have a good cry, and then I'll be ready to go for a ride in the park with your other son." She turned toward the door and waited, blinking back tears. She refused to look at Lady Ramsdale. If she did, she might break. And she just didn't want to do that. Not now.

"To the right, up the stairs, and then take a left," Lady Ramsdale said quietly.

"Thank you," Cecelia said.

☙

Cecelia rushed past Marcus in the corridor. He reached out a hand to stop her, but she pushed her shoulder closer to the wall and stepped around him. "Not now, Marcus," she spat at him. "Mind your own matters," she snapped, and she continued on past him. Marcus stood in the corridor and watched the sway of her hips as she stormed away from him.

He was minding his own matters. She was his matter, for God's sake.

"Marcus," a voice called from the morning room. His mother stuck her auburn head out the doorway and pointed a finger at him. "I'll see you for a moment."

He didn't really have a moment. He had to see why Cecelia was in such a temper. Usually when they fought, she would throw things at him and then she would get over it. Since she'd thrown food, they should have been over it. But she obviously wasn't.

"She's still angry at me," he said as he sat down across from his mother.

"And she has every right to be."

He heaved a sigh. "I know."

"What are your intentions toward her, Marcus?" she asked.

"I don't have any intentions toward her. Aside from keeping her from falling in love with Allen." He murmured the last, and his mother's brow shot northward.

"And what if she did fall in love with Allen?"

"I would be crushed. Absolutely crushed." He couldn't think of a better way to describe it. "I made a mistake when I left her. It was a quick decision, and I was blinded by the warmth of my family." He sat up straighter and picked at an errant string on his trousers.

"Your family will still be here," she said, laying her fingertips upon his knee.

"I know that now. But I didn't know it then." He got to his feet and began to pace. He stopped to look at his mother. "My task now is to undo all the harm that I caused before some other man realizes how amazing she is and snatches her away from me." He pointed a finger at his mother. "And if Allen lays a hand on her one more time, I'm going to chop it off with a dull pair of scissors."

"Allen laid a hand upon Cecelia?" His mother looked briefly worried. But it passed.

"They were holding hands when I walked into the breakfast room."

Recognition dawned in her eyes. "And that's why she was throwing food at you this morning. Because you made an arse of yourself when you thought they were holding hands." A grin tugged at the corners of her lips. This wasn't funny.

"I don't know what you think is so amusing."

"Made you see red, did it?" she asked, her eyes twinkling.

"Red, yes. And I was about to see purple and black, because I was this close," he held his thumb and forefinger a small space apart, "to knocking the grin right off his face."

"Your brother means you no harm," she chided. "If anything, he's simply trying to help you realize what you're missing."

"He means me no harm?" Marcus pressed a hand to his chest. "I stole his title and his birthright. And I do not deserve it. I didn't sit at father's knee for twenty-odd years and learn everything that Allen did. Yet I'm the oldest, so I have to step into his future."

"And give up your own," she said quietly. "I'm sorry this has been so difficult for you."

"Difficult doesn't begin to describe it," he growled.

"It's our fault. We put you in this predicament." Her shoulders slumped. He didn't want to console her right now.

"Do you want to help me?"

She looked up quickly. "Help you with what?"

"Winning Cecelia back." He hadn't planned to do it. But then he hadn't planned to shove her away, either. "I need her more than I need a title. Or money. Or land. *Or air.*"

His mother laid a hand upon her chest. "Marcus, that's the sweetest thing you've ever said."

"If she heard me, she'd gladly volunteer to deprive me of air and smother me with a pillow. I believe she hates me."

"She doesn't hate you," his mother corrected. "But she is rather angry."

"Do you think I can't tell that?" he barked. At her

shocked expression, he worked to soften his tone. "I'm sorry, but I only have a few weeks before she will go back home."

His mother's brows drew together. "Marcus, are you under the impression that you can't go back to the land of the fae?"

"It's not worth going back there if she won't accept me in her life." He flopped in a chair rather ungracefully, suddenly feeling like the air had been let out of him.

"We have a lot of work to do," his mother said. And she pulled a writing desk into her lap. "Let's make a list, shall we?"

She smiled. And hope bloomed within Marcus for the first time in months.

Five

CECELIA CURLED INTO A BALL ON HER BED AND HUGGED a pillow to her middle. She wasn't a crier on a normal day, but she hadn't anticipated how difficult it would be to see Marcus. To be forced to be in the same house with him.

A knock sounded against her door and she jumped to sit on the edge of the bed. She swiped furiously at her eyes and crossed to the mirror, where she adjusted the hair that covered the tips of her ears. When she was satisfied, she called, "Come in."

The door opened a scant inch, and Cecelia held her breath. Certainly, Marcus wouldn't come to her chambers, would he? A brunette head poked through the door, and Cecelia's heart leaped in her chest. "Ainsley!" she cried.

The brunette streaked across the room and ran directly into Cecelia's embrace. Cecelia set the girl back from her. "What are you doing here?"

"I'm here to see you, you ninny," the girl said with a laugh. Then she threw her arms around Cecelia again.

"But how did you get here?" Ainsley hadn't

traveled with the wind the way that Cecelia had. She
had to have come a different way.

"I went by way of the fish, if you must know."

Cecelia's mouth fell open. No one went the way
of the fish except the garden gnomes and people who
wanted to negotiate. "What was that like?"

"A harrowing experience that I never want to go
through again," she admitted with a laugh. "Father
thrust me behind him and wouldn't let me so much
as look over his shoulder. The fish traded passage for
a watch fob Father carried and a few cravats he had in
his luggage. It was the strangest experience."

Ainsley pulled Cecelia into her arms for another
quick hug and then set her back. "You look dreadful,
by the way," she said candidly.

"Thank you," Cecelia said in a monotone.

"Only a good friend will tell you when you look
positively wretched," her friend reminded her.

Ainsley had been her best friend for longer than
Cecelia could remember. She knew everything about
her, and what she didn't know, Ainsley would soon
pry from Cecelia's locked jaws.

"How's Marcus? Have you seen him yet?" Ainsley
asked.

"Mr. Thorne is well," Cecelia said.

"So, that's why you look like something the dog
dragged to the door." Ainsley flopped ungracefully
onto Cecelia's bed and kicked her slippers from
her feet. "I hoped I'd find him maimed by one of
the gavels in the House of Lords. Or trampled by a
hansom cab. Or bitten by a rabid dog." She shrugged
and smiled. "I assume I can't look forward to seeing

him drooling and slobbering all over himself just before he dies a slow and painful death."

Ainsley was nothing if not candid. But she did make Cecelia laugh. "I can't believe you're here," Cecelia said with a sigh. A heavy weight had lifted from her shoulders the moment Ainsley walked into the room.

Ainsley's brown eyes sparkled with mirth. "Perhaps we can hide some perfectly dreadful plant in his tea leaves that will make him use the retiring room over and over and over."

Cecelia threw a pillow at her best friend. "I don't want to cause him harm. I never did."

"Yet he saw no reason not to rip your heart from your chest." Ainsley tapped a long, slim finger against the tip of her nose. "Justice is sweet. And mine." She cackled like a witch.

Cecelia began to drag a brush through her hair. "So, tell me, please, why you're here."

Ainsley sat up quickly, as though she'd forgotten something. "We're here to see my grandmother." She looked down her nose at Cecelia. "You know, that woman who never knew I existed until recently. I'm still not certain she likes me, by the way."

"How could anyone not love you?" Cecelia scolded.

Ainsley's gaze grew somber. "I could ask the same of you."

Cecelia shrugged. "I couldn't force him to love me." She bit back a grin. "Although he did get rather upset when he caught his brother holding my hand this morning."

"What!" Ainsley shrieked as she flopped back onto the bed. She sat up again just as quickly. "How could you have all this information and not share it with me the moment I walked into the room?" Her brown eyes narrowed. "Is his brother handsome?"

"Allen looks very much like Marcus. They're only a year apart in age. And he's very nice. Quite mischievous. I believe he likes to antagonize Marcus."

Ainsley looked overjoyed. "I like this Allen already."

"You'll like him even more when you meet him."

"Does he live here, too?"

"No, neither of the brothers lives here. They have bachelor's quarters in town." Probably where they took their whores. Cecelia's gut clenched at the thought of Marcus availing himself of all the loose-moraled women in London. "Allen is very handsome. Like Marcus. You'll like him."

Cecelia hoped Ainsley liked him. Because she could sense that, deep down, Ainsley wanted to find her own happy ending. But being half fae and half human, Ainsley didn't know where she belonged any more than Marcus did.

"You'll be staying at Ramsdale House, won't you?" Cecelia asked. She tented her hands. "Please say yes. If they have no room, we can share."

Ainsley waved a breezy hand in dismissal of that idea. "No need. My trunk was already delivered to the room next door." She smiled broadly. "I'll be here to help you with Marcus."

"And I'll introduce you to Allen."

"Mmm," Ainsley mumbled.

"What?" Cecelia asked. "I think you'll like him."

"You also said I'd like Robert Winstead, and he liked to pull the wings off helpless flies."

"We were six!" Cecelia complained.

"He still does it!" Ainsley exclaimed. "And he picks at his underarms and then sniffs his fingers. It's disgusting."

Cecelia dissolved into a fit of giggles. Goodness, she was glad Ainsley had arrived.

A knock on the door jerked them from their laughter. "Could that be Marcus come to fetch you?" Ainsley whispered dramatically. "Perhaps he wants to kiss you."

Cecelia was sure that kissing her was the last thing on Marcus's mind. "Come in," Cecelia called.

A maid poked her head in the door. "Lady Ramsdale would like to see you below stairs in the parlor, miss," she said. Then she curtsied and backed out of the room.

"How do you like Lady Ramsdale?" Ainsley asked.

Aside from pouring her heart out to her this morning, Cecelia hadn't spoken to the lady very much. "She's seems right enough." She pulled her hair into a knot at the back of her neck. "Are my ears covered?" she asked as she arranged her hair to cover them.

Ainsley joined her at the mirror. "Yes, are mine?" She looked up at Cecelia. "One has to be careful to maintain appearances in this world, doesn't one?" she asked.

"Yes, appearances are everything."

⁓

Standing across the parlor from his mother, Marcus pulled his watch fob from his pocket and glared at it. "Claire should have been here by now," he groused.

"She has twins, Marcus," his mother scolded. "She's allowed to be late on occasion." Just then, a picture frame appeared on the wall. "Speaking of the twins," she said, clapping her hands together with excitement. Marcus would never get used to the way Claire could come and go through paintings. She'd been able to do it ever since she was a child, and she availed herself of every opportunity to use her power now. Claire could paint a picture of a room and then walk into that room as though through a portal.

His sister's head appeared in the painting, all strawberry blond curls and flashing eyes. "Don't just stand there," she barked, holding out a squirming baby. "Take one of these."

She leaned over the edge of the painting, and Marcus had no choice but to take the babe. He held it far away from him and grimaced. Babies smelled bad, and they made a lot of noise. Claire disappeared into the painting and came back with another bundle, this one wrapped in a blanket, sound asleep. Cindy was only quiet when she slept, and that never lasted long.

"I only have two hands," Marcus complained.

"Oh, my," someone breathed from the doorway. Marcus looked over to find Cecelia looking toward the painting and then over at the struggling bundle in his arms, which was starting to turn a little purple.

"Some help here," Claire said sharply as she held Cindy out.

"Here," Marcus said, as he thrust little Lucius toward Cecelia. The baby's little body floundered, and he grew even redder. Cecelia winced and reached for him. Marcus's mother reclined on the settee and didn't lift a finger. "Take one," he said, "so I can get the other one."

"I think I'd rather have the one who's not screaming," Cecelia said, and bypassed the squirming baby. She took the one from Claire with a grin and made a little *tsk, tsk, tsk* sound in the baby's direction.

"Don't wake it, unless you want it to scream," Marcus warned. He'd spent enough time with Cindy to know. Once the child was awake, she would do nothing but make noise.

"Speaking of screaming," Cecelia said, as she nodded toward Lucius, who was turning a startling shade of purple. "You should do something about that."

"I plan to," he said smugly. "As soon as his mother gets herself through the painting." He shot Claire a heated glare. She climbed over the border of the painting as though she was climbing through a window and landed in the parlor. Then she reached a hand back into the painting and pulled Lord Phineas, her husband, through the opening. The man landed awkwardly beside her and smoothed his disheveled hair.

Marcus still stood with his arms outstretched. If he wasn't mistaken, Lucius smelled worse now than he had when they'd arrived. "Someone take this," he said. But no one came forward.

He looked over at Cecelia, who'd taken Cindy and sat down on the settee with the baby burrowed tightly in the crook of her arm. He sat down beside her and tried to balance Lucius on his knee. But the little guy was not happy. Not at all.

"He doesn't like me," Marcus complained.

"If you hold everyone at arm's length like that," his mother warned, "the rest of the world will dislike you just as much."

Ouch. She should just pull that knife right out of his chest. And replace it with a dull spoon. One that she could jab into the aching wound over and over. "I don't hold everyone at arm's length," he grumbled. "Just those who smell atrocious."

The soft, clean scent of Cecelia's hair rose up to tickle his nose. He looked down at her. She regarded the baby tucked into the crook of her arm with an air of contentment. His heart dropped toward his toes. He wanted that to be his baby in her arms. "You smell so much better than he does," he whispered to Cecelia with a smile.

She harrumphed at him and went back to looking at the baby. Well, that was an abysmal failure. He couldn't even deliver a compliment well. Allen came to stand at his shoulder and took the baby from his arms. Thank God. At least his brother saw fit to save him. Allen placed the baby in his mother's arms, and the little one ceased his wailing immediately.

"I told you he hated me," Marcus grumbled.

"He's not the only one," a voice said from the doorway.

Marcus looked over and couldn't keep the corners of his lips from rising at the sight of Ainsley. "Ainsley!" he cried. He got to his feet and rushed toward her. He wanted to swing her around in his arms, but the loud clearing of his brother's throat stopped him. Actually, Allen sounded like he was choking to death on a chicken bone, so Marcus turned to look at him midstride. Allen shook his head quickly. "Don't do that," he said quietly but sternly.

Marcus had forgotten the rules of this world for a moment. Instead, he took Ainsley's hand and bowed low before it. "Ainsley," he said, trying to maintain his composure. Ainsley was a sorely needed taste of home.

"Mr. Thorne," she replied with disdain.

Good God, she hated him too? "Welcome to Ramsdale House," he said.

"I'm not here to see you," she warned. "In fact, I could never see you again and be just fine."

Cecelia issued a subtle warning to Ainsley with a nod of her head. Ainsley lifted her nose in the air and ignored Marcus entirely. But she hugged Claire and Lady Ramsdale, and let Finn take her hand. Then she stopped in front of Allen and said, "Goodness, they do look quite a bit alike."

"Yes," his mother said. "The family resemblance is striking, is it not?"

Ainsley's mouth fell open in a most unladylike pant. "It's nice to meet you," she finally stammered when Cecelia made a motion for her to close her lips.

Allen bowed over Ainsley's hand. "Miss…?" He asked the question subtly with a raised brow.

"You may call me Ainsley, Allen," she said. His brow shot up even farther. And then he bowed over her hand.

Claire clapped her hands together. "I believe we've a mission today. Who's coming?"

"You're not taking the children?" Marcus asked.

"Now we know how to get Marcus to stay at home. We should take the children everywhere we go," Ainsley whispered to Cecelia. She laughed and covered her mouth.

"The children are staying with me," his mother said, as she took the baby Cecelia held in her free arm. "You all run along now. Have a good time. Find a killer. Take a walk in the park, if it's not too late. Then come back and get the children."

Everyone knew that Claire wouldn't leave her children for long, not even with her mother. "Who all is going?" Marcus asked.

"You, me, Lord Phineas, and Cecelia, since she speaks French." Claire patted her husband's arm. "Finn doesn't want me searching for killers without him."

"Can I go?" Ainsley asked.

Claire shrugged. "I don't see why not."

"Mr. Thorne, would you like to join us?" Ainsley asked.

Allen tugged at his cravat, and Marcus forced himself not to roll his eyes. "I'm not certain that would be wise," Marcus said.

"Why not?" Allen barked.

Marcus heaved a sigh. "Because you're not fae?"

Finn clapped Allen on the shoulder. "We humans have to stick together. I vote that we take him."

"I just came to collect Cecelia for our ride in the park," Allen said. His brother raised a brow at Cecelia.

"I'm so sorry, Allen," Cecelia rushed to say. "We have a mission." She shot a quick glance at Marcus. "But we'd love for you to join us."

Marcus thought Allen looked much too pleased by that invitation, damn his hide. "That settles it." Claire reached into the painting and pulled out a separate painting of Sainte-Chappelle. She hung it on the wall and then said, "Pick me up and put me in, Finn. It's so much easier than climbing."

Lord Phineas didn't even blink before he picked his wife up and put her feetfirst into the painting. She held a hand back through the void and pulled him through with her. Then she held her hand through again. "Your turn, Ainsley?" Allen asked.

Ainsley lowered her eyelashes coquettishly. "Don't just stand there. Be a dear and pick me up."

Allen looked more than a bit uncomfortable, but he picked her up and gently shoved her through the painting as she held Claire's hand. Then he followed.

"Cecelia?" Marcus asked.

"That won't be necessary," she said, as she hitched her skirts up a little higher and climbed in all by herself.

"You could have just let me do it!" he called behind her.

"If I'd wanted you to touch me, I would have," she called back.

Good Lord, he was in for a long afternoon. He took Claire's hand and dived headfirst into the painting.

Six

CLIMBING INTO A PAINTING WAS EASIER THAN CLIMBING out of one. Climbing out when someone could be watching was particularly precarious. Claire went out first and reached a hand in to pull the others free when she saw that the way was unobstructed. Then she hid the painting, their way home, in the bushes behind a nearby building.

Cecelia brushed the dust from her dress and looked around. Sainte-Chappelle was a sight to behold when one was inside, with all its glass windows. "Beautiful," Marcus breathed.

"Yes, it is a lovely building," Cecelia replied.

Marcus looked down at her, his dark eyes sparkling. "I wasn't referring to the building."

Cecelia's heart dropped toward her toes. Allen made a gagging sound with a finger in his throat, which made Ainsley laugh loudly.

"Quite nauseating, isn't it? Unrequited love?" Ainsley asked of Allen.

"I have a feeling this love isn't unrequited," Allen whispered back, but he was close enough that Cecelia could hear him.

"It should be after what he did," Ainsley said. She was nothing if not stalwart in protecting Cecelia's heart.

"Men make mistakes, my dear," Allen informed her. "It's the unfortunate nature of the beast. Particularly aristocratic men. They're unfortunately addled when it comes to things not pertaining to titles, land, and fortunes. Matters of the heart trip us up much more than transfers of holdings or a bet on the books at White's."

Ainsley snorted. "Aristocratic men are imbeciles, you say?" She rocked her shoulder into his. Shock crossed his face at her audacity, but he quickly hid it. He was raised to be such a gentleman. And a gentleman did not correct a lady. Particularly not one whose only fault so far was a familiarity with his person.

Allen adjusted his jacket. "Not imbeciles, I'd say." He leaned closer to Ainsley. "Although my brother might fall into that category if he doesn't marry that lady as soon as possible."

Cecelia heard him this time and cringed. That would never happen.

"When the two of you are finished with your flirting, let's go and see if we can find Mayden," Claire said to Allen and Ainsley, and Ainsley's face reddened prettily. The tops of Allen's ears turned pink.

Lord Phineas coughed into his hand to cover a laugh. Marcus turned away, but not before he grinned at his brother.

"If we could be serious for a moment," Claire scolded, as she held out two miniatures, keeping a third for herself. "This is what the Earl of Mayden looks like. In case you need to show him to anyone."

"Is that safe?" Cecelia asked as she looked down at the miniature.

"Probably not," Lord Phineas said. Claire and her husband knew Mayden's sordid history personally since the earl had made an attempt on Finn's life the year before. "So, be careful."

"I think we can cover more ground if we split up," Claire said.

"I'm going with you," Lord Phineas said to his wife as Claire slid her arm into his. She smiled up at him.

Allen bowed to Ainsley and said, "Shall we take a stroll about town?" Ainsley flushed again and laughed lightly as she curtsied.

That left Cecelia with Marcus. *Oh, joy.* Cecelia looked over at him and grimaced.

"Don't worry. I promise not to bite." He held out his arm for her and arched a brow in question.

"I learned to walk when I was a year old, Marcus. I don't think I've forgotten how." She started in the other direction.

৵৯

Good God, the woman would drive him absolutely mad. First she wouldn't let him put her into the painting, and now she wouldn't even take his arm. She was angry, and she had a right to be. But would she ever get past it? "Do you even know where you're going?" he called to her retreating back.

"Somewhere you're not," she called back.

"We'll all meet here at dusk," Claire called to the group. Cecelia didn't slow down to answer. But

Marcus called back his agreement, and then he ran to catch up with Cecelia.

"Where shall we start?" he asked. She was walking so fast that he was finding it hard to breathe.

She turned to face him. "A better question is where we should end. Here looks to be as good a place as any." Marcus's gut clenched. "Stop trying to open the door to the past. Your future is much more important, Marcus."

It wasn't. The only thing that was important was her. "Can't I have both?" he asked. He waited on tenterhooks.

"I don't see how."

Marcus looked at the crowd in the street and took Cecelia's hand in his, pulling her between two buildings. She tried to step around him, but he pushed her back with the size of his body. This might be his only chance to talk to her. He wasn't going to give up the opportunity.

Cecelia pushed against his chest, but he put one hand on either side of her head, flat against the wall, and leaned into her. She froze. And looked everywhere but at him. "Stop it," she protested, gritting her teeth. She glanced back and forth up the alleyway. "Someone will see."

"Then let them see, blast it all. I don't give a damn." He turned her head with his crooked finger beneath her chin. "You're the only thing that matters to me. I need you to know how I feel."

"Marcus," she protested, pushing against his chest, but he just leaned more heavily against her. "We're supposed to be finding Mayden."

"We'll look for him in a moment." He touched the side of her face. God, she was so pretty. Her eyes closed and she leaned her cheek into his palm. "We need to talk."

❧

The last thing Cecelia wanted to do was talk to Marcus. She was still smarting from his set down, and she didn't want to hear anything he had to say about the matter. Six months. It had been six months since she'd felt the beat of his heart beneath her hand. Since she'd felt the brush of his breath across her cheek. Since she'd had him this close. But this wasn't friendly, playful Marcus. This one was completely serious. And obviously mad if he thought he could handle her in such a way.

"Move, Marcus!" she cried, shoving his hand from where it cupped her cheek.

"No."

He didn't say more than that. Just that single word.

He took a deep breath, as though he needed to collect his thoughts. "I let you go once. I'll never do it again. Not willingly. Don't ask it of me." His eyes danced across her face. "Give me an opportunity," he begged.

"I can't." Her voice shook. "I have my reasons, Marcus. I just can't."

"Tell me what they are. Aside from the fact that I'm an idiot."

He wouldn't like her reason. He wouldn't like it at all. But she had to tell him something.

She pushed him back and he moved marginally. "You're too close for propriety," she warned.

"I just want another chance," he said again.

He'd had his chance. He had. And then he gave it up. So, she moved on. She had moved on, hadn't she? Truly? She'd gotten over him. She'd gone on with her life.

She'd wanted this more than anything for six months. But now, now she wasn't free to accept him, even if she wanted to. She had to return to the land of the fae to care for her father. She wanted more than anything to accept Marcus. But she couldn't.

"Why is this so easy for you?" she asked him. "And why the sudden change of heart?"

"I haven't had a change of heart. My heart's the same as it was," he said. "I loved you then, and I love you now."

Cecelia's heart would leap from her chest if it beat any faster. Either leap or break into a million pieces. She suspected the latter.

"It's too late."

His face fell, his eyes wary.

"Why is it too late? You're here. I'm here. Let me kiss you, Cece," he said. His head descended toward hers.

She couldn't have stopped him even if she'd wanted to. And she didn't want to. It had been so long since he'd kissed her.

"Why do you want to kiss me?" she asked, her voice quavering.

"Stop asking questions you already know the answer to," he growled. Then he touched his lips to hers. His touch wasn't tentative the way she remembered. His breath blew across her lips, and then he was opening her mouth with his tongue and sweeping inside. Cecelia's knees buckled, and she grabbed on to his forearms to hold herself upright. But then he was there, taking the weight off her legs as he pressed her against the building with his body.

His hips pressed hard against her stomach, his chest heaving against her breasts. There was nothing gentle in his kiss, which was the opposite of the softness she would have expected from her best friend. It was lusty and urgent. And delightful.

He drew her lower lip between his and suckled gently, and it was all Cecelia could do to stay on her feet.

The noise that escaped his throat was primal. His hands left the wall beside her head and dropped to draw her to him. His mouth continued to plunder. He licked across her mouth and inside, nibbled and sucked her lips, and stole her wits with the noises he made.

He pressed hard against her stomach, his hands sliding down to cup her bottom and draw her up and against him to where he was hard and pulsing beneath his trousers.

"Cece," he whimpered. "Tell me it's not too late."

Cecelia pulled away, unwound his arms from around her, and stepped to the side. She wiped the back of her hand across her mouth and wished for some magic dust that could take her back in time. A time before that kiss. A time before he'd taken that step. Because he thought she was free to accept him. And she wasn't.

"I can't," she said. She adjusted her clothing and tried to calm her breathing.

He tilted his head and regarded her solemnly. At least his breaths were as shallow as hers. He wasn't unaffected by the kiss. That much was obvious. "Don't tell me you didn't enjoy that," he said, his brows narrowing.

"I won't lie to you, Marcus. About anything." He stepped toward her again, hope blooming on his face. But she couldn't let him hope. "That kiss affected me." A winded chuckle left her throat. It certainly had.

"Good."

He sounded pleased with himself.

"Yours was my first kiss all those years ago."

"I know." He looked even more pleased. Damn him.

"But it won't be my last."

His mouth fell open. "What?"

Cecelia heaved a sigh. "I waited for you. I waited for months. I hoped with all my heart that you were going to come back. That you were going to come to your senses and come back to me. Return to the land of the fae. But you didn't."

He had the nerve to look contrite. "I was occupied here."

"When your grandmother asked me to come and help you, I couldn't say no, but I should have." She began to pace and wring her hands. "I should have said no, because I knew it would be hard to see you."

"It doesn't have to be hard," he said, smiling. Goodness, she loved that smile.

"But it is hard. It's like someone putting a tray of biscuits before you but telling you that you can't eat them. And then you're past the point of starvation, and the biscuits start to taunt you."

"I'll last a little longer than a tray of biscuits," he said with a laugh. "And I'm attainable."

"Not for me," she sighed.

"Why do you have to keep denying this?" he bit out. "I made a mistake. Now stop punishing me. You love me. And you want me. That kiss told me everything I needed to know." He reached out to touch her, and she let him cup her cheek. "You waited for me all these years. Now it's time to stop waiting. We can be together. We can get married."

"We can't," she said, a sob building within her. "I'm not free to accept you." She had to take care of her father. He was her priority now.

His face fell. And his mouth fell open. "What?" He took a step back from her.

"I'm not free to accept you, Marcus. Because I had to stop waiting. I had no choice. You gave me no indication that you would be returning. That you still thought of me, much less wanted to marry me. So, I stopped waiting. I am no longer free to accept you."

If the ground didn't open up and swallow Marcus, he would be sorely disappointed. Because there was nowhere to go to get away from her words. There was nothing he could do, no place to run, nowhere to hide, no way to block out the pain.

"There's someone else." There was no emotion in the words. He understood. "I always thought we would marry." He felt like a deflated balloon—empty and lifeless.

"So did I. But then you left me."

"I did." He did. Oh God, he did. This was all his fault. He dragged a hand through his hair, upsetting the queue at the back of his neck. The leather band fell to the ground as his hair spilled out around his face. He ran a hand through it again. Damn it, he was a ridiculous fool.

"And I moved on." She stood up tall and didn't back down.

"You've kissed someone else?"

"That's not it." Her face colored.

"How was it?" he asked. It was crude of him. But he had to know.

"Things are fine at home. I just…" Her voice tapered off.

He chuckled. If any kiss with someone else was just fine, he didn't have anything to worry about. "Kisses shouldn't be fine. They should be earth-moving. They should make the ground beneath your feet tremble. They should be like the one we just shared."

"That can't happen again." She looked him in the eye as she said it. "I owe him more than that."

"Who is it?" It didn't matter. He would hate anyone who had her heart.

"It doesn't matter. All that matters is that I am not free to marry you. I belong in the land of the fae."

"No, you don't," Marcus snarled.

"Yes, Marcus. I do. I won't change my mind."

"We'll see about that." He turned and walked away from her. If he didn't, he'd try to kiss her again, and she wasn't prepared for that. But one thing was certain. He would never allow her to marry anyone else. Never.

Cecelia watched him walk away and heaved a deep breath. Then she sank back against the wall to try to compose herself. That hadn't gone well. Not at all. She never should have allowed that kiss. But she'd missed the feel of his lips on hers. She'd missed the warmth of his embrace. She'd missed *him,* for goodness' sake.

It wasn't as though he'd given her much of a choice, either. But from now on, she had to keep her distance from Marcus Thorne. She shouldn't want what she couldn't have. Her father was at home, and he needed her far more than Marcus did. She picked up the leather queue from the ground and followed him into the street. He had to fix his hair before someone noticed the tips of his ears.

"Marcus," she called to his retreating back. He turned back, his eyes flashing.

"What?" he barked.

She held out the leather tie. "Your hair."

He stalked back toward her, gathering his hair into a queue at the back of his neck. He took the tie from her hand and bound it. He felt for the tips of his ears, and she reached up to adjust his hair to cover them.

"There," she said, dusting her hands together. "Finished."

He took her chin in his hand and looked into her eyes. "Not even close."

Seven

AINSLEY GRUMBLED FROM THE PARK BENCH WHERE SHE waited. "It's dusk. Where are Claire and Lord Phineas? We've been waiting for hours." She flopped back against the bench and laid the back of her hand against her forehead.

Allen pulled a watch fob from his pocket and glanced down at it. "We've been waiting for five minutes," he corrected.

"Well, it feels like hours," Ainsley grumbled. "My feet hurt."

"Mine do, too," Cecelia admitted, settling down beside Ainsley.

Marcus leaned close to Cecelia's ear so that only she could hear. "If we were married, I'd feel led to rub your aching feet for you," he murmured. His eyes looked down the bodice of her dress. "Among other places."

Cecelia was certain she'd flushed scarlet, if the look on Ainsley's face was any indication. Ainsley picked up a hand and started to fan Cecelia's face. "Goodness." Ainsley laughed. "What did he say to you?" she asked.

"Nothing that bears repeating," Cecelia replied. He'd been doing this all afternoon as they scoured the streets of Paris for the elusive Earl of Mayden, who was nowhere to be found. Not a single person had recognized the miniature.

Marcus had started out by brushing her elbow, and then he'd drawn her to his side and told everyone they met who spoke English that he and his wife were searching for her long-lost cousin. He'd slung his arm around her shoulders and pulled her to him, and had kissed her soundly on the cheek. And all it had served to do was make Cecelia angry. How dare he? She picked up a rock from the ground beside her foot and threw it at him. He deflected it with a laugh.

"Perhaps another time," he suggested with a cheeky grin. Cecelia almost smiled along with him, but then she remembered that she wasn't supposed to find him charming. But he *was* charming. No matter how much she dearly didn't want him to be.

They'd met up at the bench across from Sainte-Chappelle at dusk, just as Claire had instructed, but Claire and Finn were nowhere to be found. "Do you think they're all right?" Ainsley asked.

"As long as she has Finn with her, you needn't worry," Marcus said. Finn had laid down his life for Claire's the year before and would do so again. And again. And again. "Maybe they stumbled upon some important information about Mayden?"

Ainsley's brows drew together as she asked, "What if this isn't the place where Claire sent him? He could be anywhere by now."

"He could," Marcus admitted. "But I've seen with

my own eyes the damage Mayden could do. He's hurt enough people, countless people. We'll have to keep searching if he's not here."

The sun was setting, and Cecelia was hungry. Her stomach protested loudly, and she laid a land over her belly to stifle the noise.

Marcus chuckled. "It's getting late. We need to get you fed."

"I'll survive," Cecelia replied. It was too late for him to try to take care of her now.

"I won't," Ainsley complained, which made Allen smile. "I'm going to swoon and fall into the dirt due to excessive hunger." She blinked her dark lashes at Allen. "Will you catch me if I do, Allen?" she asked.

"As a gentleman, I would be obligated to catch you, Ainsley," he said with a wink.

"Obligated?" Ainsley complained. "That's the only reason you'd do it?"

Allen's cheeks colored. The man had blushed more today than he probably ever had in his life. "That's not the only reason," he admitted quietly. And Ainsley suddenly grew as somber and quiet as he was. What was that all about? Ainsley and Allen? Already?

Marcus grunted. "I'm a little hungry myself."

Allen said blandly, "I doubt there's a soul here who would try to catch you if you swooned, Marcus. So buck up."

"I would let him fall," Ainsley said with a grin.

"So would I," Allen admitted.

Cecelia raised a hand slowly, as though being called on by a tutor. "I would feel inclined to do the same." She shouldn't have said that, but she couldn't help it.

Marcus feigned pulling a knife from his chest. "Remind me not to call on any of you if I'm ever in trouble."

Allen grumbled. "I suppose I'm honor bound to catch you if you swoon." He looked put out by the thought. "Mother would be cross with me if I didn't."

"Father might take away your allowance."

"I daresay he would applaud me if I told him the circumstances." Allen laughed.

Marcus shrugged. "That may be true."

"Do you two always bicker like this?" Ainsley asked. "With such good natures?" She looked from one to the other. Cecelia had wondered the same.

"Things were tense when we first met," Allen admitted. "But our circumstances can't be changed. So, I've learned to tolerate him." He waited a moment and grinned.

Marcus scoffed. "He barely tolerated me in the beginning." He twisted the signet ring that he wore on his finger. The ring was a symbol of him becoming a viscount, if Cecelia was correct. "Father gave this ring to me as a gesture of goodwill when I agreed to succeed him," he said quietly. "But I'd rather have had a puppy." He grinned. Goodness he was handsome when he smiled.

"Oh, a puppy," Ainsley crooned. "I wanted a puppy once."

Marcus's brows drew together. "What on earth would you do with a dog?"

Ainsley heaved a sigh and then went on to explain to Allen. "We travel too often to keep pets. They become a burden."

"You don't have staff to care for them when you're gone?" Allen asked.

"Yes, but then I'd miss the dog." Ainsley rolled her eyes. "I don't believe leaving things you love behind to go from world to world is good for anyone," she said quietly. She looked at Marcus and then down at the ground where the toe of her slipper drew a circle in the dirt.

Silence fell on the foursome like a heavy cloak. Allen cleared his throat to throw it off. "It's well past dusk," he informed them. "I hope Claire and Lord Phineas are well."

Just then, Claire and his lordship walked toward them down the lane.

"Where have you been?" Marcus barked. His mood was sufficiently sour after Ainsley's comment. Ainsley was right, but she didn't have to say it the way she did.

"We've been hunting for Mayden. We found a woman who thought she recognized the miniature, but nothing came of it." Claire shrugged. "We should get back. I'm hungry. And I want to see my children."

Finn retrieved the painting from the bushes, hung it on the wall, motioned toward the painting, and scooped her up in his arms to put her through. She reached back to pull him in. Ainsley followed, assisted by Allen. And when Cecelia would have climbed over the edge of the painting, Marcus scooped her up and jostled her in his arms until she looked up at him.

"Stop working so hard to hate me," he said quietly. Then he stuffed her into the painting and followed her into his mother's parlor.

❧

Cecelia was driving him mad. He'd been with her the whole day. He'd pretended to be her husband, and she'd still treated him like an interloper. Perhaps that was because she loved another. Perhaps it was because she was still sore at him because he'd left her. But he wouldn't leave her again. Not for anything. She might as well get used to having him in her life, because she was stuck with him.

But there was still the question of the man back home. He had to find out who it was so he could take measures. He also needed to approach her father so he could ask for her hand. The man would probably say no, after the way Marcus had broken her heart. And he would have every right to. But she belonged with him, and Marcus wouldn't take no for an answer. He could have her. He could have the title. He could have the land of the fae. He could have his family and his missions. He could. If she'd just accept him and what he had to offer her.

What did he have to offer her?

His father broke into his reverie. "Woolgathering?" Lord Ramsdale asked quietly, as he sat beside his son at dinner. Dinner had been waiting when the six of them returned.

"I suppose," Marcus admitted.

"Want to talk about it?" his father asked.

"Perhaps another time." He stabbed his fish with his fork and took a bite of his potatoes.

"I'm here to talk anytime you need me," his father offered.

Marcus knew that. He did. But what Marcus wished for more than anything was to have his grandfather to talk to. His grandfather had taught him everything he'd known, and Marcus had been destined to follow in his footsteps, all the way to his place with the Trusted Few.

"I miss Grandfather," Marcus admitted.

He regretted the words as soon as they left his lips. He didn't intend to make his father feel inadequate. "I'm sorry," he rushed to say. But his father held up a hand.

"It's all right," he soothed. "He raised you. He helped to form you into the man you are now. Things didn't get fouled up for you until I came along."

"Fouled up." Marcus snorted. "That's a good way to describe it." He inhaled deeply. "She says she's obligated to another," he told his father quietly, glancing at Cecelia where she was seated at the other end of the table. She looked up at him from beneath her lashes and then looked away quickly when he saw her watching him.

His father's brows drew together. "Do you know this person?"

"She hasn't said who he is. But she's promised to stay in the land of the fae for him." He took a sip of his wine.

"Hmm," his father said quietly. "Do you think she loves another?"

Marcus shook his head. He couldn't be certain. When he'd kissed her, she didn't act as though she loved another. But then again, she'd always been the one for him. The only one. So, he had no comparison to make. "I think she loves me. But she's angry."

"At least you're aware of it." His father chuckled.

"Most men are without a clue. We walk around as if we're on top of the world, while the ladies want to remove our stones with a dull knife."

Marcus choked on a piece of bread. "Beg your pardon?" he gasped out.

"Don't ever assume your stones are safe, son," his father said as he clapped Marcus on the shoulder. "Not when a woman has been scorned."

༄

Ainsley leaned toward Cecelia and whispered, "What happened between the two of you today? I've been dying to ask you."

"Nothing," Cecelia lied. It may as well have been nothing. Because nothing was what could come of it. But heat crept up her cheeks as she remembered that kiss.

"You don't flush when 'nothing' has happened, Cece," Ainsley scolded. "Tell me. You know you want to."

"I told him," Cecelia muttered.

"Told him what?" Ainsley's brow puckered.

"Told him that I can't accept him. Because I'm not free to do so."

"Since when?" Ainsley's silverware clattered to the tabletop.

"Since my mother died and my father fell apart," Cecelia hissed back.

"So you lied."

"I didn't lie. Not really. I told him I'm not free."

"But you are."

"My father needs me right now."

"You can't give up your life for your father," Ainsley groaned. "I can't believe you let Marcus think that." She stabbed at the air with the tines of her fork, punctuating what she would say next. "You"—stab—"shouldn't"—stab—"have"—stab—"lied."

Cecelia heaved a sigh. "It's the only way."

"Sometimes the truth is the only way, Cece," Ainsley said quietly.

Eight

CECELIA SAT DOWN ON THE GARDEN BENCH AND tugged her shawl more tightly around her shoulders. The night air was chilly, and her heart felt even colder. She'd made a mistake in letting Marcus kiss her. She should have soundly trounced him, rather than ever letting his lips touch hers.

She'd dreamed of another kiss for as long as she could remember. And it had been all she'd expected it to be. It was all she could think about. After dinner, she'd made her excuses, claiming to be tired. But she really just needed some time alone. She'd put a candle in her window to summon Milly and walked into the garden to wait for her to appear.

Cecelia sat back and looked up at the stars. They seemed brighter at home, although she knew these were exactly the same as the ones she'd looked at her whole life.

She took a deep breath. She'd gotten herself into a perfectly wretched position.

"That kiss in Paris was beautiful," a voice said from behind her.

Cecelia closed her eyes and wished for Marcus to go away. She didn't want to face him right now. "A gentleman would never discuss such things," she scolded.

Marcus chuckled and dropped onto the bench beside her. "It's a good thing I've never been a gentleman then, isn't it?" He sat forward with his elbows on his knees, his hands dangling between his parted thighs. "Did it mean anything to you?" he asked, not looking at her. His hair was unbound and curled around his face. He was so handsome when he was unguarded like this. Like he was at home. Perhaps this was home now?

"I never know what to expect when I go on a mission," Cecelia said with a shrug.

"Stop being obtuse," he chided. "You know I'm not referring to the mission." He still didn't look at her. He looked at everything else.

"Marcus." She sighed.

He leaned back, put his arm behind her on the back of the bench, and then slid over so that his thigh touched hers. "How many nights have we spent beneath the stars like this?" he asked.

"One too many, if you count tonight," she said, her tone purposefully caustic. She tugged her shawl from beneath his thigh.

He sat quietly for a moment. "What will it take?" he asked.

"For what?" She knew what he was referring to. But oblivion was so much easier.

"For you to forgive me." He didn't elaborate. He just looked into her eyes. His were black in the darkness of the night.

Cecelia groaned, flinging her head back in frustration. She sat back up and said, "You're forgiven." If what he wanted was absolution, then maybe now he would go away.

"I'm going to tell you something that you might not like," he warned.

"How will that be any different from a normal day?" she asked.

"I am very angry at you for not accepting me."

Cecelia's back straightened. "What right do you have to be angry?"

He laughed, but it was a sound with no mirth. "None, apparently. But I'm still hurt by it." He was suddenly, clearly serious. "I always thought it would be me and you until the end of time."

"Things change when time and space separate people."

"Things don't change that much," he ground out.

Marcus didn't know about her mother's death. He didn't know about her father's problem with drinking too much. He didn't know that her father needed her until he could heal. He didn't know anything about her obligations. "You have no idea," she finally said.

His brows rose and his eyes flashed. "Beg your pardon?"

"We were once fated for marriage. But things change. They change in irrevocable ways." Her voice rose. But she didn't care. "I believe you weren't in a rush to marry me because you knew I'd always be there. That I was yours for the taking. That I would go wherever you led and do whatever you want to do. I was easy. So, you just didn't care to try."

He made a noise at the back of his throat. "I can

assure you that nothing with you has ever been easy. Including this."

She snorted. She couldn't help it.

"When you loved me, I threw it all away. But some day, you'll love me again."

"I can't, Marcus," she said. "You didn't care enough."

"No one will ever care more than me. Not even him."

"Him who?"

"See," he laughed. "You don't even care enough to know his name. Yet you've promised to marry him?"

"Oh, him," she said. "I didn't understand what you were saying."

"Who is he?" Marcus tensed, his back straight.

"He's no one." She heaved a sigh.

"He's someone if you've promised your life to him," Marcus mumbled.

"Oh, good Lord," Cecelia said, getting to her feet. "Will you stop it? Envy is not a pretty color on you."

"Get used to it. Because I'll wear it as long as you're promised to someone else." He stood up and got close to her, so close that she had to take a step back. But he just followed. "I will never stop. I will chase you until I can't chase you anymore."

"I don't want to be chased," she whispered.

"You want to be married. And to have children. And to have a home of your own." He brushed a lock of hair behind her ear. "You want me."

She shook her head. This was going nowhere. "I'm going to bed." She pushed past him toward the garden gate.

Marcus spun to chase her. "Tell me who he is." He tugged gently on her elbow.

"Who?"

"The man who will keep you from me."

He was never going to let this rest, was he? Ever. Cecelia squeezed her eyes closed. "There is no one, all right?" she cried. Her voice broke, and she hated herself for it. But the subterfuge wasn't fair to either of them.

"What?" He smiled slowly, his eyes lighting up there in the darkness of the night. "There is no one else?"

Cecelia steeled herself with a fortifying breath. "No. I just told you that to make you leave me alone."

Talking about her father hurt too much. She didn't have to tell him about that yet, did she?

✎

He would never, ever, ever leave her alone. Not now. Not a chance. "I'll never leave you again," he promised. Hope bloomed within him.

"I haven't said I'll accept you back in my life," she warned, holding up a finger to stay him.

He smiled. He couldn't help it. "You lied to me about your availability." The joviality in his voice made his comments sound like a song.

She blew a lock of hair from her forehead with an upturned breath. "And I'm pretty sure you lied too," she said. She looked away, suddenly appearing uneasy. "How many women have there been since you've been here, Marcus?" she finally asked. "I have a right to know."

A laugh bubbled up within him, but he tamped it down. "There's only you, you ninny," he said, flicking his finger against the tip of her nose. "How could I possibly be with another when you're all I can think about?"

Marcus drew her into his arms, with her protesting all the while. He laughed at her reticence, but he needed to hold her. "You had better not be lying," she murmured against his chest. "I will find out if you are."

"Cece," he said. He didn't know how to tell her everything that was in his heart. But he felt it was imperative that he try.

"Let me show you." He reached into his pocket and pulled out a vial of faerie dust. He tilted it back and forth in his hand, and Cecelia watched the glow of the flakes. He dumped a lump of it into his palm and blew it into the air. He said the words, "Show my love my heart."

The dust began to swirl and formed a picture of Marcus with his ring on the day his father gave it to him. The words "faith," "trust," and "honor" appeared in the apparition. But then they were replaced by sorrow. Sorrow, despair, and dissatisfaction trumped happiness, and the second words gobbled up the first in their greedy jaws. Marcus wiped a tear from the corner of Cecelia's eye. He swiped a hand through the dust and it dissipated, falling to the floor of the garden like sparks from the grate. Dust didn't lie. He'd been as torn in two as she had over their separation.

"I had a lot to think about when I first came here."

"Your sisters?" she asked.

Yes, he'd had to get his sisters out of one scrape or another. But then he'd gone home and his grandfather had died. And he'd taken some part of Marcus with him. "My sisters, and then my parents." He'd wanted so badly to have parents. "I felt like I needed to make them love me, since they hadn't done so my whole life. And I worried that the only way to do that was to dedicate myself to their way of life." He brushed a lock of hair behind her ear. "That's the crux of it. And I'm sorry."

She said something quietly against his chest.

"What was that?" he asked, pulling back from her.

She looked up at him, her blue eyes like limpid pools he could fall into. "I am not ready to forgive you yet."

"My father warned me that you wouldn't be so easy to sway."

She elbowed him in the ribs. "You talked to your father about us?"

"Who else am I going to talk to? Allen? He'd just as soon take you from me as help me."

"Allen's not so bad." She took his hand and led him back to the bench. She sat down and pointed to her lap. "Come on. Put your head here." She motioned him forward with wiggly fingers.

Oh, thank heavens. He could breathe again. He stretched out on his back and laid his head in her lap. The firmness of her thigh made him feel like he was coming home. She didn't put her hands in his hair right away, and he needed for her to touch him. He wouldn't feel complete until she did.

"Tell me what it was like for you when I left," he said. He might as well hear it. He would have to hear it so he could help her get past it, because the fact that she wasn't touching him, aside from letting his head lie in her lap, was telling. She still had some reservations.

"Someone took away my best friend," she said. "Only it wasn't like he was stolen. It was like he ran away from me. He went as quickly and as far away as he could. He went to a different world. I had no one to tell my secrets to. No one to tell me ridiculous tales just to make me laugh. No one to talk to about the horrible happenings in my life…" Her voice tapered off.

"My tales are not ridiculous," he grumbled playfully. He lay on his back and looked up into her blue eyes. "I'm so sorry," he said. "Can you ever forgive me?"

Her hand finally lifted, as though of its own accord, and she began to slowly run her fingers through his hair. "Perhaps someday," she said, but a smile broke across her face.

He snorted. "I don't expect you to make it easy."

Her eyes met his. "I'd say I've made it pretty easy so far."

"So," he prompted, "there was no one else back home who took your attention?"

She looked away from him for a moment, so he jostled her arm. She looked down at him and lightly tapped his forehead. "Be quiet and look at the stars," she said.

"I'd so much rather look at you," he breathed, cupping her cheeks with his hands. She looked into his eyes, her hair falling around her face. He brought a lock of it to his nose and sniffed it. She smelled like sunshine. She always had.

"Stop looking at me," she groused, but she turned her head and kissed the palm of his hand. The heat shot straight to his groin, and he raised a knee in hopes she wouldn't notice how she affected him.

"Cece," he whispered.

"What?" she whispered back dramatically.

"I want to kiss you," he said softly.

"You already did that," she replied just as quietly.

"I want to do it again and again, until I get it right."

"I'd say that last kiss was right." Her skin flushed and she closed her eyes.

"I was afraid I would do it wrong," he confessed. "I've wanted to kiss you since the moment I saw you in the ballroom. And every day before that. Every day we've been apart."

"That kiss was a welcome surprise," she admitted. "But you didn't give me much of a choice."

"We can practice," he suggested, a grin tugging at the corners of his lips.

"Maybe," she said with a wistful sigh.

"Maybe?" Certainly she wasn't serious.

"I think this courtship thing is supposed to go slowly."

If it went any more slowly, Marcus would lose his mind. He'd tasted her. He'd finally kissed her and had her back in his arms. And now she wanted to go slowly. "How slow?" he asked.

"I don't know." She shrugged. "Perhaps I should ask your mother how things are done here." She laughed. "Though perhaps not about kissing specifically."

"Are you serious? My mother would be overjoyed that I'm kissing you." He pulled her hand down to lie flat on his chest and covered it with his. Her fingers played in his hair. "She helped me make a list of things I could do to win you back."

"And just what was on this list?"

"I'll never tell."

She slapped his chest. "Tell me!" she cried.

"I may need to use that list in the future," he said with a laugh. "In the odd instance that I make you angry at me."

"I would say that's a given," she warned.

"You won't leave me, will you?"

She quieted for a moment, "Will you leave me?"

"Never again," he swore.

"Promise?" she asked, her voice quiet.

"I swear on my life." He sat up and turned to her, sliding as close as he could without pulling her inside him. He tugged her legs over his lap and turned her to face him.

"Marcus," she complained.

Her skirt showed her trim, silk-clad ankle, and Marcus moved to toss her dress back down. "I'll never make it to the reading of the banns," he swore.

"What?" Her brows drew together.

"In this world, you have to declare your intent to marry. And there's this thing called 'the reading of the banns' that takes three weeks. If you don't want to wait, we can get a special license."

"Did I say I would marry you?" she teased.

"I'll drag you kicking and screaming to Scotland and marry you over an anvil if I have to," he warned. He lowered his voice to a whisper as he cupped her cheek in his palm. "I think we should practice that kissing thing from earlier, just to be sure we did it right."

His lips touched hers, and she sat forward to reach

him. Marcus was almost certain he couldn't do this
wrong, but her response to him was a salve to his soul.
She murmured against his mouth, and when he drew
her bottom lip between his, she gasped and wrapped
her arms around his neck, hitching herself higher into
his lap.

❦

Ronald stood in the foliage and looked everywhere
but at Marcus and Cecelia. He kicked at a rock with
the toe of his boot and started to walk away. But when
he turned, he bumped directly into a body. A small
body. One proportionally his size. One that smelled
like violets. One that smelled like home. "Millicent,"
he gasped. "What are you doing here?"

He hadn't seen Milly in months, and by the look
on her face, she didn't intend to let him forget it.
"Cece sent for me," Milly admitted. "What are you
doing here?"

"I've brought a mission for Marcus. What kind of a
mission are you on?"

"You know I can't tell you," she began.

"You know you will," he cajoled, stepping closer
to her. He reached out to touch her, and she swayed
toward him. "Are you well?" he asked. He lowered
his hand just before he embarrassed himself and
brought the gnome to rest in his arms. "Tell me,"
he prompted.

"It has to do with her father."

"Is he unwell?"

She shook her head. "I can't tell you."

"Will it ruin Marcus?" Ronald asked.

Milly put her hands on her hips and glared at him. "You worry about your family, and I'll worry about mine," she snapped.

"Milly," he cajoled. "They just found their way back together." He pushed the foliage to the side. "Look at them."

Marcus and Cecelia were locked in a passionate embrace. "Go and get your faerie, will you?" Milly asked. "I need to take mine with me." She shot him a glance. "In other words, get yours off mine."

Ronald would have liked nothing more than to have his whatever on hers. But he assumed she meant Marcus and Cecelia. He wouldn't separate them. Not right now.

"I won't like what you're planning to do, will I?" he asked.

"You won't like it at all," she said with a heavy sigh.

"There's no way around it?"

"None."

"Will she be coming back?"

"I know not the future," she said softly.

He reached out and took her hand in his, rubbing his thumb along the back of it. "When can I see you again?"

She shook her head. She nodded toward Marcus and Cecelia. "I'll come back for her later."

"Please don't."

"I can't help it. She's my family. I have to take care of her. The Trusted Few have called."

"She better be here when he wakes up tomorrow," he growled.

"We shall see," she breathed.

"Young love," he said with a laugh that sounded forced, even to his own ears.

"I don't remember what that's like," Milly whispered.

Ronald did. He turned to pull Milly to him, but she was gone.

Nine

CECELIA CLOSED THE DOOR AND LEANED HEAVILY against it. She raised a hand to her lips and smiled. No one had ever told her that kissing in the garden could leave a person with aching lips. Among other parts. Marcus had pulled her into his lap and proceeded to kiss her senseless. He'd licked and nibbled and sucked, and then he'd done it some more. She laughed lightly to herself and spun around.

"Had a good night, did you?" a voice said from her window. Cecelia raised a hand to her heart, startled at the sudden interruption.

"Milly," she breathed. "Thank goodness it's you," she said. "You'll never believe what happened."

"I'm quite aware of what happened, miss," Milly said. "I stopped in the garden to find you." The gnome glared across the room.

"What?" Cecelia asked, as heat crept up her cheeks. "We didn't do anything wrong."

Milly ground her teeth. "Wrong is in the eye of the beholder," she warned.

"It was just a kiss," Cecelia grumbled. "You could pretend to be happy for me."

"I would be happy for you if I thought your relationship had a chance to flourish." Milly's frown was disturbing.

"What do you mean?"

"You're needed at home," Milly said. "There's no time to pack your things. We'll be traveling tonight."

"What?" Cecelia gasped. "I can't possibly go home now. I'm not supposed to return until the moonful."

"It's your father," Milly said quietly. Her eyes filled with tears. Milly had been with Cecelia's family her whole life. She sniffed the tears back and straightened her spine. "Your father is unwell."

"What's wrong with him?"

"He's unwell," Milly said with a shake of his head. "And he's unable to fulfill his duties as one of the Trusted Few."

"Is he drinking again?" Cecelia asked. Of course he was. Milly's face revealed every thought that entered her pretty little head.

"He's unwell."

"He was fine when I left. Dry as a desert in summer. He hasn't drunk for more than a month." Her father had been surprisingly healthy, not the way he was in the months following her mother's death.

"He took your leaving hard," Milly admitted.

"But he knew I would be back."

"Your father doesn't like to be alone," Milly said.

That much was true. He never had liked to be alone. When Cecelia's mother was alive, he'd drink occasionally. But he was a funny drunk. He wasn't angry or mean. He simply drank, had a really good time, and then went to sleep. Her mother would tuck him into bed, and then she would apologize to the community for whatever he'd done or said, and then he would not drink for a few days.

After her mother died, he'd changed. Drinking no longer made him amusing. He was cruel. He did things that were disturbing, like break things. And he got into a fight or two. To tell the truth, Cecelia was relieved when they'd asked her to go to the other world to help out with Marcus. She'd assumed Marcus's grandmother had called for her specifically to give her some respite from her father. Everyone who lived among the fae knew how desperately she needed a holiday. Was that too much to ask?

"What did he do this time?" Cecelia bit out.

"He harmed someone," Milly admitted.

"Did he punch someone? It wasn't Mr. Randall, was it?" When they drank together, the two of them could get into all sorts of scrapes.

"It was Mr. Randall, but your father didn't punch him. It was worse."

"How much worse?" Cecelia dropped onto the side of the bed, her limbs suddenly as heavy as two anvils. She'd gone from buoyant to weighted in a matter of moments. Only her father had a knack for doing that.

"Mr. Randall was injured in their altercation. And they had to use the healing waters to help him."

The healing waters were for emergencies only. Only the dying were permitted to drink from the pool.

Milly grimaced as she went on. "They fought, and

Mr. Randall hit his head." She held up a hand to stop Cecelia's next words. "He's recovering, but slowly. And the Trusted Few have decided not to let this be brushed under the rug. Your father will stand trial."

"But it was an accident," Cecelia protested.

"They don't consider it to be an accident when it happens this many times."

"He's just lonely," Cecelia rationalized. She could rationalize this, couldn't she? Her father was a harmless sot. Most days. She raised a hand to her own cheek. There was the time… But that was neither here nor there.

"The Trusted Few have called for you to come home. Tonight."

Cecelia nodded. "Let me write a note for Marcus," she said.

The wind that the Trusted Few had sent for her blew through the open window. "We don't have time. They're sending the wind to pick you up."

The wind only swirled, carrying the fae back and forth from the land of the fae, on the night of the moonful, unless there were special circumstances. "This is worse than I thought."

"Yes, it is," Milly confirmed. Her face fell. "It's pretty bad."

"What about his seat with the Trusted Few?"

"It's falling to you."

Cecelia laid a hand upon her chest. "Me?" she cried.

"You're his only child. His seat automatically falls to you."

"I'm seven-and-twenty. I can't rule the land of the fae. Not like those crusty old men." She couldn't rule alongside them. She simply couldn't. It wouldn't work out.

"They wouldn't be so adamant about this if Marcus hadn't given up his seat," Milly informed her.

Cecelia had nearly forgotten that Marcus had given up his place within the governing body of their world.

"With his seat empty, they can continue, though they'll be limping. But with two seats empty, they cannot continue." Milly cocked her head to the side. "Do you intend to relinquish your seat?"

Cecelia raised a hand to her mouth and nibbled absently at a fingernail. She had a lot of decisions to make. "Can I do that?" she asked.

"You can do anything you want." Milly's voice showed no inflection. And that was telling all by itself.

The wind tugged at the hem of Cecelia's dress, and her hair began to pull toward the window. "The wind is persistent tonight," she said.

"Yes." Milly arched a brow at her. "It won't last long. If you don't catch the wind now, we'll have to go by way of the fish."

Milly went by way of the fish all the time. But Cecelia had never done so. "I suppose we should hurry," Cecelia said. "Will you come back tomorrow with a note for Marcus?"

"If possible, yes," Milly said.

Cecelia nodded.

"There's no time to gather your things," Milly warned.

"Blast it," Cecelia swore. She took Milly's hand and let the gnome guide her to the window.

"Jump with me," Milly said.

Cecelia arched a brow at her.

"Have I ever let you down?" Milly asked.

Cecelia threw one leg over the windowsill and jumped. The wind caught her, swirling her hair and her dress until she settled within it. Milly held tightly to her hand.

"I'm sorry it's come to this," Milly said.

Cecelia could barely hear her over the wind. Over the breaking of her own heart. "I'm sorry too," she whispered. She'd never been sorrier.

Marcus stepped into the breakfast room with a smile on his face. His lips were still tender from the night before, and he drew his lower lip between his teeth to worry it. He'd never imagined that kissing Cecelia could feel quite so... right. The feel of her in his arms, and those little noises she'd made. The way that her breasts pressed against his chest while her hands played in the hair at the nape of his neck. It was making him hard all over just thinking about it.

Marcus froze in the doorway as Ainsley and Allen sprang apart. Ainsley looked down at her plate, and Allen looked decidedly uncomfortable.

"Do you want me to leave and come in again?" he asked. A grin tugged at his lips.

"That won't be necessary," Allen said. He smiled at Ainsley from beneath lowered eyelids, and her face mirrored his, all rosy and uncomfortable.

"The two of you are thick as thieves, I see," Marcus said as he filled a plate at the sideboard.

Allen grinned widely. "Do you really want to talk about relationships right now, Marcus?" he questioned.

"Why shouldn't we?" Marcus asked.

"Because my bedroom window just happens to overlook the garden," Allen said with a raised brow.

"Oh," Marcus said, a laugh erupting from his chest. "I hope you didn't overlook the garden for very long."

"Long enough," Allen murmured. He reached beneath the table to take Ainsley's hand, and she turned even rosier. "I hope you plan to marry the chit," he said.

"She's not a chit. She's to be my wife. As soon as she'll have me."

"Congratulations," Ainsley said with a cheeky grin.

"Thank you," Marcus said back. He couldn't stop smiling today. He just couldn't. His life was too perfect. He had his family. He had the fae and his missions. He had Cecelia, and he had his parents' love. Things couldn't get any better. "Have you seen Cecelia?" he asked.

Ainsley shot a worried glance toward Allen.

"What's wrong?" Marcus asked.

"Nothing that we know of," Ainsley said cryptically.

"Then why the long face?"

"Ronald and Milly are here. And Cecelia is gone."

Marcus wiped his mouth with his napkin. "Gone?"

Ainsley looked down at her plate.

"Gone where?" Marcus asked, throwing his napkin down.

"We don't know," Ainsley replied. "Milly and Ronald are in with your parents."

"Where?" He jumped to his feet.

"In the morning room," Allen said. He looked down at Ainsley and shook his head. "Don't say any more. You'll worry him needlessly."

Ainsley just nodded.

Marcus strode toward the morning room. Cecelia was probably there with the gnomes and his parents. She had to be.

He stepped into the room to find his father pacing from one end of the room to the other. "Someone had better tell me what's wrong." Marcus snapped. "And it had better be soon. Where is Cecelia?"

Ronald sat in the big, purple high-backed chair and swung his feet, eating a scone. "Millicent is the only one who knows where she is, and she's not telling." The gnome began to grumble. "Makes me want to toss her over my knee."

"I'd like to see you try," Milly spit out.

"Would you two stop it?" his father said with a heavy sigh. "This is getting us nowhere." He turned to face Marcus. "It appears as though Cecelia has returned home."

Marcus's knees buckled beneath him and he sunk into a chair. "What?" he breathed. After the night before, she wouldn't have left. And she wouldn't have gone without saying good-bye and telling him when she would return. Would she?

"She received a summons late last night," Milly said. Ronald was the only one who called her Millicent. Marcus still didn't understand that.

"A summons home?" Marcus asked.

"A summons to the sit on the throne as the Queen of England," Ronald said caustically. Then he rolled his eyes. "Of course, it was a summons home."

"Ronald," Marcus's father warned.

The gnome settled down. But then he faced Milly. "I asked you not to do this."

"It couldn't be avoided," Milly said, her gaze downcast.

"She left," Marcus breathed.

"Yes," his father confirmed.

"But she'll be back," Marcus said. Of course she would be back. She wouldn't leave him. Not after last night.

"I sincerely doubt it," Milly said.

She'd left him. She'd really done it. She'd sat in his lap and kissed him, and they'd talked long into the night. And then she'd gone straight to her room.

"Did she leave this morning?" Marcus asked.

"Last night," Milly said. "Late."

After their talk. After they'd spent so much time wrapped in one another's arms. "She's gone," he said aloud.

"Marcus," his mother began, her voice soft. "I'm so sorry."

"So am I." Marcus got to his feet, although he worried his knees would betray him.

He was sorry he'd ever kissed her. Because now their last kiss together would be the kiss he'd never forget. He'd relive every moment with her in his arms for the rest of his life. But she was gone. This time, she was the one who'd left. Was she still angry over what had happened before? It was the only way to explain her sudden disappearance.

She'd wanted to leave him. To make him feel as wretched as he'd made her feel. Only she'd done so with a purpose? That couldn't be the case. She wouldn't be so cruel. Would she? He quit the room. His mother and father followed him down the corridor until he turned the corner. He needed some time to think.

❦

Milly looked at Ronald, whose anger flashed in his eyes like sparks from the fireplace. "You should have told him," Ronald said.

"I can't. They're my family. Their secrets are mine."

"I wish they weren't mine."

"What do you mean?"

"I wish I didn't know their bloody secrets."

"I don't understand." Ronald had always been cryptic, but she could usually keep up.

"I saw the bruise on her cheek. A week after Marcus left. Her father, in a temper." He patted his cheek as though he could feel it. "You shouldn't have sent her back there."

"She's strong. She can take care of herself. And her father is not a bad man. He just has a problem."

"A problem he can't control," Ronald shouted.

Milly startled. But Ronald didn't scare her. She was more afraid that someone would hear. "No one else knows about that."

"She covered the bruise well. But I could still see it," Ronald admitted. "I'm worried for her."

"I'm on my way back there now," Milly said, getting to her feet.

"But even you can't watch her all the time."

"I can watch her most of the time."

"Her father needs some help."

"So does she," Milly said. "Do you think Marcus will go to her?"

"I think Marcus is hurt by her disappearance. And I'm going to tell him if you don't."

"You can't!" Milly cried. "It's not your secret to tell. It's hers."

"She won't ever tell him."

"She gets a seat with the Trusted Few."

"If she can't govern her own life, how will she ever govern the land of the fae?"

"I don't know," Milly said quietly. "I need to get back to her."

"Be careful," Ronald warned.

Milly nodded.

"I'll miss you," Ronald said softly.

Tears pricked at the backs of Milly's lashes. She nodded and threw herself from the open window. Sometimes, she wished for an easier life. But then she wondered what on earth she would do with one.

Ten

CECELIA CLOSED THE FRONT DOOR BEHIND HER AND walked into the drafty old manor house. She'd only been gone a few days, yet already it appeared disused. Perhaps it was just because she didn't want to be there. She wanted to be anywhere but there.

"Father!" she called out as she walked down the corridor toward his study. Before her mother had died, Cecelia would have laughed all the way down the corridor because she knew she'd find her mother perched on the edge of her father's desk, and her father would be trying to make *her* laugh. Now her father didn't laugh at all. Nor did he try to make anyone else do so. She raised a hand to her cheek.

He couldn't help what he'd become, she supposed, but she didn't have to like it, did she?

"Father!" she called again. A servant bustled into the corridor with a wet rag in her hand that smelled vaguely of spirits.

"Miss," the house faerie said, dropping into a curtsy. She pulled the study door shut as Cecelia tried to look around her into the room. "I didn't expect you to come home today. Is everything all right?" she asked.

The maid took Cecelia's elbow to guide her from the door. But Cecelia stood firm. "Where is my father?" she asked.

She reached for the door handle, but the maid covered it with her hand. "You don't need to go in there today, miss," she warned quietly. She wouldn't look Cecelia in the eye.

"Is he foxed?" Cecelia asked.

"Well," the maid began.

"Tell me!" Cecelia snapped.

"Beyond foxed, miss," the maid admitted. She rushed on to say, "But you need not worry yourself with it. We have it all under control."

Not worry herself with it? How could she not worry herself with it? It was her father, for goodness' sake. He seemed to want nothing more than to pickle himself on a regular basis.

"Step to the side," Cecelia ordered.

The maid danced in her place.

"Now," Cecelia said succinctly. She didn't need to raise her voice. Not doing so in this situation was just as powerful. The maid took one small step to the side.

Cecelia turned the knob and opened the door slowly. "I told you to get out!" her father bellowed. Then a glass smashed on the wall right beside her head.

"Father!" Cecelia warned.

The broken man who sat crumpled at the desk wasn't her father. He wasn't. His eyes weren't laughing, and his face was tarnished by days of beard growth. He may as well have died when her mother did. Sometimes Cecelia wished he had.

"Cece?" he asked. "Is that you?" He could barely hold his eyes open.

"Yes, it's me."

He reached out a hand to brush a lock of hair from his forehead. He grabbed her hand and pulled it to his cheek, which was wet with tears.

"You left me," he said softly.

"I'm back now," Cece whispered, shushing him. "Everything will be fine."

"Where did you go?" her father asked.

"I had a mission," she said.

"Did it go well?" he asked. He propped his chin in his hand and spoke to her with his eyes closed. It was all he could do to hold his head up. Apparently, she wasn't worthy of him even opening his eyes.

"As well as could be expected," she sighed.

"I thought you left me," he said softly. His voice broke. "Just like she did." He swiped at his eyes. Her father was emotional when he was foxed.

"I have to leave from time to time," she warned. His chin fell off his hand, and she slid beneath his arm to help him to his feet. If she wasn't mistaken, he would soon fall on the floor and then he'd be there for the rest of the night, since she wouldn't be able to get him up. Since he had a tendency to get violent, the footmen wouldn't come to help. Not anymore.

"Did you see your fellow?" he asked, looking down at her as she struggled with his weight toward the door.

"I don't have a fellow, Father," she said.

"Marcus? Didn't you see him?" he asked as she sat him down on the edge of his bed and bent to pull off his boots.

"I saw him," she said as he fell back onto the bed. "He wants to marry me," she said more to herself than to her father.

Her father's eyes were closed, and his head lolled to the side. "Can't leave me, Cece," he murmured.

"I know." Cecelia knew. She knew all too well.

Marcus paced across his chambers, trying to figure out what the devil he'd done wrong. She'd been so soft and warm in his arms the night before. What had changed from that perfect moment to the sun's awakening in the sky? Perhaps she'd had a chance to reconsider. But even if she had, she should have left a note.

A knock on his door jerked him from his pacing. "Enter," he called absently.

Tatten, his father's butler, opened the door. "Your father would like to see you in his study, sir," the man said.

Why would his father want him now? "Did he happen to say what he wanted?"

The butler shook his head. "He did not. He has his steward with him, and they were deliberating over some ledgers."

The last thing Marcus wanted to do was pore over his father's books. But now he remembered that he had an appointment with his father to learn more about the running of the estate. "I'll be there in a moment," he said to Tatten.

Tatten looked about the room. "Will you be staying at Ramsdale House much longer, sir?" he asked.

Marcus's head shot up. "Why do you ask?"

The butler arched a brow. "I was inquiring so I can find an appropriate valet for you, sir, if you intend to remain."

"Did you get one for Allen?"

"The younger Mr. Thorne uses your father's valet when he's in residence." Of course he did. He was at home here after all. He'd grown up here. Marcus had not.

Marcus shook his head. "I won't be staying long." Not now that Cecelia was gone. He'd be going back to his bachelor's quarters. Until then, he could shave himself, couldn't he? He hadn't become so high in the instep as to need help with every little thing, had he?

"As you wish," the butler said.

"Do you know where Miss Hewitt's room is located, Tatten?" Marcus asked suddenly.

Tatten stood a little taller. "I know where every room is located, sir."

"Show me," Marcus said, striding toward the door.

The butler fell into step quietly beside him and motioned toward the guest wing. "She's not in the household wing?"

"No sir," Tatten said.

"Well, hurry up about it," Marcus urged. This was the first remnant of hope he'd grabbed hold of all day. Perhaps if he took a look at her room, he might understand a little more about why she left.

Marcus followed until Tatten stopped at a doorway, and then he knocked softly and pushed the door open.

Marcus held up a hand to stay him. "That will be all, Tatten," he said.

"As you wish," Tatten said flatly. He bowed and then turned away down the corridor. Marcus closed the door behind him.

"What the devil were you thinking, Cece?" he whispered to himself.

Her brush still lay on the dressing table, along with a neat stack of hairpins and a bottle of perfume. He pulled the stopper and sniffed. It smelled like sunshine. Like her. He put it back on the table. Her trunk lay at the foot of the bed, and the top was still open, her shoes and other odds and ends littering the interior. Her dresses still hung in the wardrobe, several of them in fact.

How odd that Cecelia would go home and leave all of her belongings behind. Perhaps she planned to return? And to return soon, if the status of her belongings was any indication.

The door creaked open and Marcus turned to scold Tatten, but a dark brunette head came through the doorway. "Marcus!" Ainsley cried, laying a hand above her heart.

"Ainsley," Marcus muttered absently. "What brings you here?" he asked as he picked up a slipper from the trunk and dangled it from his fingers.

"Not molesting Cecelia's things, that's for certain." She put her hands on her hips and glared at him. "You should respect her privacy, Marcus," she warned.

"Why are you here?" Marcus asked again.

Ainsley sighed heavily. "I just wanted to see if it was true."

"If what was true?"

She scratched her head. "If she really left," Ainsley clarified. "I'd hoped the gnomes were wrong. She needed to be here. More than anyone else, she needed to spend some time in this world."

What the devil did she mean by that? He dropped the slipper back into the trunk. "Did she say anything to you?" he asked. He watched Ainsley's face closely.

She winced. "It's what Cecelia doesn't say that you have to pay attention to."

"Why would she leave her things here?" he asked.

"That would only happen if there were an emergency and she had to leave," Ainsley said.

"What could be such an emergency that she would leave without saying good-bye?"

"Only the worst kind," Ainsley whispered.

"Tell me what you know, Ainsley," he warned.

But she was already walking out the door. "It's not my secret to tell."

"Does she have a fiancé at home?" Marcus blurted out. Perhaps there really was someone in the land of the fae.

"No one at home has her attention the way you do, Marcus," Ainsley said. She knew something. Marcus could tell.

"Please tell me what you know," Marcus pleaded. Much more of this and he would be on his knees begging.

"They sent the wind for her."

Marcus spun around quickly. "Last night?"

"Yes, late."

The fae only sent the wind to and from the land of the fae in dire emergencies. "What was the emergency?"

"I don't know," Ainsley whispered, squeezing her eyes shut.

"But she, specifically, was needed." It was like putting together the pieces of a puzzle. But too many pieces were missing.

Ainsley nodded. "Apparently." She met his gaze. "Things have been different at home since her mother died."

Cecelia's mother had died? When?

He didn't even get to ask the question before Ainsley said, "Right after you left six months ago."

Marcus sank down onto the side of bed, afraid once again that his legs would not support him. Cecelia hadn't told him that her mother had died. It had been more than six months, and he hadn't even paid his respects. "How?"

"A carriage accident when she was on a mission in this world."

"How is her father doing?"

"Poorly."

"Is that why she had to go back? For him? He's not ill, is he?"

"He has been ill for a while. But it's not my story to tell." She squeezed her lips shut and refused to say more.

"Can you tell me anything?" Marcus was desperate.

"Can you go to the land of the fae? Can you set all this to the side and go to her?"

"I can't go until the moonful, if then." He couldn't walk away from his obligations to find a woman who might or might not want to see him. He had too much to learn here. And he wasn't at all certain of Cecelia's feelings toward him.

"Then you don't deserve her," Ainsley spit out.

Then she turned on her heel and quit the room.

"Good God," Marcus breathed. He scrubbed a hand down his face. "What do I do now?"

❧

Ainsley barreled directly into a hard chest and threw her hands out to catch herself. But strong arms wrapped tightly around her instead. "Ainsley?" the man asked. "What's wrong?"

It wasn't an aging butler who'd caught her. It wasn't a startled maid. If anyone had to see her upset, she supposed it might as well be Allen. "Nothing," she squeaked.

He set her back from him momentarily and looked down at her, his dark eyes piercing a little too deeply for comfort. "You lie poorly," he warned. Then he pulled her back into his arms and didn't insist she say a word. He didn't try to coax any thoughts from her. He didn't try to trick her into baring her soul. But that just made her want to do it more.

He inhaled deeply and held her tightly against him. She fit beneath his chin like he was made for her. Was he? She lifted her chin and looked up at him. "You want to kiss me, don't you?" she teased.

"No," he blurted out, setting her back from him. Ainsley felt the loss of him immediately.

"Yes, you do," she teased.

"Where did you learn to do that?" he asked.

"Do what?" She had no idea to what he was referring.

"You shock people so that they'll forget what they were trying to wheedle out of you."

"You were trying to wheedle something out of me?"

"Not yet," he said, a grin forming on his lips.

"You want to wheedle something out of me."

He cocked his head to the side as his brows drew together sternly. "I want a lot of things from you," he said. "But I intend for you to give them to me willingly. Otherwise, I don't want them."

Ainsley's heart leaped. "You have a plan?"

"A rather decisive one," he admitted.

"Tell me about it," she whispered.

He lowered his voice, too. "If I did that, I wouldn't have the element of surprise, would I?" He nodded toward Cecelia's closed door. "Where were you rushing off from?"

"Marcus," Ainsley said on a heavy sigh. "He's a dolt."

"I won't argue that." He grinned. "What did he do that was so doltish?"

"It's what he won't do." She shook her head. "You wouldn't understand."

"Try me," he said.

"Well, Cecelia is gone. And I think he should rush off to find her. To help her."

"Does she need help?"

"More than you could ever know," Ainsley whispered.

"Is she in danger?" His face grew serious.

"I can't tell her secrets." She crossed her arms and glared at him. But he didn't turn away from her, not like men usually did. He stood his ground.

"If that's the best you can do, you don't stand a chance in this relationship," he warned.

"This is a relationship?" she squeaked.

"It will be," he said.

Ainsley's belly dipped into her drawers. "All right," she replied.

"All right, you'll tell me what's wrong?"

"No. All right, this is a relationship." A grin tugged at her lips. She'd never wanted anything more.

"Good," he said, slinging an arm around her shoulders as he began to lead her down the corridor.

"Shouldn't we kiss on it to make it official?" she asked, her cheeks burning.

"Later," he said. "Right now, we need to help Marcus."

"How do you propose we do that?"

"We don't. But Mother and Father will know what to do."

Allen stopped at the morning room and stuck his head inside. "Could we talk with you for a moment?" he asked his mother. She set her embroidery to the side and motioned for them to sit.

Allen looked at Ainsley quickly.

"First, I plan to court Miss Packard," Allen said, looking his father in the eye.

Lady Ramsdale's face glowed as she clasped her hands to her chest.

But he rushed on. "And Marcus is an idiot. He's in need of an intervention."

Lady Ramsdale was slightly taken aback. "I assumed he would rush off to the land of the fae to retrieve his lady."

Allen shook his head. "No, he's being a bit thickheaded."

"What else is new?" his mother asked, pinching the bridge of her nose between her thumb and forefinger.

"He needs steering."

"His sisters are good at steering."

"His sisters could wrap him up in spiderwebs and haul him back to the land of the fae," Ainsley muttered.

Lady Ramsdale snickered and held up one finger. "I believe we can do better than that."

"I'd kind of like to see him tied up in"—he looked at Ainsley—"spiderwebs, you say?"

Ainsley nodded. "They're tremendously sticky."

"I can imagine," Allen said, visibly impressed with her knowledge. She grinned.

"So, what would you like to do?" Lady Ramsdale asked her son.

"I have a plan," Allen began slowly.

Eleven

MARCUS HAD THE WEIGHT OF THE WORLD ON HIS shoulders. He'd spent the morning with his father's steward and the afternoon riding with the foreman in the fields, taking a look at the land. He'd met with his tenants and made a list of the things they needed. One needed another roof. And still another had a drainage problem, with standing water in his fields. He'd met their wives, and he'd given treats to their children. He was tired, yet now he had to dress for dinner with his family. At least he'd stayed busy. He hadn't had more than a moment to worry about Cecelia or the fact that she'd returned home without him.

Marcus dressed for dinner and then stepped down the main staircase, but when he got to the bottom, he stopped, because milling about the front entryway was his entire family.

His mother supervised the stacking of trunks, and his sisters each held at least one of their offspring in their arms, or two in Claire's case. At least the infants weren't screaming at the moment.

Ainsley riffled through a trunk of her own and then tugged on her gloves.

The Duke of Robinsworth looked bored as his servants brought his trunks in through the front door, and Lord Phineas looked content as he kissed his wife on the forehead.

"Are you going somewhere?" Marcus asked.

His mother looked up. "Oh, yes, darling. We've planned an impromptu trip. We hope you don't mind. Cook will serve dinner to you in your chambers, if you've need of it."

Need of dinner? He hadn't eaten all day. Of course he had need of dinner. "Where are you going?"

His mother smiled. "We're going to the land of the fae for a bit. It's of no importance. We won't be gone long. You'll barely miss us."

"What's the occasion?" Marcus asked.

"We just remembered it's your grandmother's birthday. And the only thing she wanted this year was to eat her birthday dinner at her own table." His mother laughed. "Such a simple request, really. We couldn't tell her no."

He made a sweeping motion across the room. "You're all going?"

His mother beamed. "I mentioned to your father that we should go, just the two of us, and then we sent word to Sophia and Claire about our proposed absences, and they sent word that they would like to go too. And we can't leave the children behind." She bent and placed a kiss to Lucius's head.

"Will you take him?" Claire asked.

"Absolutely not," Marcus said. With all the women

in the room, certainly one of them could relieve Claire of some of her burden. The lad's father took him instead, laying him upon his shoulder.

Lady Ramsdale bustled forward and kissed Marcus's cheek quickly. "We'll miss you, darling. But we'll be back soon. You'll be fine without us, won't you?"

"Of course," he said quietly. "But how do you plan to go to the land of the fae today? By way of the fish?"

"It was actually Claire's idea." His mother beamed. "We'd originally planned to go by way of the fish, since that's how we went last time."

"We're going through one of my paintings," Claire chirped. "Then we can return whenever we like."

"Won't the Trusted Few be angry?" Marcus asked. They liked nothing more than order. And this certainly wasn't orderly.

"They'll have no idea how we secured passage. We'll just be there one day."

Allen chimed in, "And I've never been, so I'm looking forward to it."

What? "Allen's going?"

"Yes," his mother said with a smile.

"But he's not fae."

"Neither are Robinsworth, Lord Phineas, or Lady Anne." Lady Anne, the Duke of Robinsworth's daughter, poked her head out from behind Sophia.

"Hello," she chirped.

Marcus's mother's brow furrowed. "You'll be all right here by yourself, won't you?" she asked.

"I suppose," Marcus said quietly. They were all going to the land of the fae and leaving him behind?

"Excellent, darling. We'll see you when we return.

Do send word if you need anything." She turned and motioned to a servant, who propped a floor-to-ceiling-sized painting against the wall. It was a painting of their manor house in the land of the fae. It was home. Claire went first, carrying one of the babies. Then she held her hand out and took the rest of them, one by one. They each called out salutations as they exited the world of the humans. The servants even bustled through with their trunks.

"I'm a little nervous," Allen admitted when it was his turn. But Ainsley took his hand and smiled broadly at him. It appeared as though Allen would follow her anywhere, and then he did.

The room was quickly emptying of people, and Marcus felt nearly as empty as the room. They all were going home. They were going to the one place he dearly wanted to be.

Yet he had obligations here, didn't he?

His dad looked at him and said, "The steward will be waiting for instructions from me and will take care of anything that comes up. But you can guide him if you feel the need to do so."

Marcus nodded. "But…" he started.

Then it was his father's turn. "I'll see you when we return," he said, and he clapped Marcus on the shoulder.

The room was empty. His entire family was gone. Even Ainsley and Allen were gone, along with his two younger sisters, who'd never been to the land of the fae. Good Lord, the fae didn't know what they were up against. His family would wreak all sorts of havoc. Havoc of unmentionable proportions. Marcus scrubbed a hand down his face.

He turned in a circle, looking at the empty room. But that's all this place was. An empty room. Suddenly, a hand appeared in the painting, reaching out. He knew it was Claire's. Did she think they'd left someone behind? They hadn't. They'd taken everyone. Except him.

Marcus steeled himself, adjusted his waistcoat, and reached for her hand. It was risky, he knew, but he dearly wanted to go. It was just for a short while, right? And they could come back as easily as they'd left. He clasped Claire's hand in his and she gave it a gentle squeeze, and then he walked into the painting with his family. He left it all behind. He left this world, his obligations, and his destiny. And he went home.

When he stepped into the painting, he took a deep breath and came out on the other side. He looked up at the stately old mansion and took another, fuller breath. He could breathe again. He was home. He looked around. His mother laid a shocked hand upon her chest. "Marcus, what on earth are you doing here?" she asked.

"I thought I might join you," he said.

His mother smiled broadly at him, took his face in her hands, and kissed his cheek. "I'm so glad. But won't you be missed? All of your obligations?"

"It's nothing that can't keep," he said. It was. Right?

❦

Cecelia knew the moment the air shifted at the dinner table. Her father had gone beyond the point of abashedly tipsy. He was now obnoxiously foxed. It had started with a sherry before dinner. Then he moved on to whiskey, since sherry was a lad's drink, he'd said. She'd tried to steer him toward something as innocuous as wine and had even asked the footman to make a pot of tea. But her father would have none of it.

"I can hold my spirits," he slurred.

It had been the most trying of days. She'd battled with him at every turn and had to cajole even their most stalwart of servants to remain with the household. "This is the last time, miss," they'd said. And it had been more than one. The butler met her eyes across the dining room. The pity she saw there shocked her. It was like a stab to the heart. This man they'd once revered, and her, their darling girl, the girl they'd all played a part in raising—they all pitied her now. And pity was something she simply could not tolerate.

"You should go to bed, Father," she warned.

The butler stepped forward and raised his brows in question. She shook her head quickly in the negative. "Not yet," she mouthed. He was one of the few people who could handle her father. But he was also much more likely to get punched than any of the others. Probably because he didn't give up. If it took overpowering her father to get the job done, then that's what he would do. He was a reed of an old man, but he was stalwart, and she had a feeling she would be in his debt before the night was out.

"I miss her," her father said as he lifted his glass to his lips and tipped it back. It was empty, but that didn't stop him from trying to drain the last drop.

He clunked the glass on the table, signaling for more in the rudest way possible. She shook her head at the butler.

"It's time for bed, Father. Things will look brighter in the morning." Cecelia pushed her uneaten food to the side and stood up.

"I'll go to bed when I'm good and ready," he said, getting to his feet. He nearly fell over, and the butler stepped forward to catch him. But her father was already belligerent, so he shoved the kind man to the side.

"Father," she warned. She made her voice purposefully chipper. "Mother once told me a story about you taking her to the top of Mount Angel. Can you tell me the story while we walk?"

He scratched the top of his head, his eyes glassy and unfocused. But a smile broke across his lips. It was a watery smile, but a smile nonetheless.

"Can you tell me the story, Father?" she asked.

"I dragged your mother all the way to the top of that blasted mountain. She complained the whole way. But we got to the top, and the sun was setting, and the hues were all golden and yellow. Then they turned to purple, and we sat in the grass and planned our lives."

He heaved the glass in his hand against the wall, and it shattered, the pieces falling like broken dreams to the Aubusson rug.

"Why did you do that?" Cecelia cried, covering her head with her hands. He didn't have to be this way. He chose to be this way. He chose it every time he took a drink. Every time he let the memories overwhelm him.

"She left me," he said, smashing his fist into the wall. He pulled back scuffed knuckles and grimaced at what he'd done. But he didn't apologize. He never apologized until the next day. When it was too late.

"She didn't leave you, Father. She died. It wasn't voluntary." Cecelia couldn't count the number of times they'd had this same conversation. And it always ended the same. Poorly.

"You miss her, don't you?" he slurred, holding on to the wall as he walked down the corridor. At least he was walking toward his chambers and not toward the common rooms. The butler walked a few feet behind him, and Cecelia was somewhat comforted by his presence.

"I miss her every day," Cecelia said softly. There had never been a kinder or gentler woman. Never. But she was gone. She'd died. And she'd left Cecelia with her father. It was growing harder and harder to forgive her mother for dying.

What an absurd thought. Her mother hadn't chosen to leave them.

Her father turned to the butler and said, "Get me a bottle of scotch, would you? Have it delivered to my chambers."

Her father would probably be just fine all alone with a bottle in his chambers, but she couldn't feed his habit. She just couldn't.

"The delivery didn't arrive today, sir," the butler said. "I could brew a pot of tea. Or perhaps some coffee. Or chocolate?" Her father liked chocolate.

"When did I get such poor staff that a delivery can't be arranged?" her father mumbled. "Worthless, the lot of them."

Actually, it was her father who was worthless. He

was nothing. Not anymore. The man who'd once swung her so effortlessly from his shoulders now was a shell of a man. At the door of his chambers, Cecelia leaned over and kissed his cheek. "Mr. Pritchens will help you prepare for bed, Father."

His gaze didn't meet hers, but he did nod. That was more than she got most days from him. "Mr. Pritchens is a dolt."

Mr. Pritchens was standing directly behind them. Cecelia just heaved a sigh, opened the door to her father's chambers, and then watched him walk inside.

"Go to bed, miss," Mr. Pritchens said, touching her elbow lightly. "I'll take care of Mr. Hewitt."

"Thank you," Cecelia whispered. And then she fled. She fled because she didn't want to help her father fall into bed fully clothed. She didn't want to see him without any dignity at all. She didn't want to see him. She didn't want him to be her father, but that was neither here nor there. She was stuck with him, like it or not.

A soft knock sounded on the door just as she walked past it. She looked up only briefly and kept walking. Whoever was calling could return on the morrow, couldn't he? It was late. Cecelia doused the lights and turned to walk up the stairs to her chambers.

A maid passed her in the corridor. "There's someone at the door. Would you tell whomever it is that we're not available?" Cecelia told her.

The maid curtsied and said, "Yes, miss." She turned away and then back quickly. "Can I get you anything, miss?"

"A new life?" Cecelia said with a chuckle. But it was a sound without any mirth.

The maid pinched her lips together in a thin line. "Would that I could, miss," she breathed. Then she turned to go and answer the door, the knocking growing louder.

Cecelia called back to the maid, "If it's not too much trouble, could you call for a bath to be brought to my chambers?"

"Yes, miss," the maid said as she bustled away. "Right away, miss," she called over her shoulder.

◦◦◦

Marcus shifted from foot to foot in the doorway of Cecelia's father's home. Hope spilled from his fingertips as he touched the heavy knocker, lifting it and letting it drop. The lights had been doused moments before, but it was still early. The sun had barely set, only two hours before. Surely, Cecelia wasn't in bed yet. Though the thought of her in bed wasn't entirely unpleasant. He immediately imagined her warm beneath her counterpane, dressed in a gown made of linen with long sleeves and ruffles at the neck. Her gown would be twisted around her legs, which might even be parted in sleep, one knee pointed up.

He was growing hard just standing there. He adjusted his stance and the fit of his trousers, as he raised and lowered the door knocker again. He could just admit himself, he supposed. He'd done it before. But that had been for dinner parties or soirees when Cecelia's mother was alive. Not since then. Of course, he hadn't been home since then. So he couldn't compare.

The door opened slowly, and a harried maid blew a lock of hair from her face. "Mr. Thorne!" she cried.

"Good evening. Is Cecelia about?" he asked. His heart was beating like a team of runaway horses.

The maid glanced toward the stairs and back at him. "She said she doesn't want to see any visitors tonight, Mr. Thorne. I'm sorry."

He pointed to his own chest. "Did she say me specifically?" Of course, she wouldn't do such a thing. Would she? Perhaps she was angry at him after all.

A couple of burly footmen walked toward the stairs carrying a tub and buckets of water up the steps.

"She said she didn't want to see anyone today, Mr. Thorne. She's had a long day of it." The maid glanced down the corridor toward Mr. Hewitt's suite of rooms. "And it might be a longer night," she said, but it came out as a frustrated breath.

"Is everything quite all right?" Marcus asked.

"Quite," she said.

But household staff wouldn't say if something wasn't all right, even if the walls were caving down around their ears.

"Would you like to leave a note?" she asked.

"No. I'll call upon Miss Hewitt tomorrow," he said. He turned to walk away.

"I'm glad you're home, Mr. Thorne." Marcus turned back to face her. But she wasn't smiling. She was doing the opposite, and she worried the edge of her apron. "I hope you can help to set things to rights."

She closed the door softly, and he stood there until he heard her footsteps fade away.

Something was wrong. Something was very wrong.

He wouldn't be able to sleep until he saw Cecelia. So, he waited for a moment and then slowly opened the front door, looking left and then right to be sure no one was around. His Hessians made soft knocks against the oak floor, so he sat down on the lowest stair to pull his boots from his feet. He set them in the dark corner behind the stairs and quickly climbed the staircase in his stockinged feet.

He knew which room was Cecelia's. He'd played in it when he was small, and he'd steered clear of it when he was older, because being caught in Cecelia's chambers past a certain age was inappropriate and her father would have thrashed him.

The house no longer smelled like freshly oiled wood and clean linen. It smelled like dust and discomfort. What had changed? Had Cecelia's mother's death changed the household this much?

He stopped outside Cecelia's door and listened intently. A splash of water and the clank of a bucket against the floor were all that he heard. Was Cecelia taking a bath?

He scrubbed a hand down his face. Good God, the woman would unman him and he hadn't even seen her yet. It had been less than a day since he'd seen her, yet he ached to look into her eyes, to hold her in his arms.

The idea of Cecelia naked in the bath, with nothing but clear, clean water tickling her skin, was enough to steal the breath from his lungs. But then he heard her sniffle.

He opened his mouth to call out to her as he stepped into the room. It was the poorest of form for him to spy on her and for her not even to know he was there. But there was a privacy screen between them. He stepped to the edge of it, his feet still quiet, and prepared her name on his lips. But then he saw her reflection in the looking glass. She was curled into a ball, her face buried between her bent knees and her shoulders heaving.

Good God, what was he to do? He couldn't rush to her. He couldn't take her in his arms, not as he was. What on earth was making her so sad? It wasn't him, was it? Perhaps it was. Perhaps he was the last person she ever wanted to see.

His heart ached with the need to go to her. But she laid her head back against the rim of the tub, and he couldn't tell if the wetness on her face was from the bath or if it was from her crying.

The knob on the door turned, and Marcus dashed to hide behind the curtains that hung from Cecelia's bedposts. He'd hidden here plenty of times when he was younger and they played hide the slipper. Only now he didn't feel quite as well concealed. He held his breath until the maid stepped behind the screen with Cecelia.

"Shall I help you with your hair, miss?" the maid asked.

"Yes, please," Cecelia muttered.

She sounded like all the fight had been leached out of her. Perhaps he'd just caught her at an unguarded moment. This wasn't his Cecelia. His Cecelia rarely ever cried. She hadn't even shed a tear when she'd fallen from Mr. McGregor's apple tree when she was nine. She'd cut her arm badly but never shed a tear.

Marcus untangled himself from the bed curtains and

tiptoed to the door, where he let himself out into the corridor and crept back down the stairs.

He reached into the shadows for his boots, but a crash from down the corridor caught his attention. Without even thinking, Marcus walked toward it. Perhaps Mr. Hewitt was injured. He'd never forgive himself if he left the man there hurt. But as he went around the corner, the sound of a scuffle met his ears.

Good God, it was like Bedlam. He looked into Mr. Hewitt's chambers, where he was being held down by two footmen. And Mr. Pritchens, the stately old butler who never had a cross word for anyone bellowed at him, "We will not allow you to do this. You will leave her be." He pulled a flask from his interior coat pocket. "Here." He shoved it at Mr. Hewitt, who took it like a man who was dying of thirst. "Drink it all. Then go to sleep," the butler warned. He brushed a lock of hair that had tumbled from his perfectly combed head back into place. Mr. Pritchens never looked disheveled.

Something was wrong. Something was very wrong.

Marcus turned to walk back down the corridor. But the sound of his soft footsteps drew the butler into the corridor and there was nowhere for Marcus to hide. "Who goes there?" Mr. Pritchens asked.

Marcus turned, forcing himself to grin and be friendly, though it was the last thing he felt like doing. "It's just me, Mr. Pritchens. I came to give my regards to Mr. Hewitt."

Mr. Pritchens looked down at Marcus's stockinged feet and back up at his face, his brow furrowed. "You had to remove your boots to give your regards?" he said.

"It seemed prudent at the time," Marcus said with a shrug.

The man nodded.

"Is all well?" Marcus asked, motioning toward the door with his hand full of boots.

"As well as any other day." Mr. Pritchens breathed out on a sigh.

"What has happened here since I left, Pritchens?" Marcus asked.

The man lifted his nose into the air and regarded Marcus as though he might as well be an ant beneath his shoe. "What's happened is that someone has broken into the family home where he has not been invited." He motioned toward the door. "I'll see you out."

He brushed at that errant lock of hair again, and Marcus noticed that the butler's jaw was darkening to the color of a cold grate.

"I'll find out what's going on here, Pritchens," Marcus warned.

"I certainly hope you do," Mr. Pritchens said, and then he gave Marcus a gentle shove out the door and closed it behind him.

Damn. What a mess. He'd been gone for just over six months, and now that he was home, nothing was as he'd left it.

Even Cecelia wasn't the woman he'd left behind. She was naked in the bath. And crying. And her father was foxed. And Pritchard had given him a flask while footmen held him down. And Pritchard had been hit in the jaw.

And Cecelia was crying.

Something was very wrong if Cecelia was crying.

Twelve

CECELIA DRESSED SLOWLY, DONNING HER FAERIE CLOTHing with care. One good thing about being at home was that she could do away with the long dresses and bonnets. She could let hair hang freely over her shoulders, and she could tuck it behind her ears. She shook her skirt out over her knees. Fae dresses were made for usability. They were designed with strips of fabric that fell to the length of one's knees, and the pieces tore off when one got stuck sliding beneath a windowsill or through a keyhole. They were fitted to the skin, with no excess of material.

With her silk stockings tied up with red garters, she slid her feet into her fae slippers. She was ready. She was ready for anything that could happen today. Anything at all.

She stepped into the breakfast room and forced herself not to react when she saw her father at the head of the table, with his head buried in his hands. He groaned aloud and rubbed the heels of his hands into his eye sockets.

"Long night?" she asked.

He looked up slowly, like the light hurt his eyes.

"I don't remember most of it," he admitted.

He never did. That's what made his crimes so heinous. He couldn't properly apologize because he had no idea what he'd done wrong the night before.

Mr. Pritchens stroked a finger along the line of his jaw, almost absently, as he stared a hole into her father's back.

"I believe you had too much to drink. Then you proceeded to break some glasses and punch a hole in the wall, and you had to be restrained in your room until you drank enough that you fell asleep." She looked over her shoulder at Mr. Pritchens. "Is that about it?" she asked.

The man nodded. "Quite right," he clipped out.

"I'm sorry," her father said, not looking up from where his face rested in his hands.

She didn't respond. He deserved a solid dose of reality. He deserved to feel as miserable as they all did.

She filled a plate for herself and sat down at the table. After a few minutes of stilted silence, she asked, "What are your plans for the day?"

He heaved a sigh. "I have none."

Mr. Pritchens spoke up. "I believe you're to pay a visit to Mr. Randall today."

Her father snorted. "I'm the last person he wants to see."

"Probably," Cecelia agreed. "But you should visit anyway."

"We'll see," her father said. He raised an inquiring brow at her. "What are your plans today?"

"I believe I have to see how much damage you've

caused, find out what the repercussions will be, and try to fix everything you've fouled up." She took a sip of her tea. "That should take the whole day. And perhaps tomorrow." And the rest of her life.

"I'm sorry," he said blandly.

"Don't be sorry," she snapped. "Change."

He threw his fork down with a clatter. "You think I haven't tried?"

"Try harder."

She hated to be so callous. But this problem wasn't going to solve itself. He had to participate in his own care. He had to help them. He had to have a reason to help them.

She leaned forward, catching her father's dark gaze with her own. She forced him to look her in the eye by not breaking contact. "If you can't clean yourself up, I'm going to leave."

He snorted. "And go where?"

She tossed her napkin into her plate and got up from her chair. "Anywhere but here," she said as she left the room.

There was room for her in the human world, she was certain of that. She could be a governess or a nanny. She could even marry a rich lord and have his children. She'd have to clip her wings to do so, but maybe leaving home was what she needed. Right now, she couldn't get far enough away from her own life. She needed someone else's. Desperately.

Cecelia had to go pay a call on Mrs. Dalparsons. She was the only one in the land of the fae who might know what to give her father to keep him from drinking. She specialized in herbs and potions, and she knew what to give for every ailment. And if anyone ever had an ailment, it was Cecelia's father.

She went out the front door, her skirts swishing about her knees, and looked up at the bright sun. The land of the fae didn't have the same soot-washed streets as London. It didn't have the litter or the dull gleam of disuse. It nearly sparkled. And she usually sparkled with it. But she couldn't find a single spark within her. She drew in a deep breath and then nearly choked on it when she saw Marcus coming up the lane. He had to be a figment of her imagination. His body was limned by the rising sun, and he was hatless, his hair loose about his shoulders.

Her breath halted in her throat, and tears burned at the backs of her eyes. She blinked them back and stayed put. She wouldn't run and fling herself into his arms. She couldn't let him know that she needed him that much. But she needed him. Good God, she needed him.

"Marcus," she said as he walked closer to her. His grin was almost infectious. "What are you doing here?"

He lifted a stalk of wheat to his lips and then talked around it. "This is kind of like déjà vu, isn't it?"

"I don't know what you mean."

He mocked her tone. "What are you doing here?" He changed to his own deeper tone. "Looking for you, you ninny." Her tone. "Why are you looking for me?" His. "Because I can't live without you."

He held his hand to his heart and looked at her, and then reached for her. She didn't even think twice before she took his hand. It swallowed hers as he came to stand beside her on the top step. Then he sat down and tugged on her fingertips until she sat down beside him.

His knee brushed hers, the warmth of his leg seeping through his trousers and the skirt of her dress. "My parents came for a visit. It's my grandmother's birthday, apparently."

Her heart sank.

"I think it was a trick," he admitted, grinning, "because her birthday isn't until January."

"But that's why you came."

He shook his head. "No. I came for you. Because I can't live without you."

He looked out over the fields and down the lane, spinning his wheat stalk between his fingers like a pinwheel.

"Marcus," she began.

"You left without even a note."

"I was going to send one," she rushed to say.

He nodded. "Milly told me. She refused to give me one. Said I would ruin you."

She swallowed past the lump in her throat. "You ruined me a long time ago," she admitted.

He chuckled. "And I thought I was the one ruined."

She chucked his shoulder with hers. "We're a sad lot, aren't we?"

He put a hand to his chest. "I'm not. I'm happier than I've ever been. I'm sitting in the land of the fae with the woman I love." He smiled at her. "What do you want to do today?"

What had she planned today? She couldn't remember, so she shrugged instead. "What do you want to do today?"

He threaded his hand beneath the hair at the back of her neck and pulled her so close that his next words brushed her lips, as surely as any kiss would. "I want to take you somewhere we can be alone, and then I want to hold you close and never let you go."

She nodded, her nose brushing against his, they were that close. "All right."

⁂

Marcus held her close to him, so close he could feel the beat of her pulse in the air between them. She'd said, "all right," like he'd made the most reasonable request in the world.

"I'm going to marry you," he warned.

"Don't ruin the moment," she whispered with a grin. "Just let me enjoy it." She held up a single finger. "One day. Give me one day." She poked that finger into his chest. "One day with you."

He nodded and pulled her to her feet. It was one day that would start the rest of their lives. "One day," he repeated like an idiot as he walked side by side with her down the lane. She turned around backward and walked that way, looking at him like he'd hung the moon and the stars.

"Am I forgiven?"

She smiled and shook her head. "Don't ruin it," she warned.

He held up both hands as though in surrender. "Not ruining it. Yes, I nearly forgot."

"Where are we going?" she asked, her grin cheeky and infectious.

"We're going to take a walk in the woods until we

get to my grandfather's hunting lodge," he said. He could barely speak past the lump in his throat. But she was so damn beautiful walking backward in front of him, all of her attention focused on him, her smile so bright that it outshone the sun.

"Then what?"

"Then we can play cards."

She frowned, her lip turned down in a pout.

"We can organize the cabinets and wardrobes in the lodge?"

Her lip poked out even farther, and he wanted nothing more than to kiss it. But that would come later.

"We can walk in the woods down by the stream and watch the sunset."

Her pout disappeared. She liked that idea.

"We can lie on the settee and take a nap."

She smiled. She really liked that idea.

All he could think about was lying with her on the settee and pulling her into his arms, and maybe even falling asleep with her head on his chest. His trousers were growing unbearably tight at the thought of it.

"I could undress you slowly and make love to you." He choked out the last, nearly overcome by the emotion. Her smile faltered and turned into an expression he'd never seen on her face before. It was unadulterated lust. And she liked the idea, if the flush creeping up her chest and neck was any indication. But that could also be the exertion of the walk.

"I like that idea best," she said, and she turned around and fell into step beside him. She was quiet as they crossed the hills and dales, and his feet were aching by the time they reached the hunting lodge, but it was worth it.

"You remember this place?" he asked.

"Of course," she chirped. It had been a long time since they'd been there. Too long.

"I want to talk about the future," he said as they crossed the threshold, but she held a finger to her lips and didn't let him utter what he was thinking.

"Not today," she warned.

"Today, Cece," he began to argue.

She slammed her hand against the doorjamb hard enough to make him jump. "Not today!" she cried. "Today isn't for regrets." Her voice dropped to a whisper. "Just let me live. For today. Please," she said.

"All right," he agreed. And then he reached for her.

Thirteen

CECELIA FELL INTO HIS ARMS AND LET HIM PULL HER even closer as soon as the door closed behind her. She needed this. She needed one day, one hour, one minute she could call her own. Her heart didn't have many desires. Not anymore. But she wanted this. She wanted him. And she would have him this day.

His mouth touched hers, his hands bracketing her face as he licked gently across her lips. She didn't want gentle. She wanted Marcus. And they'd spent enough time kissing in the past that she knew he was holding back. So she stepped up on her tiptoes, pushed her body closer to his, and slipped her tongue into his mouth.

The velvet rasp of his tongue against hers left her quaking in his arms, but she forced herself to take him farther, to pull him deeper into her. She pulled his tongue between her lips and suckled it gently. He groaned at her need and showed her his own. He put inches between them that she didn't want, and she protested, moaning low in her throat until she realized that he was unbuttoning his coat and shoving it from his shoulders.

He was still wearing the trappings of the other world, so she began to unfasten his waistcoat and helped him shove it from his shoulders.

When he wore nothing but his shirtsleeves, he put his hands at her waist and kissed her, at once gentle and tender yet raging with the fire of a thousand grates, and she thought she would melt right there in a puddle of lust if he didn't end the torment soon.

"Marcus," she protested against his lips.

"Too fast?" he asked, pulling back ever so slightly.

She laughed. It was an uninhibited sound, and she barely recognized it in herself. "Too slow," she warned instead.

She raised herself on tiptoe, and his hands slid down to cup her bottom. He hoisted her in his firm grip and she threw her legs about his waist. "Let's move to the bedchamber, shall we?"

"I thought we might just do it on the floor." She giggled against his neck. He groaned and kissed her again, not even looking where he was going.

She would have been fine with the floor, but she assumed this was supposed to be done in a bed when one did it for the first time, wasn't it? She laughed at her own silly thoughts.

"I love that sound," he said, and she could feel his smile against her lips.

"What sound?" she mouthed back at him.

"When you're happy. It makes me happy."

"Just today," she whispered, pulling back and looking into his eyes.

"Just today," he whispered back, but he smiled at her like he knew a secret she didn't know.

He lowered her to her feet and stood her beside the bed, and her traitorous legs nearly buckled at the thought of what they were about to do. "Marcus, I'm scared," she whispered.

But suddenly he was there. He was brushing the hair back from her face and pulling her into him, like they were one person, and the thoughts of moments ago passed. This was Marcus. She had nothing to fear.

"Have you ever done this before?" she blurted.

He stilled.

Oh, no. He had. He'd done it without her. He'd done it with someone else.

He brushed her hair back and looked into her eyes, his brown eyes so full of longing that it stole her breath. "I've never done this before," he admitted. He kissed her forehead with tender lips and breathed heavily against her skin. "How could I have ever done this without you? I've waited for you my whole life."

"Are you afraid?" she asked.

He took her hand and placed her palm on the center of his chest. "Terrified," he admitted, and his heartbeat kicked like a mule in his chest.

"What if I'm really bad at it?" she breathed. It was a ridiculous question she knew, but she was suddenly consumed with worry.

"Not possible," he said with a chuckle.

He turned down the counterpane and looked at her as he reached behind him and pulled his shirt over his head.

"Oh, my," she breathed.

His naked chest was dusted with a light down of dark hair that was springy and curled against the tips of her fingers. She let her fingers trail through it slowly, until he took her hand and stopped her exploration.

"What's wrong?" she asked.

"I'm afraid of what will happen if you keep doing that," he said, his voice muffled by the way he kissed the side of her neck, his lips trailing across her skin, leaving a cool, wet path behind.

"What do you mean?"

He chuckled. "Nothing."

❧

She was wearing entirely too many clothes. And it was his job to remedy that situation, if he could just think of the best way to do so. Instead, he sat down on the side of the bed and tugged his boots from his feet, and then he began to unfasten the fall of his trousers. He pushed his stockings down his feet and shoved his trousers down until he wore nothing but his small clothes. She reached out to touch him, her inquisitive fingers hesitant but searching. She pressed the head of his manhood with the pad of her thumb and he squeaked like a mouse. A very lusty mouse, but still a mouse.

He'd taken himself in hand enough times to know that he was very close to spending. Painfully close if the ache in his stones was any indication. She squeezed him between her thumb and forefinger, and he bit his lower lip to keep from coming.

It didn't work. He was painfully erect. And weeping, if the way his smalls were dampening was any indication. Her pretty little brows drew together, not understanding at all what was happening.

"Very normal reaction," he grunted.

Then he pulled her to stand between his spread legs and began to tug her dress up. It was made of spider's thread so it could grow and shrink with her, and it slid over her head like shedding a second skin, leaving pink skin behind. Her breasts were pert and round and perfect, and he pulled her close so he could lick across one distended tip. The sound that left her throat was painful in its intensity.

He'd never last long enough like this. He turned and lay back on the bed, bringing her over him as he did so. She looked down at him, her hair falling like a cloud over them both, tickling his chest. He tucked his hands behind his head and looked up at her. Her breasts were unbound, and the curly patch of hair at the apex of her thighs called to him. But if he so much as moved, he would disgrace himself. He knew it. He shut his eyes tightly. She was naked but for her stockings, and he wore nothing but his smalls and he was afraid to touch the woman he loved because he couldn't control himself.

He wanted this to be pleasant for her. He wanted her to find joy in it. He wanted to make it perfect.

But then she touched him. She reached her hand inside his smalls and took him in her grip. He protested, grabbing for her hands. "I just want to see it," she whispered, laughing in that way only Cecelia could.

He shoved his small clothes down over his hips and off his feet, and kicked them to the side. She laughed, but then she grew completely serious. She came up to sit beside him on the bed, crossing her legs and putting a pillow in the center to protect her modesty, he assumed.

"Quite daunting, isn't it?" she asked, looking down at his manhood, her lip drawn between her teeth as she appeared puzzled.

"Yes, you are," he laughed.

"Me?" she cried, laying a delicate little hand on her naked chest. "I'm not the one who's all purple and… hard."

Yes, he was hard. Good God, he was hard.

"Can I touch you," she breathed.

He swiped a hand down his face. "I wish you wouldn't," he grunted.

But she paid him no heed. She reached out one tentative little finger and brushed the weeping slit, swirling it around the head of his manhood. "Cece," he warned, raising a knuckle to his mouth and biting down.

"What?" she whispered back, a shaky giggle tainting her mirth.

"You're going to unman me," he warned.

"That sounds like fun. How do I do that?" she breathed.

But then the dam burst. With her sweet little hand holding his manhood, squeezing him tightly, he couldn't keep from coming. He spent, his essence hitting his belly as he grunted. The damage was done. He'd come without even being able to get inside her. So, he did what any man would do. He wrapped his fist around hers, and worked it up and down his shaft as he grunted, his seed spilling across their fingers as he worked her hand up and back. She squeezed just hard enough that it hurt like the devil, in a really good way. He looked up, wanting to make eye contact with her, but she watched his manhood, her mouth hanging open as he came.

He reached for her, pulling her down to kiss him in one harsh move. She kissed him back, apparently emboldened by his response. Her tongue slid against his, and he pumped out the last of his seed as she lay on her elbows on his chest, kissing him with passion. She finally pulled back and looked at him, her hand stilling on him when he couldn't stand any more.

"That wasn't supposed to happen," he said by way of apology.

"I think it was," she whispered with a giggle.

"Not until I was inside you," he said. He sat up and reached for his shirt and used it to clean their hands. Then he crossed naked to the washstand and pulled out a cloth. There was fresh water in the pitcher. Why was there fresh water in the pitcher? It didn't matter. He wet the cloth and walked back to her, offering it to her, biting his lips together to keep from apologizing again.

She pointed toward his manhood. "It appears not to have affected your rigidity." Her face flushed crimson as she cleaned her fingers. He took the cloth and wiped his belly.

He would probably never soften again, not while she sat naked like that. He climbed over her, pulling the pillow from her lap as he pushed her to lie back on the bed. "That's the beauty of the male appendage. It can disgrace you one minute and then be ready to do so again in a moment, apparently." He couldn't keep from laughing.

But she wasn't laughing. She was smiling, yes, but it was a silky siren's smile, one that shot straight to his groin, and then he didn't worry about having embarrassed himself. He was going to be inside this woman, and he was going to do it soon.

He lay atop her for a moment, looking down into her inquisitive face. "I love you so much it hurts sometimes," he confessed.

She closed her eyes tightly and wouldn't look at him. "One day," she whispered.

So he would give her one day.

He cupped her breast, plumping it in his palm as he thumbed across her nipple. She squirmed and he settled more firmly between her thighs. Drawing her nipple between his lips, he tongued it gently, and a little noise left her throat. She arched her bottom upward, rocking against him.

"Does this feel good?" he asked.

"I didn't give you the Spanish Inquisition when I was exploring your body, did I?" she said with a grin.

"How am I supposed to know what pleases you if you don't tell me?" He blew against her puckered little nipple, which was the same color as her pretty little lips, and saw that her nipples were growing just as rosy as her well-kissed mouth.

"You please me," she said again.

"I let you explore me," he warned, and then he sat back and settled his shoulders between her thighs.

"What are you doing?" she shrieked.

Her thighs were perfect. They were fleshy and supple and strong. And he wanted them wrapped around his hips. "Shhh," he crooned. "I let you look around. Now you have to do the same."

He shoved her thighs wider, though she protested

for a moment. "Pretty," he breathed, and she shivered as she clenched the bed linens in her fists.

He used one finger to strum up and down the weeping slit, and he applied pressure until he found the center of her and then slowly slid one finger inside. She gripped his finger like a silken glove, and he was glad he'd come in her hand, because he would never have survived the tightness inside her if he hadn't. She cried out as he slid his middle finger in and out of her, and he let her pick the speed with which he entered her. His thumb pressed above her slit as he tried to find purchase inside the silken depths of her and she froze.

"What's wrong?" he asked, stopping.

"Do that again," she coaxed.

"Do what?" He had no idea what he'd done.

She reached her fingers into her wet curls and touched the swollen spot at the top of her cleft. "Here," she said. "Touch me here."

So he did. He pressed his thumb against the rigid little bump and she groaned. So he did it again. She began to thrust against his questing finger and he pushed a little harder and worked his thumb in small circles.

"Yes," she cried. She was so wet that his hand glistened with the essence of her, but he'd never seen anything so beautiful, never felt anything so right as being inside her. "Don't stop."

There was no way he would stop. But he did climb back up her body so he could look into her face as she squeezed his finger and he strummed across that place that made her so happy. Though happy really wasn't the right word. Hot. Molten. Spilling. And then she broke. With a keening cry, she arched her hips, and her body began to quaver. She spilled very similar to the way he had, and he watched her face as he worked her, as she shook in his arms, as she came for him, as he took the essence of her inside himself in the most elemental of ways.

She stilled in his arms and blew a lock of hair from her eyes. Her face grew rosy and she tried to roll into herself for modesty's sake, but he'd seen everything now. "No," he warned as he settled back between her thighs and pressed against her heat.

"I didn't mean to do that," she said, somewhat chagrined.

"Now you know how I felt," he said with a laugh.

"What's good for the goose and all that," she warned.

But then he pressed into her softness and she stilled, but she parted her thighs more, allowing him to settle more firmly. He slid inside her heat, watching her face as she took him into her body. He pushed in slowly, afraid he would hurt her. But she didn't complain. His arms shook under his weight as he impaled her, and she just pushed him on, lifting her hips to take him inside. Good God, this woman was his. She stilled suddenly when he hit a barrier.

But then he pushed past it with one quick thrust. A tear rolled down her cheek, and she turned her head into his arm. He moved to pull back, but she wrapped her legs around his hips to keep him there. "Don't go," she said. "The pain has passed."

"Are you certain?"

She nodded. Her blue eyes met his, and he couldn't have retreated if he wanted to.

He pushed until he was seated fully inside her, and it felt like a piece of his heart broke apart and it was hers. He moved inside her, tilting her hips by grabbing her bottom so he could go deeper. She cried out, but this time she was clutching his forearms and kissed the side of his wrist where it rested by her head. They were wicked little nips of teeth and tongue, and he felt the need building within him again.

"Yes," she cried.

And this time, when he topped that peak, he took her with him. They crashed together like waves upon the seashore. They moved together like one, and he poured himself into her, taking part of her in return. It was a part he would never give back. Never. Ever. He stilled, softening inside her, and then he withdrew and rolled to the side, taking her with him to lie on his chest.

⁂

Cecelia settled the side of her face on the springy hair that matted his chest. But part of her was broken. Where she'd been whole, she now was in pieces. Tears formed in her eyes, and she tried to blink them back, but she couldn't. And then suddenly, a sob erupted from her throat, and she buried her face in Marcus's chest, trying to take his strength inside her. He would give it to her, she was sure, if he knew how much she needed it. And she dearly needed it. She needed it so badly.

"Please tell me I didn't hurt you," he said, his voice rough and abraded as she sobbed into his chest.

"You didn't," she gasped out. But the sobs hadn't

stopped. He pulled her to lie on his chest, and she straddled his hips like she would her favorite horse. She settled into him, letting him support her weight. She let him do this for this one day, this one hour, and this one minute. She let him hold her. She let him carry her. She let him have her as no one else ever had. And no one else ever would.

He held her until the tears subsided, stroking her naked back as he crooned to her. Until finally she stopped. Then he pulled the counterpane over them both, and she fell asleep on top of him. And he let her. She burrowed into the space where his neck met his shoulder and put her hand above his heart, and to the rhythm of his heartbeat, she fell asleep.

Fourteen

Marcus rolled to the side, lowering Cecelia gently to the bed, and she burrowed into him, even in her sleep. God, he loved this woman. She'd cried until she'd exhausted herself, great sobs heaving from her tiny frame until she'd finally stilled on top of him and rested.

She rolled toward him, looking for the heat of his body like it had always been hers to claim. And he supposed it had. He was hers. She was his. He'd been an idiot for the space of six months, but things were well now. Things were as they should be. Now she just needed to marry him and everything would be perfect.

He placed his lips tenderly against her forehead and pulled back, sliding from beneath the counterpane. He pulled on a robe that hung on the edge of the bed and walked out to the kitchen. He hoped he could find something in the kitchen to eat. It had been a while since anyone had been in the cabin, but surely there were some supplies. He stopped in the threshold of the kitchen when he heard whistling.

"You're at the wrong place at the wrong time,

Ronald," Marcus warned. Ronald stepped from behind the counter, an apple clenched between his teeth.

"Never a wrong place. Not when you need help." The gnome winked. "Who do you think left the fresh water for you?"

The sorry little sot.

Ronald brushed a hand through the air, dismissing Marcus with a simple gesture. "There are always consequences for your actions," the gnome warned, talking around a bite of apple. He nodded toward a basket on the table. "I brought sustenance for you."

"Thank you," Marcus grunted, not yet willing to be as appreciative as he should.

"I had to tie Millicent up and put her in the closet to keep her away from here."

Marcus's head jerked up. "You did not."

"Truthfully, I just sent her on a wild-goose chase. Said I'd seen the two of you down by the shore." He shot Marcus a telling glance. "It won't be long before she shows up here."

"Keep her away. I promised Cecelia one day." He riffled through the basket, pulling out cheese and meat and some warm shepherd's pie. "Who baked?"

"I stole it from Millicent's house," the gnome said with a shrug. "She won't mind once she realizes it's for her girl. She'll get over the fact that you'll be partaking of it, too." He snickered.

"What were you doing at Milly's house?" Marcus asked.

"Stealing shepherd's pie," Ronald said crisply.

"And?" Marcus smiled. The thought of a romance

between Milly and Ronald made him want to laugh out loud. Those two had been at one another's throats for years and years.

"And it's none of your concern," Ronald growled. "Who knows? We might plant a seed in the ground and see if we can grow any little garden gnomes."

The idea whirled like a tornado in Marcus's head. "That's how…" At Ronald's scorching glance, he didn't finish his thought. But he still wondered. "How long have you known Milly?"

"Forever," Ronald said, tossing his apple core into the rubbish bin.

"And you two have never…" He let his thought trail off again.

"Again, mind your own matters," Ronald chided.

"And you should do the same." Ronald knew what they'd been doing. He probably knew that Cecelia was naked in Marcus's bed right now.

"Milly and I married centuries ago," Ronald said quietly. "She's mine. I'm hers. End of story."

Married? They were married. "What?" Marcus gasped out.

The gnome shrugged. "I love her. She loves me, most of the time. We each have obligations. We see one another as time permits. The life of a gnome is a solitary existence. But we make do."

"But you rarely get to see her."

"Absence makes the heart grow fonder and all that," the gnome said. He started to sift through the basket, looking for more to eat. Marcus jerked it from his reach.

"But Milly hates you," Marcus wondered aloud.

"Hello Pot. My name is Kettle," Ronald said drolly. Then he sobered. "So, Cecelia must not hate you anymore."

"Not right this moment," Marcus said, tensing at the thought of Cecelia ever hating him.

"She came right out with it and told you she loves you." Ronald narrowed his eyes at Marcus.

"Not yet." She hadn't. He'd said it multiple times that day, but she hadn't said it yet. But she would. She couldn't avoid it. "She asked me not to ask her for anything today."

"That makes a lot of sense, seeing how much you love her." Ronald snorted. Marcus really loved the little garden gnome at times. And really despised him at others.

"She's had a tough go of it," Marcus said. "She asked me for one day. Then we'll marry and set things to rights."

"She said she'll marry you?"

"Not in so many words." She had never really agreed, had she? She hadn't.

"I think that she had her way with you, and now she'll dispense with you and go back to her sorry life." Ronald hitched up his breeches and glared at Marcus.

"Her life's not sorry, you little…" He reached for the gnome, but Ronald had always been too fast for him.

"Her life is sorry, and if you knew anything about her, you would know how hard she's had it since you left." He shook a finger at Marcus. "I'm warning you, lad, take great care with how you go about this." He gestured to the cabin. "All this is fine and good, but real life will rear its ugly head before you know it."

"This is real life," Marcus grumbled.

"No, it's the life you want. It's not real life. There's a difference."

Ronald crossed to the window and threw open the sash.

"There's a perfectly good door, you know," Marcus said.

"Why use a door when there's a perfectly good window?" The gnome glared at him for a moment and then turned and flung himself out the window.

Good riddance.

Ronald had no idea what he was talking about. This wasn't a storybook life. This was real life. This was his life with Cecelia. This was real. Wasn't it?

Cecelia stood beside a frozen lake, her arms flung out to the sides as she looked up at the night sky. Her father stood on one side of the lake, beckoning her to come to him. Instead, she fell back into the icy waters. She let them slide over her skin and suck her under the lake's surface, until there was no air left to breathe.

Cecelia awoke with a start. There was coldness all around her, but she was safe beneath the comfort of Marcus's warm counterpane. Yet an icy, cold something pressed against her back. She leaned back to look up at Marcus's face, where he rested on his elbow, looking down at her. "You're freezing," she complained, pulling the counterpane closer about her naked shoulders. She looked down and realized she was completely naked. Then she looked over at him, and so was he. The only heat in the room was what crept up her face, apparently. "Where have you been?" she asked, looking everywhere but at his smiling face.

"I went to find food," he said, snuggling his cold body closer to her. He flung one leg over her thighs and nudged her hip with… that couldn't be…

"And took a dip in an icy loch, did you?" she asked. "You're freezing."

"I lit a fire in the kitchen and one in here," he said, cupping his hand over a yawn. Then he looked down at her. "Did you sleep well?" he asked.

She nodded. She'd slept better than she had in a very long time. She looked toward the window. The light was waning. Hadn't it been morning just a short time ago? "What time is it?" she asked.

"Dusk," he said. His voice sounded like it had been dragged down a gravel road.

She sat up, and the counterpane fell below her chest. She snatched it back up with a gasp. "I slept that long!" She flung her feet over the side of the bed and started to get up. But he wrapped a strong arm around her waist and drew her back to him. She didn't protest. Not really. She wanted to stay with him forever, never to go home. But reality would intervene before long.

Cecelia lay back against his arm, which had slipped beneath her head somehow. She turned to face him, their noses no more than inches apart. "Did you sleep well?" she asked.

"Not as well as you, I'm afraid." He picked up a lock of her hair and toyed with it. "I love you, you know," he said softly.

"Not today, Marcus." She held up one finger. "One day. You promised," she reminded him.

"I'll never stop telling you, Cece," he declared, and a lump formed in her throat.

Her stomach grumbled and she laid a hand upon it. "Oh, dear," she said with a laugh. This was Marcus. He wouldn't care if her stomach grumbled in a very unladylike way.

Marcus jerked the counterpane from around her shoulders and shoved it down so he could trail a finger over her belly. "Hungry, are you?" he asked softly. Then he bent and pressed his soft lips to the tender skin just above her hip.

"Mmm-hmm," she murmured. Though she was not thinking about food at the moment. "Unless you had something else in mind," she teased.

"I have a lot of things in mind," he said with a laugh. She covered her breasts with her hands, and he looked up at her and rolled his eyes. "I think we're past that point, don't you?" He climbed up her body and whispered in her ear, "I've been inside you, Cece."

Her heart leaped and a throbbing began between her thighs. "Yes, you have."

"And I plan to do it again," he murmured, kissing across the sensitive skin of her belly, until he could come up and kiss her lips quickly.

"Thank goodness," she breathed.

He looked at her askance. "Do you want to eat first?"

"I want to do that and then eat and then do it again," she said with a giggle. He wouldn't hate her audacity, would he? If the way his eyes smoldered at her suggestion was any indication, he didn't dislike it at all.

"I do like it when you take me by the hand and lead me," he whispered, his fiery lips kissing just above the spring of hair between her thighs.

"Marcus," she complained.

"What's good for the goose and all that," he said, mocking her earlier words. He slid his fingertips into her heat and began to stroke her from top to bottom. He slid a finger inside her quickly, rimming her entrance, and that brought her wetness up to that pulse point at the top of her sex. "I think I know how to please you," he whispered with a smile, his touch growing more insistent.

"Yes, you do…" she gasped out.

Her breath hitched in her throat, and she was no longer able to respond to him, aside from a moan and a squeeze of his arm.

"I do like exploring you," he said, as he bent and drew her nipple into his mouth.

"I like your exploration," she managed to squeak out.

"I can tell," he said. But he pulled his hand back and moved to lie between her thighs. "But I can't wait one more moment to be inside you."

"Please don't wait," she said, although she already missed his touch. He spread her thighs wide and looked down at her, licking his lips in a most carnal manner. He left a little space between them when he entered her. This time was still slow and soft, but he filled her fully and completely, rotating his hips around as he was seated fully inside.

"God, that's pretty," he groaned as he looked down at the place where they were joined. She flung an arm over her eyes to keep from seeing him, and he just chuckled. But then one hand snaked between them, and he began to rub that pulse point he'd discovered as he moved inside her. He took her slowly, building in speed as she urged him on.

"Don't stop," she said, her hips arching to meet his thrusts.

❦

Marcus watched her face as he brought her higher and higher. He had to bite his lip and think about ices at Gunter's and the cold water in the morning that he poured from the pitcher in his chambers. It wasn't working. His balls ached with the need to spend inside her. Every thrust was pure heaven, and the way she arched to meet him nearly undid him.

But he continued, rolling his fingers over her pleasure center as he moved in and out, in and out, in and out, and then with a cry, she reached out, and he caught her hand in his. She spasmed on his manhood like a tight fist, and he rode out the storm with her squeezing him, her body quaking in his arms. He came inside her, soaking her walls with his release. And he'd never felt so at peace as he did in that moment when he collapsed on top of her and pushed her damp hair from her face. He'd made love to her twice. He'd taken her innocence, and she'd taken his, just as it should be.

He rolled off her and flopped onto his back. "Did you know Ronald and Milly are married?"

She lifted her arm from her eyes and looked over at him, her blue eyes clear in the waning light. "No," she said, and she laughed. "I knew she had an odd obsession with his whereabouts. They don't spend much time together." She nodded her head. "That makes sense, now that you mention it."

"Do you think they're faithful to one another?" Marcus couldn't help but ask.

"I think I don't want to think about Milly and Ronald doing what we just did," she said with a shudder.

"He said they might plant a seed in the ground and see what grows of it."

He leaned over Cecelia and laid his face on her stomach, looking up over the swell of her breasts to see her face. She didn't stop him, and she twined her fingers with his. He kissed the soft skin of her belly tenderly.

"Milly and Ronald with a child. I shudder to think," she said, laughing.

He kissed her stomach again, imagining the swell of unborn life that could be theirs, and he smiled. "I want a child. Or two. Or ten."

She nodded, but she didn't respond except to say, "You always did."

The fingers of her free hand toyed with his unbound hair. "You don't?" he probed.

She held up a single finger. "One day," she groaned. "You promised me one day."

"One day," he agreed. He would give her one day. And then he would ask her all the questions he needed to ask her. And he needed some answers from her. But they could wait as long as her one day. "I'm hungry," he said, reaching for the basket he'd set beside the bed. "And I might just use you for the plate."

"Promises, promises." She giggled.

She sounded like his Cecelia so he didn't want to ruin the moment, but he wanted some answers now. Some things could not wait. "What made you cry earlier, Cecelia?" he asked as he set a wedge of cheese on her belly and popped a blueberry into her mouth.

She thought for a moment as she chewed. But then she spoke. Her voice was clear. "I was broken. And you put me back together." She touched her fingertips to his bent knee. "Thank you," she said softly, but her voice was clear. It was so clear that it reached into his soul and squeezed his heart.

"You're welcome," he said. And then he proceeded to paint her with clotted cream and lick it off. And she didn't protest even the slightest bit.

Fifteen

Cecelia let Marcus help her back into her clothing, with plenty of pauses for kisses, nips, and licks of
appropriate body parts. Then he pulled her between
his thighs and brushed her hair until it was silky soft
and didn't look like he'd tumbled her. Several times.
She looked much more at ease than she had when
they'd arrived at the cabin, and that said a lot to him.

She could be happy with him. He could marry her
and life could be perfect.

"Where will you tell your father you've been all
day?" he asked gently as he turned her to face him and
laid his forehead against her stomach, so tightly that his
nose was pressed into the soft flesh of her belly. His
hands held tightly to her hips. Fear gnawed at his own
belly, and he really didn't want to take her home. He
wanted to hide out there with her forever. He wanted
to live in that tiny cabin and never leave it again, with
Ronald bringing them necessary food and supplies.
But such was not to be his lot in life.

She shrugged. "I hadn't planned to tell him anything.
His opinion no longer matters to me." Her voice was

suddenly dull and lifeless, and he wished he had never brought it up.

"What does that mean? How could that be?" he murmured, looking up into her face, his hands still resting on her hips, still holding her close to him.

"My day isn't over yet. If you try to ruin what's left of it, I won't forgive you," she warned.

He nodded at her. He would get to the bottom of this. If it was the last thing that he ever did, he would figure out what the rift was between her and her father.

"Do you know the time?" she asked.

He pulled his watch fob from his pocket and looked down. "Well past the dinner hour. Your father is probably worried sick." He stood up and pulled her toward the door. "Come along. I'd better deliver you home."

She nodded as she looked longingly around the room. "It's time to go home," she said quietly.

But she wasn't broken. Not the way she'd been when he'd brought her there. She had seemed like a kite caught in a summer storm when they'd arrived. And now she was the gentle sun he'd always known, shining directly into his life.

They walked back to her house hand in hand. No one was on the roads between the cabin and town, and even if someone had been, they could have said they'd taken a walk. Rules were a little more lax in the land of the fae. They weren't lax enough to allow for what they'd done that day, but they could take a walk without a maid. After all, they were trusted to go on missions together.

Responsibility was earned in the land of the fae, as was trust. And if one proved oneself, one gained more and more freedom as the years passed. Not so in the other world, where status was all that mattered.

They walked slowly up the stairs at the front of her house and stopped at the threshold. Cecelia reached up and cupped his face in her palm, looking deeply into his eyes, hers as dark as night in the quiet of the evening. "Thank you for today," she said softly, and she leaned forward and kissed him. No, this wasn't a lusty mesh of teeth and tongue. This kiss was affectionate and comfortable.

"You're welcome," he said softly.

Mr. Pritchens should have come to open the door for her by now. Where was the man?

A thud sounded from the other side of the door.

"What was that?" Marcus asked.

"One of the maids moving furniture to clean behind it, I'm sure," Cecelia said with a breezy wave of her hand.

"At this time of the night?" He reached for the door handle, but she covered his hand with hers.

Her eyes looked everywhere but at him as she rushed to say, "You know, I forgot that I'm supposed to be staying the night at Ainsley's house."

He pulled back a little to look down at her face. "Why are you staying there?"

"We wanted a little time to catch up. And she wants to talk to me about your brother. I'm pretty sure there's a courtship going on there that no one knows about."

"Allen and Ainsley," Marcus said with a snort. "There's a match for you." He shuddered to think of how arguments in their household might be won, with two such strong-minded individuals in residence. Ainsley had a tongue sharp enough to cut glass, and Allen was no slouch when it came to quips. "They'll kill each other within a year," he said with a laugh.

She started down the steps. "Ainsley will be waiting for me," she said.

"Are you certain you want to go there at this time of the night?" It was well past dinnertime.

Well, she certainly didn't want to go home, not with the evidence of her father's drinking audible from outside the house. She didn't want Marcus, of all people, to see what her father had become.

By now he would be deep in his cups and belligerent. The thump they'd heard was probably her father throwing himself at one of the footmen. Or shoving furniture. Or trying to thrash Mr. Pritchens. Pity washed over her. Poor Mr. Pritchens. He'd been forced to deal with her father all day while she'd had a wonderful day with Marcus. She couldn't leave the poor butler with her father the rest of the night. But she couldn't let Marcus go inside the house, either. Not now.

"Walk with me to Ainsley's house?" she asked, tugging his fingers to get him away from the door.

"I certainly wouldn't let you go alone," he grumbled. He probably knew something wasn't right. He was a smart man. It didn't take a genius to realize that something was off.

They walked in silence down the lane until they came to Ainsley's father's house. It was small and quaint, and what it lacked in grandeur it made up for with happiness.

Marcus knocked on the door and waited with her for the butler to open it. "Miss Hewitt," the man said, shocked at her arrival.

"Miss Hewitt is here to see Miss Packard," Marcus said.

She could speak for herself. She really could. Cecelia squeezed Marcus's hand and said, "I'll see you tomorrow." Without waiting for his response, she slipped through the door, closing it solidly in Marcus's bewildered face.

She leaned against the closed door as Ainsley's butler looked at her as though she were bound for Bedlam. But just then, Ainsley skipped down the stairs in her nightrail and robe. She stopped on the middle step and said, "Cece, are you all right?"

The butler watched the two of them closely, and Cecelia nodded her head toward him to warn Ainsley not to say anything that could get back to her household.

"I'm sorry I'm late," Cecelia said. "I know you said to come after dinner, but I got busy with Father and we lost track of time."

Ainsley nodded slowly. "I'm glad you finally arrived," she said. She pointed down the corridor. "I was just on the way to get some warm milk. Come with me."

Cecelia nodded at the butler and walked behind Ainsley, her arms crossed over her chest. She was suddenly freezing. Her perfect day appeared to be over. Reality was returning to the forefront of her life. When no one was about, Ainsley began to warm some milk on the wood stove and asked, "Who are you avoiding? Your father or Marcus?"

Cecelia rocked her head side to side as though weighing her next words. Perhaps she was. "Both?" she asked. "Make one of those for me, will you?" She pointed to the pan of milk.

Ainsley nodded. "I came to see you today. Your father said you were out."

Cecelia nodded. "Was he foxed yet?"

Ainsley shook her head. "Not yet."

"Good."

"Where were you?" Ainsley asked cautiously.

"I went with Marcus to his grandfather's cabin in the woods and we stayed there all day."

Ainsley's jaw dropped. "You didn't!"

Cecelia couldn't bite back a smile. "I did!"

"What did you do there?"

Cecelia grinned. "We didn't play cards," she laughed.

"And?" Ainsley prompted as she poured warm milk into a cup and handed it to Cecelia.

"We didn't organize the wardrobes."

"Did you clean the linens?" Ainsley giggled.

"The linens!" Cecelia cried. There was bound to be some evidence of their day because they hadn't changed the linens. What the devil was she going to do? She supposed that could wait until the morning. No one would be there before tomorrow.

Ainsley's brow arched. "And why are you worried about the linens?" she prompted.

Cecelia said quietly. "You know, they say it hurts the first time, but it really didn't. Only for a moment." An uninhibited tear rolled down her cheek.

"Oh, Cece," Ainsley crooned, pulling her friend into her arms. Cecelia could always count on Ainsley. She didn't ask too many questions. And she always knew when to keep her opinion to herself and just listen. Ainsley set Cecelia back from her after a brief hug and said, "What was it like?"

"Beautiful," Cecelia breathed. And it had been. It had been everything she'd ever dreamed it would be. "He was warm and sweet and thoughtful, and he kept telling me over and over that he loved me."

Ainsley suddenly looked worried. "Is that why you did it? Because he made you feel like it was the next logical step?"

Cecelia shook her head. "No, I just wanted one day. And I asked him specifically if we could spend it that way. He wants to marry me."

Ainsley groaned out her name. "Cece," she said. "Of course he wants to marry you. You're amazing. When is the wedding?"

Cecelia shook her head. "We're not getting married."

Ainsley's brows narrowed. "Why not?"

"There's too much at stake. His world. My world. There's no way we could make it suit." She rushed on to clarify. "That doesn't mean I don't love him, because I do. I love him more than anything." She clutched her fist to her chest. "But I can't marry him." She took a deep breath and plunged on. "When he walked me home, my father was already foxed. I could hear furniture crashing inside."

"So you had him bring you here?"

"Well, I wanted to see you anyway. To tell you about it all."

Ainsley's face softened. "Thank you for sharing it with me."

"Thank you for listening."

"Was it terrifying?" Ainsley asked, her grin nearly infectious.

"It's a rather daunting appendage," Cecelia murmured.

"Isn't it, though?" Ainsley asked.

Cecelia put her hands on her hips and glared at her friend. "And just what do you know of it?"

"Not much," Ainsley admitted. Her cheeks got all rosy and she said, "Allen kissed me today. I mean, really kissed me. And the… umm… appendage… was hard to mistake."

Cecelia laughed. "How was the kiss?"

"Hot enough to scorch my hair," Ainsley said, holding up a lock of her hair. "Was he gentle with you?" she asked softly.

"He's Marcus," Cecelia scoffed. "Of course he was."

"At least he wasn't a bumbling idiot."

"He'd never done it before, either. So, we had to figure things out together."

Heat crept up Cecelia's cheeks. She wouldn't tell Ainsley everything.

"What if there are consequences?" Ainsley asked. "Will you marry him then?"

Consequences? Cecelia hadn't even thought about consequences. Goodness, what if they'd created a child?

"Forgot about that little detail, did you?" Ainsley chided.

"Completely," Cecelia muttered.

"Marcus is a good man. He'll take care of whatever needs to be taken care of."

Cecelia knew he would. But she really didn't want Marcus to have to take care of anything.

"I need to get home. I don't want to leave Mr. Pritchens alone with my father all night. Just in case."

"I'll have one of the footmen walk with you," Ainsley said.

"No need. There's no one about. I'll run directly home."

"Are you certain?"

"Completely." Cecelia crossed the room and hugged her friend tightly. "Thank you," she murmured.

"You're welcome." Ainsley patted Cecelia's back. "Now run home. Send for me if you need anything."

Cecelia went out the front door, holding a lantern in her hand as she walked down the road. She heaved a sigh of relief when she saw that the lights of her home had all been doused.

She slipped through the open door and closed it behind her. But she didn't realize what a mistake it was to come home until a bottle hit the wall directly beside her head and shattered all over the floor.

"Where have you been?" her father bellowed.

Sixteen

CECELIA CLOSED HER EYES TIGHTLY AND COUNTED to ten.

One.

Two.

Three.

Four.

Five.

Six.

Seven.

Eight.

Nine.

Ten.

She could count to one hundred and when she opened her eyes, her father would still be there in all his drunken glory, and she would still hate him just as much.

The first time he'd raised his hand to her was just after her mother's death. That had been a slap across the cheek when she'd chastised him for having another glass of wine.

The second time had been a little more direct and

couldn't be explained away as a rash on her face. She'd had a bruise across her cheekbone that required her to stay at home and out of sight for a sennight.

Mr. Pritchens stepped between her and her father. "Mr. Hewitt," he began, his voice shaking with rage. "Miss Hewitt went to fetch something for one of the upstairs maids. She has a terrible megrim. It was at my request."

"Are you daft, man?" her father bellowed. "We have servants for running errands."

All the servants would be in bed at this time of the night, but her father didn't know or didn't care about anyone's comfort but his own. "I volunteered," Cecelia said. "Everyone else was in bed."

"Why didn't you go yourself, Pritchens?" her father snarled. "You sent my daughter out in the dead of night to run an errand?"

Mr. Pritchens gritted his teeth and said, "I was somewhat preoccupied."

Her father kept Mr. Pritchens busy every night for what seemed like the whole night. But her father paid no heed to how much discomfort he caused everyone else.

Her father stepped forward and shoved Mr. Pritchens so hard that he thudded against the wall. Hitting her father back was like hitting a child who was having a tantrum. It did no good. It served no purpose. And no one felt good about it afterward. But when her father made a move to charge Mr. Pritchard, Cecelia felt obligated to step between them.

This time, her father's shove sent her into the wall. She stood there stunned, unable to take a deep breath for a moment. But when she could, there was no apology. There was only her father snarling, "Look what you made me do," in Mr. Pritchens' face.

"He didn't make you do anything, Father," Cecelia said, putting a hand on her father's shoulder to gently pull him back.

In the past six months, she'd done so more times than she could count. And he usually took it very well. But this time, he didn't for some reason. "He did make me do it. I would never hurt you on purpose," he bellowed, spittle flying from his lips to land on her face.

Cecelia closed her eyes and took another deep breath. She'd taken so many deep breaths lately that they should have called her Windy instead of Cecelia. Perhaps that would be the name she chose when she began a new life. One far away from her father.

"You hurt me every day, Father. Every time you do this."

He huffed. "Do what?" He jammed the heels of his hands into his eyes and scrubbed them.

But Cecelia had had enough. She stepped close to his face and screamed in it, just the way he had in hers. "Every time you do this!"

She was shocked at herself, so she stepped back and closed her eyes, counting to ten again. She didn't even see the hand flying toward her face. But she felt it. The back of his hand connected with her cheek, hitting her hard enough that it spun her head and she fell to the ground.

The last time he'd hit her, he'd been immediately contrite. Not this time. This time, he fell on top of her, intent on flipping her over, probably so he could yell in her face. But she folded her arms over her head to ward off any future blows and curled into herself. Inside herself was the safest place to be right now.

Suddenly, her father's weight shifted off her, and she looked up from between her elbows. Despite his slightness of form, Mr. Pritchens had wrestled her father from on top of her and laid him on his stomach, his left arm pulled up behind him at an almost sickening angle. Her father swore like a dockworker and threatened Mr. Pritchens.

"You don't have to dismiss me, Mr. Hewitt," the butler gritted out. "It's only because of your daughter that I'm still here." He looked up at Cecelia. "I can't keep doing this, miss," he said. "I want a peaceful existence. And this isn't it." He wrenched her father's arm higher behind his back when he began to struggle. "Stay down," he snarled.

He looked at Cecelia's face, which hurt like the devil.

"You're going to have a bruise there, miss," he warned.

She reached up and touched the tender side of her face. "I suppose I should have come home earlier tonight." She snorted to herself. Oh, the irony.

"How is Mr. Thorne?" Mr. Pritchens asked quietly. Her father had settled into a lump on the rug, with his eyes closed. He would be asleep in moments, she was sure.

She smiled at the memory of her day. "He's well."

"Nice day?" Mr. Pritchens asked, as if they were taking tea.

"The nicest," she said. And it had been. Until her father ruined it.

Mr. Pritchens removed his pointy knee from the center of her father's back, and her father didn't move. He didn't utter a sound, aside from a loud snore. Cecelia breathed a sigh of relief. Thank goodness.

"I suppose I should get him to bed," Mr. Pritchens said.

"I'll help you," she volunteered, moving toward her father. She knew Mr. Pritchens gave the staff the nights off because this became a regular occurrence with her father. It had become normal for him.

"One moment," he said.

Mr. Pritchens left the room and came back with a wet cloth, pressing it gently against the side of her face. "Ouch," she complained. Her eye was already swelling shut.

"That's going to hurt like the devil in the morning," he mused, tipping her chin up to get a better look.

"Where did you learn to fight, Mr. Pritchens?" she asked. As small as he was, he was strong. And he could take down her father. Why, he wasn't much bigger than Cecelia was.

"Necessity," he admitted.

Cecelia furrowed her brows. But it hurt to do so. "My kind of necessity?" she asked.

"Yes." He didn't say more. Just that one word.

"Yet you stay." She looked into kind, old gray eyes.

"I wouldn't leave you here for anything," he admitted. "Not alone."

"When I have my own household someday," Cecelia began, "will you come and manage it for me?"

His tired eyes brightened. "I live for the day."

She nodded.

He pressed the cold cloth tightly to her eye, and she winced again. "Keep it on there. It'll help." He patted her shoulder twice, then squeezed. "Go to bed. I'll take care of your father."

"Slap him around a few times while you're at it, will you?"

He heaved a sigh. "I would if I thought it would help." He looked Cecelia in the eye. "We're going to have to get some help for him."

She nodded. "Someone to slap the bottle out of his hand." She tried to laugh. But it came out more as a sob.

Mr. Pritchens cocked his head to the side and pressed his lips tightly together. "If that's what it takes."

"It won't help. Not unless he wants to change. He used to be an amusing drunkard."

He gently probed at her cheekbone. "Not amusing now," he murmured, anger flashing in his eyes.

"You're certain you can get him to bed by yourself?" she asked.

"Quite," he said, gritting his teeth as he looked down at her father. "Go to your chambers. I'll see to him."

Cecelia was halfway up the stairs when he called out to her. She turned back. "What should I tell Mr. Thorne when he comes to call tomorrow?"

"What makes you think he'll come to call?" she asked, her heart leaping at the thought.

He smiled. "He'll come."

She sighed heavily. "Tell him I'm not accepting callers." She turned to go upstairs.

"He'll ask for a reason," Mr. Pritchens called to her back.

"Tell him I'm ill, for goodness' sake, Pritchens," she called back. She couldn't let Marcus see her looking like this. And it would look even worse tomorrow, if history was a good indicator.

"He won't accept that."

"He won't have a choice."

Cecelia entered her chambers and looked around at what used to be her home. She crossed the room and leaned close to the looking glass. She'd seen pugilists leave Gentleman Jackson's looking less beat up than this. Her eye was a startling shade of red, and it was quickly swelling shut. She pressed the cold cloth against it, wincing as it touched the scraped skin of her cheek. Her father must have caught her with his ring.

A rising sense of elation buoyed her for a moment as she realized what Marcus would have walked into if she'd allowed him to escort her inside the house. At least he was spared from it. Even if she wasn't.

❧

Marcus broke his fast the next day to the sound of babies crying in the breakfast room. Allen stuck his fingers in his ears and made a face. "I imagined the land of the fae to be calm and serene." He raised his voice comically loud. "This is nothing of the sort."

Lord Phineas grinned. "Just wait until you have one of your own. I'll be sure to remind you of this conversation." He bounced Lucius on his knee.

"Can't you take them to the nursery or something?" Allen groused.

Claire passed Lucius to a hovering nurse, and another stepped forward for Cindy. Thank goodness Sophia and her son were still upstairs. "Take them to the nursery, will you?" Claire brushed Lucius's hair from his forehead. "And come and get me immediately if you need me."

"Yes, my lady," the nurse said.

"What are you two doing today?" Claire asked as she began to eat.

Allen looked at Marcus and grinned. "I'm going to see Ainsley. She's going to show me the sights."

Marcus snorted. "That what they're calling it these days?"

Allen flushed scarlet. "Shove it," he growled good-naturedly. He looked at Marcus. "What are your plans?"

He smirked. "I'm going to join you and Ainsley."

"If you must," Allen growled.

"I'm only joking. I'm going to call on Cecelia." His groin tightened at the thought of calling on Cecelia. "And then we're going to do whatever she had planned for herself today." He grinned at the thought. He didn't even care what it was. He just wanted to be with her. They could darn socks all day and he would be happy.

He tossed his napkin onto his plate and stood. "Speaking of which, could you make my excuses to Mother and Father? I don't want to wait for them to come down."

Claire stabbed a fork toward him. "You may want to send a calling card, first, Marcus, to be sure she's receiving callers today."

He'd never sent a calling card in his life. She would receive him. Any alternative was laughable. "Why would I do that? She's not angry at me anymore."

"Straightened all that out, did you?" Claire asked.

He grinned. They'd more than straightened it out.

Claire raised a brow at him and said to Lord Phineas, "Darling, why don't you tell Marcus where we went last night?"

Lord Phineas shot her a look hot enough to scorch paper. "I'm certain he doesn't want to hear about that."

Yet Claire continued. "I took Finn to see the cabin. You remember Grandfather's old hunting lodge, don't you?" She tilted her head at Marcus, but the wry tilt to her mouth told him she knew already.

"I remember it." He hadn't been able to stop thinking about it all night, truth be told. "You say you took Lord Phineas?"

Damn it all. The maid was supposed to go this morning to change the rumpled sheets and do the housekeeping.

"Mmm-hmm," Claire hummed.

"Damn it, Claire," he began.

Lord Phineas sat up taller and said, "Watch it, Marcus."

"Apologies," he murmured. "Stop acting like the cat that ate the cream."

"I will as soon as you admit what's going on," she shot back.

"I admit nothing," he batted out.

"I'm guessing it was Cecelia, wasn't it?" Claire asked, not the least bit sly about her probing.

"Leave it alone, Claire," Lord Phineas warned.

"Listen to your husband, Claire," Marcus warned as well.

"Oh, posh. I have your best interests at heart, Marcus." She suddenly sobered. "How is Cecelia?"

He shrugged. "She's well." Probably sore, but that wasn't anything Claire needed to know about.

"I have heard some things, Marcus," she started.

"What kind of things?" He sat back down to glare at her.

"It's all scuttlebutt, Marcus," she said on a heavy sigh. "But things are not well at home." She poked the air with her fork tines again. "Be careful, Marcus."

Marcus sighed and dropped his face into his hands, scrubbing down it. "I hate it when you're cryptic. Why don't you just say what you're thinking?" He couldn't tell if Claire was referring to the fact that he'd bedded Cecelia or that something was wrong with her. "She hasn't been ill, has she?"

"Her father hasn't been well," she started.

But Lord Phineas cut her off. "Claire," he warned.

She threw her fork down. Lord Phineas was the only one who'd ever been able to take Claire to task.

"The man is grieving, Claire," Marcus said. Surely everyone could see that.

"It's more than that." But Lord Phineas shot her a look, and she shut her lips tightly.

"Ask questions, Marcus. Lots of questions." Apparently, she was done with her cryptic ramblings, because she left the room.

"I won't stick my nose in your matters," Lord Phineas said. "But tread lightly with Cecelia, Marcus."

"You've already stuck your nose in my matters. I hate it when people say things like that but won't explain. So, out with it."

"You're straddling two worlds. And giving it a valiant effort, I might add."

"So are you." Marcus didn't understand this line of questioning.

"I'm not straddling anything. I'm a visitor here."

"And I'm a visitor in your world. Is that what you're saying?"

He took a sip of his tea. "Not at all. Your home is there. Or did you intend for it to be here?"

"It can be both."

"Does she want home to be both places?"

"I haven't asked her." He would do so today. He'd live wherever she chose. Particularly now that he had his father's blessing to do so.

"Ask lots of questions, Marcus. That's all." He grinned at Marcus and said, "And next time, change the damn linens so Claire won't speculate about who's been at the hunting lodge." He laughed as he stood up and quit the room.

Marcus adjusted his jacket and tucked his hair behind his ears. He was dying to see Cecelia, and he didn't want to wait another moment. If he was any happier, he would have to skip to her house like a child.

❧

He knocked on the door to Claire's house and made a move to step inside when Mr. Pritchens answered it. But Pritchens blocked his way. "Miss Hewitt is not receiving callers today, Mr. Thorne," he said.

"What?" Certainly Cecelia wanted to see him.

"I believe you heard me." The butler stood a little taller.

Marcus's heart clenched in his chest. "Might I ask why?"

"Miss Hewitt is otherwise occupied." But he didn't look Marcus in the face when he said it.

"What happened to your jaw, Pritchens?" Marcus asked, running a finger down his own jawline.

"Rotten luck," Pritchens said blandly.

"Sorry to hear it. Must hurt like the dickens."

"I've had worse." The man's voice retained no inflection.

"Step aside, Pritchens," Marcus said. "I'll see Cecelia now."

"No, sir," Pritchens said, his arms spanning the doorway.

"Is she sick?" Marcus asked.

"Not that I'm aware of."

"Then what's the problem?"

"She's otherwise occupied." Again, the man didn't look him in the eye.

"Move aside, Pritchens," Marcus growled.

"No, sir," Pritchens said again. Marcus knew he could take the old man.

"Did she tell you why she doesn't want to see anyone?" Marcus asked. His heart was beating like a team of runaway horses. She didn't want to see him? How could that be?

Marcus heard whistling behind him and turned around to find Ainsley walking up the stone path that led to the front of the house. "Good morning,

Marcus," she said. She had a little skip to her step as well.

"Morning," he grunted.

Pritchens smiled at Ainsley and stepped to the side, and she slid into the house. When Marcus went to follow, Pritchens stepped back into the doorway. "Why does she get to come in?" Marcus asked.

"Because she's not you?" Pritchens said very directly.

Marcus's heart was ready to break into a million pieces. "She doesn't want to see me. But no one else's visiting has been limited."

The butler refused to look Marcus in the eye. "I can't say, sir," he said. "Would you like to leave a note?"

Marcus shook his head. "That won't be necessary." His heart hurt so badly that he could barely take a deep breath.

"I'm sorry," Pritchens said quietly. "Come back in a few days."

Days? He wanted him to wait days to see her? Marcus nodded. Where there had been a spring in his step earlier, now there was none. His feet felt like they had lead weights attached to them.

They'd made love, and now she wanted nothing to do with him. It had been perfect, and now she wouldn't even see him. She wouldn't come to the door. Had he done something wrong? Had he hurt her without knowing it?

❦

Cecelia sat in her window and listened, the sound of voices below like a hatpin stuck through her heart.

Marcus's voice was soft, and he gave up easily. Too easily. But it was for the best. He certainly couldn't see her looking like this, could he? He would want an explanation. And this one couldn't be explained away as having hit her eye on the wardrobe door. This one was awful. And it was even worse that her father had been the one to deal the blow. It would be at least a week before the signs of the bruise faded.

Marcus was patient and kind. He turned to look up at her window, and she pulled herself back into the curtains. She couldn't face him right now. She just couldn't.

"Good morning," a voice called from her doorway. She turned around to find Ainsley walking into her room. Cecelia turned back toward the window. She didn't want Ainsley to see her face either, but she supposed it couldn't be avoided. At least Ainsley knew what was going on. Cecelia didn't have to explain.

"Why was Marcus being detained at the door?" Ainsley asked as she untied her bonnet and threw it on Cecelia's bed.

"I didn't want to see him," Cecelia said quietly. "Did he appear angry?"

"He was fit to be tied," Ainsley said. "I loved it." She laughed loudly. "I just don't understand it, since you were together yesterday." Ainsley's face turned crimson.

Cecelia slowly turned to face Ainsley. She wanted to wince at the embarrassment of it, but doing so would hurt too much.

Ainsley's choked gasp was all the proof Cecelia needed that her face looked as bad as she'd assumed.

"What the devil happened to you?" Ainsley asked, running to appraise the fresh bruise. She poked at it with her finger, and Cecelia had to brush her hand away.

"That hurts," she said.

"I'm not surprised," Ainsley said. "It looks like it hurts terribly."

What hurt terribly wasn't her eye. It was the fact that she could finally admit her love for Marcus, but she couldn't see him. "Ainsley," she said, her voice cracking.

"Your father did this." Ainsley didn't ask. She just gathered Cecelia in her arms, and Cecelia nodded into her shoulder. "Someone should horsewhip the man every time he picks up a bottle," she ground out.

"He's sick. I know he's sick," Cecelia explained. "He's been so sad since Mother died."

"Has he ever tried to stop drinking?"

"He's tried more times than I can count. What am I going to do, Ainsley?" she asked.

"You can't keep this a secret," Ainsley said.

"I can't tell anyone," Cecelia cried. She didn't want to see the pity on their faces. Nor the sneers. Nor did she want her father to be judged.

Ainsley wrung her hands together. "I can't, Cece," she finally said.

"What?" She couldn't have heard her right.

"I can't keep your secret. Not this time."

"I don't understand."

Ainsley took Cecelia's hand in her own and squeezed tightly, so tightly it nearly hurt. "I love you too much to let this continue." She grabbed her bonnet from the bed and put it on, tying it tightly. "I'm going to talk to Allen. I need some help with this."

"You can't, Ainsley." Cecelia rushed to follow her from the room. "You can't tell anyone," Cecelia called to her friend's retreating back.

Suddenly, Ainsley turned back to her. "I can't not tell anyone. Don't ask me to do that." Her eyes shone with unshed tears.

Then Ainsley turned and fled through the front door.

Cecelia walked downstairs, her feet heavy on the treads, and sank down on the settee. Mr. Pritchens flopped down beside her. "Finally," he breathed.

She reached out and blindly took his hand, unable to see through her tears. "Finally," she repeated.

What if Marcus was too hurt by her rejection to come and help her?

"He'll come," Mr. Pritchens said. She didn't even need to explain. "I feel somewhat sorry for your father when he does. But Mr. Thorne will come."

Seventeen

MARCUS SPENT THE DAY RIDING THE LAND. HE HADN'T checked on his holdings or the spiders that knitted their clothing or the mill or anything else in months. He still had holdings on this land, and he needed to take better care of them. He spoke with his tenants and made a list of things they needed, just as he'd done in the other world.

He'd kept track throughout the day and made a mental list of things he needed to check tomorrow.

By the time he returned home, the sun had set and it was pitch black outside. The moon was hidden behind dark clouds, and the stillness of the night was nearly ominous. Even the crickets had stopped chirping. Something was wrong. A hush in the land of the fae was never a good thing.

Marcus threw his reins to a waiting groom and walked briskly to the front door. He found his family, every last one of his family members, sitting silently in the front room. "Who died?" he asked as he looked from one to the other. None of them jumped up to tell him anything, but they all looked decidedly uncomfortable.

"Someone had better start talking!" he shouted.

His father stepped forward and laid a hand on his shoulder.

"Did something happen to Grandmother?" he asked, his chest hurting all of a sudden. He dropped into a chair.

His grandmother bustled around the corner. "I'm here, darling," she said. "I don't know why he assumed it would be me," she said playfully, her eyes sparkling.

"Then what's wrong?" he asked.

Ainsley sat forward, and she began to speak, her eyes filling with tears. She choked on the words, and Allen pulled her into his chest.

"Is it Cecelia?" he asked.

"Yes," his father said.

No. It couldn't be Cecelia. It couldn't be. "What happened?"

Ainsley composed herself and said, "She didn't want me to tell you."

"Tell me what?" Marcus barked. Someone had better come forth with some news soon, or he would go mad.

"She refused to see you this morning," Ainsley said.

He nodded. "What of it?"

"She didn't want to see you because her eye is swollen to the size of a turtle's back and she has a bruise on her cheek."

Marcus jumped to his feet.

"I had to tell you," she called to him. He turned around and walked to her, pulling her to him for a quick hug.

"It's all right. I'll sort it all out." He was trying

to calm himself just as much as he was trying to calm her.

He said to himself as he walked toward the door, "I shouldn't have taken no for an answer."

"Wait, Marcus," his father said. "I want to go with you."

"Me, too," Lord Phineas said, as he got to his feet.

Allen stood up and started for the door, as did Robinsworth.

"That bad, is it?" Marcus asked.

The women in the room looked at one another, and Ainsley was silently weeping.

"I really don't need help finding the place," Marcus said.

"I'm not worried that you'll need help with that," his father said.

"Who hit her?" Marcus asked, looking toward Ainsley.

"Her father," she whispered.

Marcus took off at a run toward Cecelia's house. Every man in the household joined him, as did his mother. "I'm going for Cecelia's sake," she explained. "Not for the rest of you."

Marcus didn't stop. He ran all the way to the door. When he got there, Mr. Pritchens was already pulling it open. He stepped to the side and Marcus said, "Where is she?"

"I knew you would come," Pritchens said, his chest swelling.

Marcus gathered the lapels of Pritchens's jacket in his hands and got in his face. "Tell me where she is," he said quietly.

A thump came from the corridor where Mr.

Hewitt's office was located. Pritchens nodded in that direction.

"Mr. Pritchens!" Cecelia yelled, as she stormed out of her father's study, but she came to a halt when she saw Marcus running toward her.

She reached up to cover her face. "Marcus," she said, closing her eyes as he pulled her hands back to look at her.

Her eye was swollen shut, and the skin around it was an alarming shade of purple. He pushed her cheekbone gently with the pad of his thumb. "I'm surprised it's not broken," he said.

He drew her into his chest. He would draw her into himself, if he could. But then a crash sounded behind them. "I'll get that," Pritchens said.

"Father, will you…" Marcus began. But Lord Ramsdale was already moving in that direction, along with Robinsworth, Allen, and Lord Phineas. They were a force to be reckoned with.

Cecelia grabbed his hands. "Don't let them hurt him," she pleaded. "When he's foxed, he sometimes does things."

"How long has this been going on?" Marcus asked. He didn't need an answer to that, since even once was too often.

"Since right after my mother died." Cecelia's voice broke, and she buried her face in his chest.

"I can't believe you didn't tell me."

"You weren't here to tell," she said softly.

She may as well have kicked him in the gut. All the breath left his body. She was right, though. He hadn't been there for her to lean upon. He hadn't been there because he had been trying to be human. "I'm so sorry," he said, his own voice breaking as he held her.

Marcus set her back from him, and his mother stepped forward. He said, "Trust me to take care of your father?"

She drew her lower lip between her teeth and said, "Do you promise you won't hurt him?"

He nodded. He wanted to kill him. But she would never leave if she thought harm would come to her father.

"He doesn't want to be like this."

"I'm going to help him, Cece."

"All right," she said with a nod.

Marcus leaned forward and kissed her. He kissed her hard, with every bit of the passion in his body. "I love you so much," he said.

"I love you, too," she whispered back, smiling through her tears.

"Go home with Mother," he said. He gave her a gentle push toward the door.

"But…" she began to protest, until his mother drew her into her arms and held her like she was her own daughter.

"We need to go," his mother urged. "Let Marcus take care of him."

"He doesn't want to be like this," she said again, panic in her voice.

"I'm not going to let anything happen to your bloody father," Marcus said. Cecelia flinched. "I promise, Cece. But you have to get out of here."

A crash sounded in the study, but Marcus wouldn't let her walk back there.

He bent at the waist and hoisted her over his shoulder. She squealed and held tightly to the back of his coat. "Put me down, Marcus," she said.

"No." There was no way he would let her stay there. Not right now. He walked out the front door and carried her over his shoulder all the way to his parents' house, where he walked through the door. She'd just about given up the fight when they arrived, and the ladies all jumped to their feet when he entered the house. His mother clucked a warning behind him.

"Claire," Marcus said, and she came forward.

"What can I do for you?" she asked. She bent over and looked into Cecelia's face. "Oh, dear, you do look dreadful," Claire said.

"Thank you," Cecelia said, her nose stuffy from being upside down. She sniffled.

"Put her down, Marcus," Claire said. "The poor thing has had enough."

"Not until she's safe," Marcus said, shaking his head. "Can you take her back through the painting to the human world? I don't want her father to be able to find her. Not until we get things sorted out."

Marcus had her thrown over his shoulder like a sack of feed, and she hadn't had enough fight in her to protest.

"You're certain you want her to go?" Claire asked.

He nodded. "It's the only way."

"We'll all go," Sophia said.

Claire nodded. "We'll all go."

"We have to get the children," Claire and Sophia said at the same time.

"Do you have the painting, Claire?" he asked, growing impatient.

She reached behind a heavy curtain. "It's been here all along."

Marcus took her hand in his and prepared to step into the painting with her. "Me first," his mother said. "You can't just thrust her in the human world with no one there."

She took his hand from Claire's and replaced it with her own, and then she walked into the painting and was gone. "Your turn," Claire said. "We'll follow in a very short time."

She patted the back of Cecelia's leg, and Cecelia laughed at the absurdity of it. "I'm glad you find this amusing," Marcus groused at her.

"I feel like a sack of grain, Marcus," she said, laughing louder. "I can't help it."

"She's delirious," Marcus grumbled. But he took Claire's hand and walked into the painting. When he got to the other side, he dropped Cecelia to her feet. She swayed for a moment as the pinkness receded from her cheeks. "Did I hurt your face?" he asked, taking her face in his gentle hands. Marcus had such gentle hands. He always had.

"I'm fine." She straightened her skirts. She was still dressed as a faerie. She would have to remedy that.

He turned to go back, but she jerked his arm and pulled him to her. His mother turned her back, thank goodness. Because she planned to kiss this man. And she planned to kiss him thoroughly. Her lips met his, and it wasn't a gentle kiss. It was a wild clash of teeth and tongues.

"I love you, Marcus," she said, pressing her forehead against his. His breathing was heavy and thick. Claire's hand was still extended through the painting, and she snapped her fingers to bring him back.

Ainsley popped her head into the painting next and said, "I'll be along shortly. I have to notify my father."

"All right," Cecelia laughed.

"I'll see you as soon as I can," Marcus said, his voice tight.

"Take care of yourself," Cecelia said.

He hugged her to him, his embrace tight enough to make her squeak. And then he left her standing there in his mother's entryway. Cecelia turned to Lady Ramsdale, who drew her into her arms.

"I think I forgot my daughters in the land of the fae," she said with a laugh.

"I'm so sorry to put you through this," Cecelia said.

Lady Ramsdale squeezed her. "You're a daughter to me, too," she said. "I can never take your mother's place, but I love you just as much as if I'd given birth to you, Cecelia."

Tears pricked at the backs of Cecelia's lashes. "I hope you do, because I plan to marry that man."

The rest of the ladies made it through the painting, all in good time, including Lady Ramsdale's daughters.

"Let's have some Madeira in my private sitting room, shall we?" Lady Ramsdale asked all the adults.

Cecelia nodded. If this was to be her new family, she couldn't have chosen a better one for herself.

Marcus let himself back in when he got to Cecelia's house. He peeked his head into Mr. Hewitt's study and found all of them, Mr. Hewitt included, playing cards. Mr. Hewitt could barely hold his head up. But he was still drinking.

"What's going on?" Marcus asked.

"Vingt-et-un," his father said. "Do you want to play?"

Marcus motioned toward the corridor. His father passed his cards to Mr. Pritchens, who took his place.

"Why are you playing cards?" he asked.

"It was Robinsworth's idea." His father shrugged.

"What's the theory behind it?"

"He's drunk and belligerent. And he's not going to get any better. So, it's best to let him fall asleep in his cups and then talk to him when he's sober. He'll be more receptive."

Marcus nodded. He really wanted to pin Mr. Hewitt to the wall by his throat. But he had promised Cecelia he wouldn't hurt her father. There would be plenty of time to talk to him tomorrow when he was sober. Then they would figure out what to do next.

&

"I want you to take all the spirits from the house," Mr. Hewitt said. "I want them removed. Every last drop."

His eyes shone with unshed tears. But Marcus couldn't drum up enough sympathy for him. Or any. He'd hit Cecelia. He'd hurt her. More than once.

The only reason he was there trying to help the man was because Cecelia had asked him to. "We won't return it to you," Marcus clarified.

"I don't want you to," Mr. Hewitt said, shaking his head.

They'd informed him of his misdeeds when he'd woken up that morning, and he'd taken it none too gently. The last thing he remembered when he woke was a rousing game of cards. He didn't remember going to sleep. Before he'd fallen too deeply into his cups, they had him write a note to himself, just to prove that he did things he didn't and couldn't remember when he was foxed.

He didn't remember writing the note, but the evidence was there in front of him when he woke.

"We won't allow you to get more," Marcus said.

"Tie me up and put me in a room," Mr. Hewitt said. "I'm a danger to myself. And to others. And to my daughter." His voice cracked. "Bloody hell," he swore. "How did it come to this?"

Marcus refused to allow Cecelia's father to justify his actions with his grieving, even though he was. He was a drunkard, plain and simple. He drank too much, and he did stupid things when he drank. Therefore, he must not drink anymore.

"There will be no servants in the house while you get sober," Marcus warned. "Not even Mr. Pritchens."

Mr. Pritchens opened his mouth to protest. "But…" he began. Marcus held up a hand, and Mr. Pritchens silenced himself.

"Mr. Pritchens has a fondness for you. And he must leave because he might see your weakness and feel the need to make you happy again when things go poorly. And they will go very poorly."

"I've stopped drinking before," Mr. Hewitt said. "It wasn't that bad."

"You suffered a great loss when Mrs. Hewitt died. And you tried to fill the void. We understand that. But if you want us to help you, we have to do it our way."

He nodded. "Let's do it."

"Get all the spirits, Mr. Pritchens," Marcus said. They dumped every drop out the window together.

"These next few weeks will be difficult for you," Marcus warned. "You'll probably vomit. You'll perspire. You'll not be able to sleep. You'll curse the day we were born."

Mr. Hewitt looked from one person to another. "You're all going to stay?" He heaved a sigh. "I feel terrible keeping you all from your families."

Marcus's father spoke up. "When this is over, my son is going to marry your daughter, so you're part of our family already."

Mr. Hewitt nodded. "What shall we do to occupy ourselves?" he asked.

"Cards?" Marcus suggested.

Everyone moved to sit down at the table.

"Where are all your wives?" Mr. Hewitt asked.

"We sent them to the human world to keep Cecelia safe," Marcus said. "They are keeping themselves busy. Probably buying bonnets and slippers and ribbons they don't need." They were more likely to be curing diseases or solving someone's problems. But he wanted to ease the man's mind, after all.

Marcus covered Mr. Hewitt's hand with his. "I plan to marry her," he warned.

"I know you will," Mr. Hewitt said. "I wish you'd done it six months ago."

So did Marcus.

Eighteen

CECELIA LIFTED A FINGER TO HER MOUTH AND ABSENTLY nibbled at a nail. She'd been waiting for what seemed like hours for Claire to walk back through the painting with her father and Marcus in tow. Marcus had sent word with Milly just days ago and said to expect them. He said her father had some business to take care of before they could leave, but that they would be along as soon as it was done.

Lord Phineas and the Duke of Robinsworth had returned to the other world a sennight ago. Marcus had stayed behind with her father to clear up his outstanding issues. There was the matter of his fight with Mr. Randall and his punishment. He was to be removed from his seat with the Trusted Few, and when Cecelia returned, she would take that seat.

She wasn't certain she could do it justice. Sometimes, she wanted nothing more than to tell the fae to go to the very devil, but she couldn't. They were her people, and she would have to go back and forth in the future. At least she would be able to represent both worlds with her leadership and fight for the interests of all.

The first motion she would make would be regarding marriage equality. Her marriage to Marcus would be viewed differently by the Trusted Few than would the marriage of two fully fae people. And she wanted that practice to cease. Her marriage would be just as valid as any other, and she wouldn't settle until the unpardonable errors were changed to reflect the need for equality. She could do good things with her seat on the bench. She really could. She was sure of it.

A knock sounded on the window, and Cecelia crossed to throw it open. "You're going to wear your nails down to the quick if you don't stop that incessant gnawing," Milly warned.

"Where have you been?" Cecelia asked. "I expected you to come yesterday with news."

Milly kicked at the oak floor with the toe of her slipper. "Something came up."

"You mean Ronald?" Cecelia asked playfully.

"Ronald has a way of stealing my attention." A blush colored the garden gnome's cheeks. "Even after all these years."

"Do you know where they are?" Cecelia asked.

"Things didn't go very well in court," Milly confessed. "They were detained for a bit."

"What didn't go well?"

"They wanted to put your father in gaol," she said. "But he made restitution to Mr. Randall, and the man was finally satisfied, so he asked for leniency."

"So all of that is resolved?"

"Every bit of it. Your future husband is a brilliant speaker. He had the Trusted Few believing that your father has turned over a new leaf. That he has changed.

He went on and on about how your father hasn't had a drop of spirits in a month."

Marcus had written to her about it, but he hadn't been very forthcoming with details.

"My father is coming here with Marcus, right?"

Cecelia was a little bit scared to see her father. She'd left him with a group of men he didn't know to dry out. It was his family-to-be, but he still could hold a grudge. He might be upset that she'd abandoned him a month ago. Although it was really he who abandoned her. He might not see it that way. "He's well now, right?"

Milly smiled. "He's well." She patted Cecelia's hand. "I would worry more about that man who is dead set on marrying you." She grinned.

"If we marry here, he'll have to wait for the reading of the banns."

"Not if he asked his father to secure a special license," Milly sang.

"He didn't!" Cecelia cried. But her heart leaped at the same time.

"Rumor has it that he did." Milly clucked her tongue. "They might send for the vicar this very evening."

Nothing would make Cecelia happier. It had been more than a month since she'd seen the man she loved more than life itself.

Claire had gone into the painting more than an hour before to bring them back. Cecelia expected them to return right away. But it wasn't to be, apparently.

Cecelia flopped down on the settee to wait. After another hour, her eyelids grew heavy. She laid her head down on the arm of the settee and waited. She tried to stay awake, but it was simply too difficult. Certainly, she would wake when Marcus came through the painting.

She let her eyes close and drifted off to sleep.

Marcus had never seen a sight more beautiful. Part of him didn't want to wake her, but she was waiting there for him. She'd fallen asleep waiting, apparently, and he loved her even more for it.

Good God, she was beautiful. Her hair spilled over the side of her face, and he reached out to tuck it behind her ear. She stirred, reaching for his hand. He took it in his and looked at her face.

Suddenly, her eyes shot open and she sat up. "Marcus?" she squealed. And she launched herself into his arms. He picked her up, spinning her around until he was certain he would make them both dizzy. "I missed you so much," she admitted when he finally set her down and looked into her face.

"Not as much as I missed you," he said. He'd missed her like he would miss his right arm if someone took it. Every day, he'd debated about going through the painting to see her. He'd considered it so many times. But there were days in the beginning when his presence was needed. And there were days at the end of his stay with her father when he didn't want to miss the healing process. He wanted to witness it all so he could recount it to her. So he could tell their children about their grandfather's triumphs. So he could tell them how strong he was and how much he'd overcome.

There was also some truth to the fact that he

wanted to see the man punished. But they'd spent hours and days and weeks talking. They'd talked about Mrs. Hewitt's death and the utter devotion Mr. Hewitt felt for her. They'd talked about how he felt when Cecelia was born. How he'd never been disappointed he had a daughter and no sons, because his daughter was bloody perfect.

Mr. Hewitt told him about the day of her birth, and how frightened he'd been the day she went on her first mission and how angry he was at himself for hurting her. It wasn't until Mr. Hewitt learned to forgive himself that he could heal. So, Marcus stayed to help him with that.

Cecelia jerked him from his reverie when she reached up and pulled him down so that his lips could meet hers. In that moment, he felt like he'd come home. She kissed him, her lips soft and welcoming, and her arms were strong and open. And he'd never loved her more.

"Where's my father?" she asked when he finally let her breathe for a moment.

"He'll be along in a moment," Marcus said. "I wanted to see you first. Your father will arrive with Claire momentarily."

She nodded.

"Cece, I love you so much," Marcus said.

"I love you, too," she repeated. "I thought I would die if you didn't come to me soon."

Marcus pulled her down to sit beside him on the couch. He took her face in his hands and said, "I want to be inside you so badly." His voice shook with the strain of his words.

"Marcus," she scolded. "You shouldn't say such things."

"But it's true," he said. And he took her hand and placed it on his trousers where he was rigid for her already. A blush crept up her cheeks.

"Will you come to me tonight?" she whispered.

He would love nothing more. "I thought you would never ask."

Claire walked through the painting, and Marcus looked at Cecelia and said, "Your father will shoot me if he catches us like this." A grin tugged at his lips.

"I doubt he could care."

After her father had sobered up, he'd threatened Marcus's very life over his daughter. And Marcus had a healthy fear of the man. Or at least of the father of the woman he planned to marry.

"Your father is coming through," he warned. He kissed her quickly and left the room.

❧

"Thank you, Claire," Cecelia said, as her father entered the room. His appearance was that of the man she used to know when her mother was alive. His face was clean shaven, and his hair was combed and slicked back with pomade. He was dressed for dinner, and he'd never looked more handsome. "Papa," she acknowledged hesitantly. She probably sounded more than a bit cold, but she couldn't help it. He'd done some terrible things. And they couldn't be taken back.

"Cecelia," he said. He smiled at her, but he didn't rush across the room to come to her. Out of the corner of her eye, she saw Claire leave the room quietly.

"You can't even look me in the eye, can you?" he asked. "Do you hate me?"

Did she? Maybe a little. She didn't answer.

He rushed on to say, "It's all right if you do. I wouldn't blame you. You have every reason."

She nodded, biting her lower lip between her teeth.

"I can't begin to tell you how sorry I am." He crossed the room to stand in front of her. "God, you look so much like your mother it hurts."

Tears threatened to spill over Cecelia's lashes. "I can't help that."

He rushed to shush her. "I wouldn't change it for anything." He took a deep breath. "I was angry at her for leaving. And I was angry at myself for not protecting her."

"And me? Why were you angry at me, Papa?"

"I was angry at you because you wouldn't let me fall into a hole and die, Cecelia. You gave me a shadow of a reason to live. And I didn't want to. I wanted to die. I wanted to go with your mother. I wanted to leave."

"You wanted to leave me?" she asked.

"You're the only thing that kept me here, Cece," he admitted. "You're the only thing."

He touched her hand tenderly, cautiously, as though he was afraid she would jerk away. She still might. She didn't trust him. She didn't trust that he would stay away from spirits for the rest of his life. She didn't trust that he would be the father she'd once known.

"I love you, Cecelia," he said. "And I don't expect you to forgive me. But I hope you'll let me be a part of your life and let me share in it."

"Marcus wants to marry me," she said cautiously.

He nodded. "He's not good enough for you," her father said.

It was almost as though a hand reached into her chest and squeezed her heart. "You can't possibly say no."

He chuckled. "I would never keep you from that lad," he said. The pressure in her chest eased. "But I stand by my comment. He's not good enough for you, because no one will ever be good enough for you. Ever." He chuckled again. "But as sons-in-law go, I suppose I could do worse."

She smiled a watery smile at him. He was feeling protective of her, was he? He hadn't felt like that in a very long time.

He took her chin in his hand and tipped it up. "I don't expect forgiveness, and I'm not asking for it. All I want is a chance. Give me a chance to be your father."

"You'll always be my father."

"I've always been your father. Now I want to be a good father." He coughed into his fist, as though he needed to clear his throat. "For the first time in a very long time, I have something to live for. Let me live for you."

She pressed a hand to his heart. "Live for you," she said.

A knock sounded on the door, and Cecelia looked over to see Marcus with his head stuck through the door. "Everything all right in here?" he asked.

Her father looked down at her and asked, "Is it? Is it all right if I stay for a bit?"

She nodded.

"Thank God," Marcus teased. "Because we were just about to call for the vicar. And I'd like to marry your daughter, Mr. Hewitt, if I have your blessing."

Her father sobered. He looked down at Cecelia. "Would you consider waiting for a month?"

"A month? Why?" Marcus said calmly.

"I just got my daughter back," her father said. "Give me some time with her."

Marcus looked at her, his brow furrowed. "Is that what you want, Cecelia?" he asked.

"Not really," she said.

"A fortnight?" her father said. "A proper courtship?"

Apparently, her father wanted things done the proper way. Marcus scowled. She asked hesitantly, "Would you mind waiting? Just a fortnight?"

Marcus bit his lips together, but then he said in a big rush, "If it's what you want." He threw his hands up in surrender.

"It's not what I want," she said quietly. "But I fear it's what we need."

Marcus crossed the room to her and took her face in his hands. "I'll provide for your every need from now on."

Her father coughed into his closed fist. "I'm still providing for her needs for the next fortnight. But you can court her."

Marcus grinned. "Courting in this world means rides in the park and dancing at balls."

She looked up at her father.

He scowled down at her. "It means riding in the park with a chaperone. And dancing at balls with a chaperone."

"Bloody hell," Marcus bit out.

Her father laughed. "You'll survive it, Marcus."

Marcus nodded. "I'll do anything for her."

"I know you will. That's why I asked." Her father laughed. And he sounded so much like the man she used to know that she wanted to grant his request.

Nineteen

Cecelia's father was determined to keep her away from Marcus, and he was doing everything he could to prevent them from spending any time alone. If he knew what they'd done at the cabin in the land of the fae, he wouldn't be so set on his mission to keep them apart. Or perhaps he would. But he would also feel the need to choke the life from Marcus if he knew, so she supposed this was for the best.

Her father had walked her to her chamber after supper the night before, and she could have sworn she heard him pacing the corridor during the night. She'd never wanted anything more than to hold Marcus in her arms. She wanted to lay her head on his chest and listen to his heartbeat. She wanted to feel his skin against hers. She wanted to hold him between her thighs.

"If your face gets any rosier," Lady Ramsdale chided from across the breakfast table, "we'll have to douse you with water to cool you off." She arched a brow at Cecelia. Luckily, they were the only two people in the room. Cecelia had risen early, hoping to see Marcus before anyone else got up. Or rather, before her father rose from bed. No one else seemed to mind the way they pined for one another. But her father had lost time to make up for, she supposed.

"Woolgathering," Cecelia muttered at Lady Ramsdale.

"Must be some rather warm wool," Lady Ramsdale shot back.

Cecelia choked on her tea.

"Oh dear, I didn't mean to make you choke!" Marcus's mother said.

Cecelia held up her hand. "It's all right," she sputtered. "You just surprised me."

"Darling, I'm not so old that I don't know what you're feeling." She looked at Cecelia over the rim of her teacup. "It certainly won't hurt Marcus to wait for a fortnight."

But what if it hurt Cecelia? "Yes, Lady Ramsdale," she said. "I know."

"Are you nervous at all about the wedding?" Lady Ramsdale asked.

Cecelia shook her head. "I am not at all anxious about that. I'm more anxious about our life after that."

"What about it worries you, dear?" Marcus's mother asked, putting her teacup down.

Cecelia shrugged. "Sometimes I worry about going from one world to another all the time. I almost think it would be better for me to give up my wings and come here. We could live a quiet life."

"You will do no such thing," Marcus said as he barreled into the room. He walked over and kissed Cecelia on the forehead. His lips were soft, and he ran a hand down her hair before he crossed to the sideboard and began to fill a plate with his breakfast. "In fact," he went on to say, "I would give up the title before I would allow you to do something that ridiculous."

"You would do that for me?" Cecelia asked.

"That and more," he said, and he pulled his chair as close to hers as it could go. "I would go to the ends of the earth for you," he said, looking deeply into her eyes. His knee touched hers, the heat of it seeping through his trousers to warm her leg.

His mother sniffled across the table and dabbed at her eyes.

"I can't imagine you without wings," Marcus said. "Preposterous."

"We already have enough magic between us, Marcus," Cecelia said with a laugh.

"As long as we don't have magic *between* us," Marcus clarified. He motioned from her to him and back. "As in keeping us apart. I would give up this world in order for you to keep your magic."

"You mean more to me."

"Oh, I can almost see it now," his mother said. "For his birthday, you'll give him your wings in a box. And for your birthday, he'll give you his ring."

Cecelia looked down at the ring that his father had given him. The family crest. "That wouldn't do either of us any good, would it?" she said with a laugh.

"So I suggest you adapt to going back and forth. Particularly now that you're both going to be seated on the bench."

"I still can't get over that," Cecelia said with a sigh.

"Does it intimidate you at all?" Lady Ramsdale asked.

Cecelia shook her head. "Not really. Maybe we can do some good. I don't think anyone young has ever been in leadership. Not that I can remember."

"You two will do wonderfully. Perhaps someday, humans who marry fae will be able to go back and forth at will. Even without sneaking into a painting."

"Marriage equality is the first thing on my agenda. I aim to rewrite the Unpardonable Errors."

Marcus looked deep into her eyes. "I plan to help you."

"We'll do it together."

Marcus certainly hoped so. "Where is your father?" Marcus asked.

Cecelia shrugged. "I suppose he hasn't risen yet. I'm not certain."

"I thought I would wake up to find you tethered to his side for the next fortnight."

Cecelia giggled. "So did I, honestly."

Beneath the table, Marcus laid a hand on her knee, and she looked up at him, scolding him with her glance. But he didn't even look at her. He continued to eat with his right hand, while the tip of his left index finger drew circles on her knee.

Cecelia worried she would grow as bright as an overripe tomato. She laid a hand on his and squeezed. But when she did, he looked down at her. His eyes held a promise. One she dearly hoped he would fulfill. Soon.

His mother jerked her from his gaze when she cleared her throat and said, "The two of you do know where babes come from, correct?"

Marcus choked on his eggs. "Mother!" he cried.

She held her hands up as though in surrender. "I'm just asking." She laughed to herself. "Do I need to remind you that babes typically take nine months to grow before they're born, and that the *ton* counts those months the way they count the money under their mattresses?"

Marcus didn't say anything. But his cheeks were rosy, and his neck and the tips of his ears were just as colorful.

"Although, I will admit," she said, "that you were special, Marcus. You only took seven months and then there you were."

"Oh, dear God," Marcus grumbled as he looked down at the table.

Cecelia clamped a hand to her mouth to keep from laughing.

"I should go get your father and let him have this talk with you," Lady Ramsdale said. She started to get to her feet.

"Please don't," Marcus cried.

His mother plopped back into the chair and laughed. "If you're certain." She heaved a sigh. "I didn't get to be your mother for a long time, Marcus. So, let me be one now." She leaned forward, her weight on her elbows, as though she wanted them to listen closely. "The *ton* can go to the devil," she said.

Then she got up and started for the door. Finally, Cecelia might have a moment alone with Marcus.

"Thank you, Mother," Marcus said.

Mr. Hewitt appeared in the doorway just as Lady Ramsdale was leaving. "Mr. Hewitt," she cried. "I'm so glad I found you. I have an emergency with my rosebushes, and I was wondering if I could prevail upon you to help me."

"Well, I…" he started, but he didn't get to finish, because Lady Ramsdale just threaded her arm through his and led him away, chattering like a magpie all the way.

"I think your mother just gave us permission to… you know."

"I don't want to talk about my mother," Marcus groaned, and he took Cecelia's face in his hands. His lips touched hers, his tongue licking over and into her mouth. Cecelia's breath rushed from her body, and she found it difficult to get it back. "I need you," he said. "Your father caught me in the corridor last night when I was trying to come to see you."

"I thought I heard a commotion out there," she said. "What happened?"

"He threatened to chop off my head. And my manhood." Marcus shivered dramatically. "And I believed him."

"He likes you."

"He might like me, Cece, but he loves you. We became good friends through his recovery, but I'll never surpass you in his heart. He'd sooner kill me than allow me to harm you." He looked into her eyes. "Or bed you."

Marcus glanced toward the door. "How long do you think we have before they come back?" He grinned, his eyes twinkling.

"Not long enough for what you want to do," she said, laughing.

"At this point, I don't think it would take me very long."

"I vaguely remember it not taking you very long that first time. In fact," she held up a finger, and he stopped her by kissing the tip of it.

"Don't remind me," he groaned.

She leaned closer to him. "I like that I can do that to you," she said quietly. Then she licked her lips.

"Don't do that," he ground out.

"Do what?" she asked, but a grin tugged at her lips. "I don't know what you're talking about." She inched her hand toward the fall of his trousers.

"Don't touch me," he warned. "If you do, that same thing might happen again."

He reached down and began to ruck her gown up in his fist, raising it higher and higher. The servant had vacated the room when she and Marcus had started kissing, thank goodness, because she wasn't about to stop Marcus. When he had her gown gathered in his fist, he bent down, his breath heavy against her neck as he breathed, "Open up for me."

His hand slid up the inside of her thigh. "Please touch me," she begged, reaching for his shoulder to steady herself.

His hand was almost to the center of her, which was throbbing and aching for him, when loud laughter from the corridor made him jerk back, pull her skirt down, and sit up. He filled his mouth with egg, and she reached for her teacup, but her hand was too shaky to lift it.

"I don't know if I can wait a fortnight," he growled.

"Oh, I am sure they're in the breakfast room,"

his mother said loudly. "They have a servant with them, so I'm not worried," she went on to reassure Cecelia's father, he supposed. The servant entered through the rear door and positioned himself beside the sideboard. He looked like he wanted to grin. But he composed himself.

"I do love your mother," Cecelia said.

"She's very good at what she does," Marcus said with a laugh.

If he wanted her nearly as much as she wanted him, he was sorely in need of attention. "I could sneak out tonight and come to you," Cecelia said.

"He'll hear you," Marcus grumbled.

Cecelia heaved a sigh. They were doomed to wait a fortnight.

❦

If Marcus got any harder, he would never be able to get up from the table. Even the servant shot him a sympathetic glance.

His mother made some more noise, and Marcus moved his chair back from Cecelia's so that their legs weren't touching beneath the table. To suit her father, he really should go sit on the other side of the table, but he couldn't get up right now if he wanted to.

"I think your mother is choking to death in the corridor," Cecelia laughed.

"She's giving us fair warning," Marcus said, rolling his eyes.

"If she hadn't, they'd have walked in while your hand was up my dress," she whispered, her face coloring prettily. He wanted to kiss her. He wanted to kiss her until they were both naked and breathless and he was inside her.

"Bloody hell," he groaned to himself.

"Might I suggest thinking about the ice sculptures your mother will buy for the wedding dinner, Mr. Thorne?" the servant said.

He motioned the servant forward. "Take Miss Hewitt's plate over to the other side of the table, would you?" he grunted.

"Yes, Mr. Thorne," the footman said with a smile.

Cecelia grumbled, but she went. The footman arranged her plate across from Marcus, and that was when her father and his mother walked back into the room.

"I'm so sorry," his mother was saying. "I thought the roses needed some attention, but the gardener must have gotten to it before we got there. I regret wasting your time."

"No harm done," Mr. Hewitt said. He narrowed his eyes at Marcus. "Everything going well, Marcus?" he asked.

Well, I had my hand up your daughter's skirt and you almost caught me, but aside from that... "Wonderfully," Marcus said. "Did you sleep well?"

Mr. Hewitt arched a brow at Marcus. "Aside from a disruption or two."

Marcus nodded.

"I hope we won't have the same interruptions tonight," Mr. Hewitt warned.

Marcus heaved a sigh. "Certainly not."

Marcus would go mad before he got to hold Cecelia in his arms again.

"Certainly not," Mr. Hewitt repeated.

His mother broke into their head-butting. "Cecelia, I thought you and I might be able to go shopping today." Her eyes sparkled at Cecelia. His mother was up to something. He just didn't know what.

"Of course," Cecelia said. "When do you want to go?"

"Claire and Sophia are coming. We can go when they get here." She winked at Cecelia.

Cecelia looked up at Marcus, a question in her eyes.

Cecelia wasn't at all certain what was going on, but something was. Lady Ramsdale came to collect her, and they climbed into the carriage. "Where are we going?" Cecelia asked as she settled back against the squabs.

"*We're* going shopping," Lady Ramsdale chirped. She looked at Claire and Sophia and raised her brow. "*You're* going to see Marcus."

"What? I don't know what you mean."

Claire pushed back the curtain that covered the window, and there stood a painting. It was a beautiful painting of a small meadow. A tree stood in the corner, and a small stream meandered across the field. A blanket lay nestled in the tall grass with a basket of food beside it. "Marcus is waiting for you in there," she said.

"He is? How did you?" Cecelia sputtered.

"Dear God," Lady Ramsdale said, throwing her head back. "If I have to wait a fortnight for you and Marcus to spend time together, it's going to be like talking to a bear. A big one. One that will bite my head off at every turn."

"He's not that bad," Cecelia groused. He kind of was. Or she could imagine he would be. And she was dying to see him alone. She'd missed him so.

"Why are you really doing this?" she asked.

Lady Ramsdale wiped beneath her eyes. "I remember what it's like to be young and in love. Embrace it, Cecelia."

Sophia and Claire looked on sympathetically. Then Claire gave her a nudge. "He's waiting for you."

"We can't give you very long," Lady Ramsdale warned. "So spend your time wisely. We'll collect you in four hours. Then I have to deliver you back to your father." She looked out, her eyes dreamy. "You can take a long walk by the stream. You can sit beneath the shade of that tree. You can talk for four whole hours." She grinned.

"Or you can just make love for four hours," Sophia said, her voice bland. "Though it's rather wretched sounding, and it makes me want to cast up my accounts. So, if that's what you're doing, I don't want to know about it when you come back."

"As if they would do anything else," Claire said, sarcasm heavy in her voice.

"This is a bit awkward," Cecelia said, hanging her head.

"He loves you. You love him. Enjoy your time together. Because you're not likely to get any more."

Claire held out her hand, and Cecelia dropped to her knees, ready to crawl into the painting.

Twenty

MARCUS JERKED HIS WATCH FOB FROM HIS POCKET AND looked down at it. It had been three quarters of an hour since he'd entered the painting. With his blasted luck, he would be stuck there for the rest of his life. It would probably serve him right. But when his mother had presented him with the opportunity to spend some time with Cecelia after having been away from her for a whole month, he'd jumped at the chance.

Her father had probably figured out their plot and foiled it. But then, out of the corner of his eye, he saw Cecelia climb into the painting. Claire poked her head in long enough to wave at him and yell, "Four hours, Marcus! And please don't be naked when I come back!"

Marcus reached down and helped Cecelia to her feet. "What is this place?" she asked.

He shrugged. "It's one of Claire's paintings. It's not a real place. You can tell by the walls."

"There are walls?" she asked, walking toward the edge. She sank her hand into where the painting ended, and her hand disappeared through the fog. "The walls are fictitious."

"All of this is," he said.

"That's some talent Claire has. How did she end up with it anyway?" Cecelia asked.

Marcus looked at her and bit his lower lip. "That's an amusing story."

He took her hand in his and walked with her to the blanket beneath the willow tree. The sky was blue and the clouds puffy and billowy, and the stream lent a low rushing noise to the background. "Tell it to me," she said as she sat down.

He sat beside her and straightened one leg before him, while keeping the other one up. He drew her to lean against his leg so that she reclined in front of him, and he tangled his fingers with hers. "It all started with Sophia."

"Sophia can walk into paintings too?" Cecelia asked.

"No, Sophia is entranced by music. It's how she met the Duke of Robinsworth. She was at a house party his mother threw when she heard music in the night. She was entranced by it, and it drew her to his chambers. They spent a lot of time together over the piano, and she couldn't resist his songs."

"I didn't know the duke played," Cecelia said.

"He doesn't do it often. But Sophia says he used to do it when he was feeling melancholy. He had a piano in his chambers."

"That's an odd thing to have in one's chambers," Cecelia mused.

"He's a bloody duke. He can have whatever he wants."

"So what does the music have to do with the paintings?"

He took a deep breath. This was difficult to explain. "It appears as though Mother and Father left a token with each of their fae children so that we could recognize them later in life. For Sophia, she was entranced by music. And the purpose was so that she would recognize the song of a loved one."

"And she recognized the duke?"

Cecelia ran a finger down the center of his chest and stole his attention. "What were we talking about?" he asked.

She laughed. "Sophia recognized the duke as someone who loved her."

"Oh, yes. He was the one. The tokens have backfired, apparently. Because by the time Sophia's token began to work, the duke was in love with her, so it was his song that entranced her. She recognized him as the one who loved her, and then they fell in love, and the rest is history."

She mulled it over in her mind, the crease between her brows growing deeper. "Wait, so you're saying that the token was so that she could find her parents, your parents, but she found the duke instead? Because he was the one who loved her and it was his song she recognized?"

"Exactly. Mother is a singer, and she thought it would be her song. But the duke fell in love with her before she found Mother and Father."

"But what about Claire and the paintings? Is that her token? The fact that she can paint?"

"Father is an artist," he went on to explain. This really was very convoluted. "They left Claire with a magical paintbrush, and when she has the paintbrush in her hand, she can walk into any painting of her choice. If it's a real place, she's in that place, like when we went to Paris and to the land of the fae. And if it's not a real place, then she goes to a place like this." He held up his hands, indicating the picturesque little field and the tree.

"I still don't understand," Cecelia said. "What does her walking into paintings have to do with your parents?"

Marcus heaved a sigh. "They left her with a painting of a tiny door that Grandmother kept in the attic. Over the door it said 'Sweet Home' in Latin. When Claire was angry one day, she went to the attic, found the painting, the paintbrush, and the door, and she went through it, hoping to escape Mother and Father's presence in the land of the fae. She didn't yet like them at that point."

"And?" Cecelia prompted.

"When she went through the painting, she tumbled directly into Lord Phineas's bedchamber, because he was 'home' for her. He was mad for her, and she was already increasing, so this all made sense at the time."

"Oh, I see," she said. "Did you get a token, too?"

"I did." He nodded.

She elbowed him in the belly. "Tell me what it is. Don't leave me in suspense."

"First, I need to tell you what we've come to know about the tokens," he said. He brushed a lock of hair back from her face. "We learned that the tokens represent home. When we were younger, that home might have been with our parents. But since our tokens took effect later, they pointed us to homes of a different sort. They took us all to the home in our hearts. The ones we love."

He reached into his pocket and pulled out his compass. "This used to point me home when I went on missions. It always did. I would leave home, and I could always find a portal by using my compass. It never failed me. Until I left you. And I found you again. The night you appeared at the ball where we were all introduced to society, I opened my compass and it pointed to you."

"I'm home for you?" she asked, sitting up, the sweetest of smiles on her face.

"Wherever you are is home. Here, there, the land of the fae… We could be on the moon and it would be home for me as long as you're there."

"But does that mean each of you were fated to fall in love with one specific person?" She didn't appear happy. Not at all.

He rushed on to say, "No, it doesn't work like that."

"Are you certain? Because that doesn't sound very fair if that's the case."

"No, no." He'd bungled this royally. "We were all in love already when our tokens took effect. I love you, Cece. The only one who doesn't know it is you. The universe already knows." He jiggled the compass at her. "The magic knows. The world knows. You need to know." He took her face in his hands and looked into her eyes.

"But it's almost like none of you had free will."

He threw up his hands. "It's not like that at all."

"Why isn't it?"

"The tokens point to who we love, you ninny." He tweaked her nose. "They are merely further proof that we are with the people we're supposed to be with. I'm supposed to be with you for the rest of my life. You're home for me."

She lay back, her head on his thigh. Usually, their positions were reversed. But he rather liked this, too. He began to pull the pins from her hair, dropping them one by one to lie beside him on the blanket. "What are you doing?" she asked.

"I want to touch you all over. And I'm starting at the top," he said with a chuckle.

"What if I wasn't the one, Marcus?" she asked. "What if your compass pointed to someone else one day?"

"My compass will never point to anyone else, Cece. Ever."

"But what if someday it magically does?"

"Then I will bash the blasted thing into oblivion. Because I know my heart better than any compass ever could."

"Hmm…" she said.

"Stop thinking," he urged. "The tokens are just further proof. They have nothing to do with how I love you or why I love you or how long I'll love you."

"How do you love me?" she asked with a giggle. She looked up at the clouds with a smile on her face rather than looking at him.

"Desperately and completely," he said.

"Why do you love me?" she asked, her smile even bigger than before.

"Because you're home for me."

Her smile softened. "How long will you love me?" she asked.

"Forever and a day."

She was quiet, and he could tell she was thinking. He nudged her head with his knee, brushing her hair back from her face with gentle fingers. "What are you thinking about?"

"I'm thinking about how much I missed you when we were apart." She turned onto her side to face him. "I'm thinking about how I felt abandoned and alone."

She might as well have stuck a knife in his gut. He could never say he was sorry enough. "When we were in the land of the fae, did you sleep with me because you were in love with me? Or because you needed to escape from your life?"

She didn't say anything for a moment. "A little bit of both," she finally admitted. "I used you shame-lessly." She giggled. "I would be angry at me if I were you."

A grin tugged at his own lips. "I would be willing to pay penance such as that anytime you choose."

"You're so selfless," she chided.

"You should have told me about your father," he said softly. "I could have helped you long before I did."

"You left me. And I didn't want to call upon you for anything after that." She shrugged. "Stubborn pride."

"I would have come back for you," he said, taking her chin in his hand so he could look into her eyes. "I would have come back for you anytime."

"I wanted you to come back for me just because you loved me. Not because I needed someone to save me."

"Yet you came for the mission to secure my place in human society."

She looked everywhere but at him. "I needed a reprieve from my father."

"You didn't want to see me at all?" He was only jesting, but he was also curious.

"Oh, I wanted to see you." She grinned. "I wanted to see you strung up by your toenails and flogged to within an inch of your life."

"You're not harsh at all, are you? Should I live in fear of you for our entire marriage?"

"Definitely!" she said. Then she raised a hand to pull him down to her. She breathed against his lips. "You should be afraid of me. Very, very afraid."

He hardened immediately.

Marcus spun around, pushing her back onto the blanket. He lifted her arms above her head and held her hands there, tight within his fists. "I think it is you who should be afraid," he said softly.

"Of who?" she asked. "You?" She grinned. "Do your worst, Marcus." She wiggled beneath him.

He couldn't let a taunt like that go unchallenged. He nestled his leg between hers so he could lie against her heat and bent to kiss her cheek. Then her jaw. Then he drew the lobe of her ear between his teeth and sucked it gently. She squirmed beneath him.

"I've thought about this for a month," she admitted.

He raised his head and looked into her eyes. "What have you thought about?"

She flushed, her cheeks flaming cherry red. "I thought about the way you kiss me." Her voice was soft and quivery.

He bent and did just that, drawing her lower lip between his teeth where he could lick across it. She let her tongue slide across his, and where he'd been only hard a moment before, he was now painfully hard. He pushed against her heat and her eyes closed.

❧

"Tell me what else you thought about when we were apart," he requested.

The words trembled on her lips. "I thought about the way you kiss your way up and down my body."

He tugged the string at the bodice of her gown, opening it down the front, and then he pushed it down her shoulders. Her chemise followed, until they both bunched around her hips. He sat up on his knees. "Lift," he said.

She did, and he pulled her gown and chemise down her body, taking her drawers with them. She covered her breasts with her hands, and he took her hands in his and lifted them back over her head.

"Tell me what else you thought about."

"I thought about when you put your fingers inside me. And when you found that little spot that makes me go mad."

He pretended to be puzzled. "What spot was that? I don't recall."

"Marcus!" she squealed. He took her nipple into his mouth and licked across it, his tongue scratchy and soft at the same time. He bit down gently on her left nipple, and heat shot straight to her groin. "Marcus," she crooned more softly.

"What?" he whispered, his mouth popping off her breast long enough to talk, but then he suckled her again, drawing on her nipple until it made her belly clench. "You were talking about this special spot that makes you go mad."

She leaned up and kissed his forehead. "If you can't find it, I can show you where it is." She laughed, throwing her head back, her eyes closed. She opened them when his head suddenly shot up and he looked her in the face. She would never live this down.

"Did a little exploring, did you?" he asked with a grin. "How did that go?"

"Well," she squeaked.

Good God, the thought of her doing that would unman him. "Did you think of me when you touched yourself?" he asked.

"Every time," she breathed, her warm words blowing across the shell of his ear.

Thank heavens. "What was I doing in your fantasy?"

"The same thing you're doing now, only you were moving down there a little bit quicker." She couldn't keep from laughing.

He kissed between her breasts and down across her belly button, stopping to flick his tongue inside it. Then he kissed all the way down to where her springy hair hid her mound. And then he kissed and licked his way down through it, until he settled with her knees over his shoulders.

"What are you doing?" she asked. But his hot breath already blew across her folds, and she was ready to beg him to touch her.

"Since you did some exploring, I thought I might do the same," he said. Then he spread her open with his thumbs. He looked up at her. "Did you make yourself come?" he asked.

She squeezed her eyes closed tightly. "Yes," she whispered.

"I want to watch you do that one day," he said as he licked her from top to bottom.

"You can watch me do anything you want," she gasped as he bumped against the sensitive spot at the top of her sex. "Right there," she said.

"Show me what you like," he said, reaching up and taking her hand. He pulled it down and placed it at the apex of her thighs.

"Just touch me, Marcus," she said. "Touch me before I go mad."

He slid one finger inside her and stopped. "Is that better?" he asked.

"Marginally," she gasped out.

"Rub yourself," Marcus commanded.

"Give me more," she pleaded. He pulled his finger from her and rimmed around the edge of her opening with it.

"So pretty," he breathed.

"Marcus," she pleaded, pushing against his hand.

"I want to look around down here," he teased. "Stop being in such a hurry."

"Marcus!" she cried. "You're not supposed to be looking around down there."

"How else am I supposed to figure out how everything works?" He slid his fingers inside her, and this time, it must have been more than before, because she suddenly felt full. She stilled. "That worked," he breathed.

"Stop playing, Marcus," she warned.

"I was an innocent before you took my virginity, silly girl," he teased. "I'm still learning, just like you."

He pressed her fingers, which still rested at the apex of her thighs, against her heat. "Show me how you rub it," he said gently.

She groaned into the side of her arm. She lay there naked, aside from her stockings, and his head was between her thighs and he wanted to map out her body parts from down below?

Fine. She would show him how she liked it. She dipped a finger into her passage, her fingers sliding along his, and brought some of her moisture forward.

"That's an interesting tactic," he said.

"Makes it slippery," she whispered, a grin tugging at her lips. This was so wicked. And if there was one thing she would never have expected to do in broad daylight with Marcus, it was explore her body.

"Show me," he pleaded, his voice sounding like it had been dragged down a gravel road and back.

She circled her finger around that little nub, and Marcus groaned. "God, I love you," he growled. "Don't stop."

Marcus licked across the center of her, kissing her nether region the same way he kissed her mouth. He worshiped her with his teeth and tongue, and his fingers slid slowly in and out of her. He crooked his fingers inside her, and she reached for his head with her free hand, sliding her fingers into his hair.

"Marcus, I'm close," she warned.

Marcus nudged at her hand with his nose, pushing it to the side as he continued to crook his fingers inside her. She ground her hips against his hand, pushing him deeper, making herself tighter. His lips replaced her finger as he uncovered the little nub that pulsed like mad with his thumb and bent to take it into his mouth. He suckled her, latching on to that swollen little spot with his mouth, abrading it with his teeth and tongue as he set a rhythm at one with the beat of her heart.

"Marcus!" she cried. "Good God, Marcus."

And then she broke. She was so sensitive that she tried to move away from him so she could come apart slowly and carefully. But he would have none of that. He hooked his arms around her thighs and held on to her hips, refusing to let her get away. And as the waves crashed over her, he gave no quarter. Her body quaked, her channel convulsing in spasms of sheer pleasure. Her sheath clenched, and she desperately wanted it filled.

"Marcus," she groaned as he finally slowed his tongue and loosened the suction on that little button of fire between her legs. "Marcus," she warned, pushing his head away, as he wouldn't let the pleasure stop rolling over her, again and again. "No more. I can't stand it."

❧

Marcus wiped his face on the blanket by the inside of her thigh and then climbed up her body to look into her face. Her arms and legs were trembling, and her breaths rushed from her body. "I love you so much," he said.

"I'll love you again when I can talk," she heaved. But she was settling into the counterpane, soft as cotton.

"I like learning about your body," he said. She grinned, covering her face with her forearm.

"Turnabout is fair play," she warned. "When I catch my breath, I'm going to start exploring your body."

"I vaguely remember you getting a good look at my body last time." He stood up and began to remove his clothes. There was something so erotic about her lying there on the blanket in full daylight completely naked. She didn't try to hide herself from him. She didn't try to roll into the counterpane. She lay there, exposed and needy, and she'd never looked more beautiful to him.

Her eyes narrowed as she looked up at him. "You made me tell you all my secrets," she grumbled.

"And look where it got us. I got to find out how you like it, and I think we get better at this every time we do it." He climbed on top of her naked, settling between her thighs. "I think we should practice, practice, and practice some more. We do have my mother's permission."

"Ick," she said. "Don't bring up your mother right now, no matter how amazing she is."

She sat up on her elbows, and he sat down on the blanket beside her so he could pull his stockings from his feet.

She rolled so that her head was on his thigh, and his manhood rocked toward her. "Goodness," she teased. "Has a mind of its own, does it?"

"Apparently," he agreed.

She arched a brow at him. "I want to kiss it," she said. She looked up and met his gaze, her blue eyes hot in the moment, full of feeling and want.

"I can't believe you would suggest such an outlandish thing," he teased. "What has gotten into you?"

"Before we go back, I hope you'll get into me," she purred. Then she leaned forward and kissed him softly. Her lips were wet and cool, and it was a short kiss. One that left him wanting. His manhood jumped toward her lips.

"Has a mind of its own," he warned her.

"I see that," she laughed. She stuck her tongue out and licked around the purple crest, her tongue tentative and shy, probably as tentative as his had been while he learned her body. "Did you touch yourself when we were apart?" she asked, her voice a hot purr against his skin.

"Only every single day," he admitted. He'd had one day with her, and then she was gone. So, he'd relived that day over and over and over in his mind.

"Show me what you do," she said.

"You're doing just fine."

"You made me show you mine."

"And I might make you show me yours again," he warned.

"Show me," she pleaded. Then her mouth closed around the crest of him. "You taste salty," she said.

"So did you," he told her. He took her hand and wrapped it around his shaft, squeezing it within his own.

"Like this?" she asked, but her mouth was full of him, the silky sweetness of her tongue nearly undoing him.

"Yes," he groaned. He put his hands in her hair and showed her how to very gently go up and down. "Take a little more," he urged.

She did, taking him farther into her mouth.

"Stop," he warned.

"Why?" she asked, talking around him.

Marcus lifted her under her arms and tossed her gently onto her back. "Not fair," she complained, as he lay between her thighs and entered in one solid thrust, driving himself all the way into her, as far as he could go.

Only once he was seated within her, his thighs firm against her bottom, did he stop. "Goodness," she breathed.

"Goodness," he repeated. He pulled back and pushed into her, filling her full. She was warm and tight around him, like a silken glove fisting his manhood.

"Deeper," she urged.

Good God, he loved this woman. The last time they'd done this, they'd both been terrified. But now it was like coming home. He pushed her legs forward toward her chest and pushed inside of her, his thrusts quick and deep.

"Oh, Marcus!" she cried.

Her breaths hit his cheek, her moans and sighs and whispers of pleasure jarring him with every thrust, wringing his own sounds of pleasure from him as he pushed in and out, in and out, in and out. She reached for him, drawing him closer to her, her legs still between them, and he went even deeper. The tilt of her bottom made it so that he could take every sweet inch of her.

Marcus kissed the inside of her calf, closing his eyes to the sensation. Her head thrashed on the counterpane. "Marcus, Marcus, Marcus," she chanted. "Please, Marcus!" she cried.

With a great keening cry, she squeezed him in

her tight grip, milking him with her pleasure. "Yes!" he cried, as he thrust through her climax, taking her higher and higher as she broke around him. And it wasn't until she pleaded for him to take mercy on her that he finished. He erupted inside her, soaking her walls, pressing hard inside her as he let her legs fall to his sides. Her thighs wrapped around his hips as she squeezed him tightly.

"Goodness, Marcus," she breathed.

Marcus couldn't move. He just collapsed on top of her, and she ran her hands up and down his back.

"Nothing could ever feel as good as you do when I'm inside you," he breathed, kissing the side of her breast in a quick, affectionate move. He rolled from on top of her and drew her to lie on his shoulder.

She looked around. "I keep feeling like someone is going to walk up and see us," she said.

"I doubt that many people can walk into paintings, Cece," he said with a laugh. "But I'm willing to take the risk."

She settled on top of him, throwing one leg across his thighs. "What are you thinking about?" he asked as his breathing returned to normal.

"I'm thinking about children we might have. The household we'll keep. I'm thinking about our grand-children. I'm thinking about all the missions we'll go on together. I'm thinking about the good we can do."

"Hmm," he hummed.

"I'm thinking about what it'll be like loving you for the rest of my life."

"Well, stop thinking about it," he warned. "Because you couldn't get rid of me now if you tried."

Twenty-One

MARCUS LOOKED AT THE PAINTING ON THE WALL AS HE dressed and he grew hard all over again. It had been almost a sennight since their trip into the painting, and Marcus hadn't been alone with Cecelia even once since then. Her father had hovered over her like a bee on a flower, keeping her from Marcus's evil clutches. Or his wayward clutches. Or his lusty clutches.

Either way, her father had kept her from Marcus's clutches. The type made no matter, Marcus supposed. Even if his clutches had been honorable, which they weren't, her father would have kept her from them. He supposed when he and Cecelia had their own children, he would feel much the same. And it was better for Cecelia to have a father who doted on her than the father she'd lived with for the previous six months.

Claire had forced him to take the painting, claiming it wasn't fit for her to look at anymore. He wanted it because he wanted to remember every minute he and Cecelia had spent wrapped up in one another. He wanted to relive every moment he was inside her. And he wanted to hear her whisper, "I love you, I love you, I love you," again and again and again. He wanted to hear it every day for the rest of his life.

A knock sounded on his door, and his heart leaped. Cecelia? No, she wouldn't be so brazen as to come to his room. Not the way her father was hovering.

"Enter," he called.

The door opened, and Allen stepped into the room. His brother brushed his hair from his face and sat down on a high-backed chair. "Something wrong?" Marcus asked.

Allen crossed one ankle over his knee and looked at him. "Can I talk to you about something?"

He smiled. "That depends. What's it about?"

He and Allen had never been close, and he'd met his brother just before he usurped his position in life, taking his potential title from him. Allen had been discomfited by him, but he'd taken it with grace. And he'd even been friendly from the start. He hadn't held a grudge, and he had done all he could to help Marcus settle into the life of a darling of the *ton*.

"It's about the fae," Allen said hesitantly.

"What about them?" Marcus asked as he tied a knot in his cravat. He shrugged into his coat and sat down opposite Allen. Apparently, something weighed heavily on Allen's mind.

"Do you think they could ever accept me? I mean, truly?"

Marcus didn't understand. "Accept you as what?"

Allen jumped up to pace. "As one of them, you dolt. As one of the fae. As one of you." He let his hand sweep up and down through the air toward Marcus's body.

Marcus laid a hand on his chest. "But I am fae."

"And I'm not," Allen bit out.

"You're half fae. Just as I am."

He showed Marcus the tip of his human ear. "But I don't have any of the traits. I don't have an ounce of magic within me. How could the world be so cruel?" His brother collapsed into the chair again, the side of his head falling to rest on his balled-up fist.

"Your mother is fae. Your father is not. So, it's not like you're not of the fae. So, what's your concern?"

"It's Ainsley," he murmured.

Marcus heard him, but he didn't want to let him get away with murmuring about it. He cupped a hand around his ear and said, "I'm sorry. I missed that."

"It's Ainsley, damn it all. I want to ask her to marry me."

"Well, I certainly hope you do, because the two of you have grown rather close."

His brother's brows shot together and he said, "Not as close as you and Cecelia."

"Don't speak of that," Marcus warned. He would hate to punch his brother in the face, but if he said the wrong thing, he wouldn't have a choice. He wouldn't let anyone speak poorly of Cecelia. "What do you know of it, anyway?" Marcus said.

"She talks to Ainsley," Allen admitted.

She did? About that? "What does she say?"

"That doesn't matter."

"Bloody hell, Allen, of course it matters," he growled.

"Ainsley is jealous," Allen said quietly.

"Jealous of what?" What on earth did Ainsley have to be jealous of?

"Of the intimacy between you two."

Oh, dear God, what had Cecelia said? "Be more specific."

"If I get more specific, you'll try to punch me in the face."

That much was true. Marcus shrugged. "What do you want me to tell you?"

"I want to go home with Ainsley. Well, I want to ask her to marry me and then go home with her. To live there. But I'm not like you."

"I don't have wings, either, Allen," Marcus reminded him. "Only the ladies have them."

"But you have magic."

He shook his head. "It doesn't matter what magic you have for yourself. It's what kind of magic you have with the person you love that will matter." He looked hard at Allen. "Do you and Ainsley have that kind of magic? The kind where you think about her even when you're not together. The kind where you want to do things and say things just to make her smile. The kind where you imagine her head on your pillow every day for the rest of your life.

"The kind where everything that hurts her makes you bleed. The kind where your breath mingles with hers and you realize you couldn't take another one unless she was guaranteed her next breath, too. Otherwise, you'd give yours to her. That's the kind of magic you need, you dolt. Not the faerie-dust and pointy-ear kind."

"Why don't you tell me how you really feel?" Allen said, smiling at him.

"Magic isn't what you think it is."

"I know she'll have to go home soon, and I want her to take me with her." He leaned forward. "I don't want her to leave me."

Marcus laughed. "You do have it bad, don't you?"

"Am I doing the wrong thing?" Allen asked.

"Why are you questioning this so much?" Marcus chided. "If you love the chit, marry her."

"You think she'll have me?" He actually looked worried.

"Knowing Ainsley, she'll make you miserable for the rest of your life if you don't marry her. You're in trouble no matter how you look at it."

"When I'm with her…" He stopped talking and shook his head. "When I'm with her, nothing else matters."

"I always thought her tongue was a little too sharp," Marcus complained.

"Her tongue is just fine," Allen said. Then he blushed profusely when he realized what he'd said. "I mean as far as what she says to me. I wasn't referring to anything else. I wouldn't know about anything else. Not with her."

His brother wasn't an innocent. He'd brought women home in the night before. Marcus could hear them in his chambers at the house they shared in Town. Allen wasn't like Marcus. Marcus had been in love with Cecelia since before he could walk. There had never been another woman for him. And there never would be.

"Have you talked to her father?" Marcus asked.

"Not yet. I plan to. I'd like to ask his permission to call on her."

"They're not going to let you into the land of the fae unless you marry her. And they're strict about human visitors even then. Things are changing in the land of the fae, but it'll take time." Marcus didn't want Allen to get his hopes up too much.

"There's no chance the fae would take our children from us, just because I'm human, is there? They wouldn't take them at birth, like they did you and Claire and Sophia?" Allen looked worried.

"I think the danger of that happening is past. Both of Claire's children are fae, and they haven't come to claim them." Though why anyone would want either of those children, he had no idea. "So stop worrying."

"What if she doesn't have the same feelings for me? You never had to worry about Cecelia's feelings for you."

"I never worried because I knew when she hated me." He laughed. "I knew when she hated me and I knew when she forgave me and I knew when she loved me again."

"You were an idiot," Allen said blandly.

"I know."

"It's a miracle she took you back."

"I know."

"There's a benefit to having a lady who has wings," Allen said shyly.

"What's that?"

"They can fly out their windows at night to come and see you, with no one the wiser."

Marcus wanted to hit himself in the forehead with the heel of his hand. Why hadn't he thought of that? "Don't steal that girl's virtue," he warned. Ainsley might annoy the devil out of him, but he still adored her, and she deserved better than someone who didn't have true feelings for her.

"You're one to talk," Allen said. He looked up at the painting on the wall, and Marcus felt a blush creep up his cheeks. "At least I don't go sneaking into paintings to get her alone with me. How did you talk Mother into that, by the way?"

"It was her idea," Marcus said with a laugh.

❧

Ainsley looked at Cecelia across the sunny parlor and said, "I think Allen is going to ask me to marry him."

Cecelia startled. She'd almost forgotten Ainsley was there. She'd sat there stitching blindly, wasting time while she waited for Marcus to come downstairs. "What makes you think that?" Cecelia asked, setting her sewing to the side.

Ainsley shrugged. "I just have a feeling. I think he's afraid."

"Of you?" Cecelia scoffed.

"Not so much of me, because when we're alone, he doesn't seem troubled by what or who I am at all. But when we're with people, he seems a little discomfited. He doesn't reach for my hand or put his arm around me or any of the things he does when we're alone." She looked into Cecelia's eyes. "What do you think?"

"I think you need not worry about his intentions. And he isn't affectionate with you in public because they don't do that in this world. Things are a little more rigid here. He was raised here, after all, so he thinks like them. You're going to have to get used to it."

"He's so proper most of the time. Like when I bump his shoulder, I can tell he likes it. He likes to play around with me. He likes to wrestle, and he tried to tickle me last night in his room."

Cecelia squealed. "What were you doing in his room?" She got up and moved to sit beside Ainsley. "Tell me. I have to know."

Ainsley shrugged. "Nothing bad. I just went to see him." She scrunched up her face in a wince. "I think I startled him when I knocked on his window in faerie form."

"You didn't!"

"I did. I wanted to see him. He'd been with his father all day, and then he missed supper. I missed him."

"Oh dear, you are in love with him, aren't you?"

Tears filled Ainsley's eyes. "I suppose I am. That's terrible, isn't it?"

"Why is it terrible?" Cecelia asked. "I think it's wonderful."

"He's not fae. I'm not even certain my father will let me have a relationship with him."

"Your father is no idiot. He'll be able to see what's between the two of you when he meets Allen." It was obvious to anyone who saw them together what their feelings were for one another.

"He's a good man," Ainsley said with a heavy sigh.

Cecelia narrowed her gaze at her friend. "But is he a good kisser?"

Ainsley blushed even more. "The best."

"Is kissing all you've done with him?" Cecelia asked.

"You're awfully curious, aren't you?" Ainsley chided.

"I told you all about me and Marcus," Cecelia reminded her.

"Well, we haven't done that," Ainsley said. "But we did sleep in the same bed last night. I meant to leave earlier, but we were lying there talking and I fell asleep."

"Mmm-hmm," Cecelia hummed.

"He's so soft and cuddly." Ainsley's blush deepened. "And so hard and rough at other times. In the best of ways," she rushed on to say. "I want to sleep in his arms every night."

"He'll ask you," Cecelia said. "But don't be surprised if he asks your father first. That's how they do things here."

"I'd like to live in the land of the fae," Ainsley said. "Do you think he'd be happy there?"

"I think he'd be happy wherever you are," Cecelia admitted. "He has stars in his eyes when he looks at you."

Ainsley's eyes filled with tears and she whispered, "I think I love him. I think I love him a lot."

Cecelia patted her hand. "I know you do."

⤝⤞

Marcus entered his father's study, surprised to see Lord Phineas, the Duke of Robinsworth, and Allen all in the same room. "What did I miss?" Marcus asked as he walked in and sat down.

"We have a bit of a problem," the duke said.

"It's not a problem. I'm going to marry her," Marcus rushed to say. "As soon as her father will let me."

The duke raised his brow and smirked. "We weren't referring to your love life, though if you'd like to discuss that, I suppose we could."

"Oh." Marcus wanted to bite his tongue. "Then to what are we referring?"

"The Earl of Mayden is back in Town," the duke said.

Marcus had met the earl the prior year, in a violent altercation with Lord Phineas, and the man was dangerous. And he was determined to hurt someone. He should have been stopped back then, but no one had been able to find him for more than a year.

"He's in London?" Marcus asked.

"He has been here for more than a month," Lord Phineas said. "All that time we were in the land of the fae, he was right here."

A shiver crawled up Marcus's spine. The earl could have harmed any one of their loved ones. "Why hasn't he made his presence known? Perhaps he has turned over a new leaf?"

The duke snorted. "He was courting someone and has recently married. She's a young American chit who just came over from Boston. Her father is incredibly wealthy and wanted her to marry a title. He didn't particularly care how impoverished it was."

"Or how corrupt it was?" Lord Phineas asked.

"This American he married, she's innocent in all of this," Marcus reminded them.

"Mayden can be charming when he chooses to be," the duke said. "He's slippery, too. And now he's back, has adequate funds, and has been seen at White's and at the track. He's spending money hand over fist. And he's also taken a mistress in Town."

"And his wife hasn't killed him yet?"

"They don't do it that way here, Marcus," his father reminded him. "It's not uncommon for a man to take a mistress, even after he's married."

Marcus couldn't imagine ever wanting anyone but Cecelia.

"His wife, and her father, for that matter, were charmed by his title. They don't know what they're dealing with. We're the only ones who know," his father reminded him.

"So he has restored his place in society now."

"He's respectable in every sense of the word," Allen said.

"So, what do we do?"

"What do you all want to do?" his father asked. "Do we wait for him to strike? Or do we try to force his hand?"

"I vote that we invite him and his new wife to the wedding celebration," Lord Phineas suggested. "There's no easier way to tell if he's turned over a new leaf. He'll show up and pretend nothing has happened, or he'll show up with demands about the fae, or he'll not show up at all."

"He has something to hold over all our heads."

"Who would believe him?" the duke scoffed. "The idea that winged people live and work among the *ton*? It's ridiculous."

"He doesn't know about wings. Or faeries. All he knows is that Claire was somehow able to shove him into a painting. But he was more than a bit mad that day. He may not even remember it." Lord Phineas shook his head. "You should have seen the look on his face. Before he tried to shoot Claire, his eyes were empty."

"So, what will we do?" Marcus asked.

"Invite him," Lord Phineas said with a shrug. "We'll all be there, and I can have all of my men attend the event."

"The wedding is at my house," the duke reminded them.

"Why is it at your house?" Marcus asked.

"Because I'm the bloody Duke of Robinsworth, that's why," Robinsworth said, grinning. "I say I want it at my house. And it's at my house."

Marcus snorted. "Sophia told you that you were hosting it, didn't she? And you couldn't say no."

"Well," he muttered, "it might have happened that way. Or it might have happened the way I said it did. You'll never know."

"Oh, we know," all the men muttered at once, and then laughter shook the room.

Twenty-Two

MARCUS WAITED BEFORE THE FOUNTAIN IN Robinsworth's serene garden, his family in attendance, along with Cecelia's father and Ainsley. It was a small gathering, and society wouldn't join them for the celebration until later. There would be dinner and dancing and… danger.

"Marcus, could I have a word with you?" Mr. Hewitt asked, taking Marcus's elbow in his hand.

"I believe my bride is about to come down," Marcus complained. "Can it wait?"

Marcus looked around. He really didn't want to go with Mr. Hewitt, but he supposed he had better. As the father of the bride, Mr. Hewitt could withdraw his blessing if he so chose. He could withdraw it despite the marriage settlement they'd agreed upon. Not that it would matter. Marcus would marry Cecelia that day and take her as his own wife even if he had to tie her father up and stuff him in a barrel for safe keeping. Well, he wouldn't do that, but he would do just about anything to make her his.

She'd been busy all week with dresses and shopping

and flowers and preparations. And they hadn't even spent any time together since their trip into the painting. He supposed it was for the best. Absence made the heart grow fonder and all that. He was feeling damn fond of her right now.

"I suppose we could talk. Can it be done quickly?" Marcus asked. He ushered his soon-to-be father-in-law toward the rear of Robinsworth's garden. "Is something the matter?" he asked. "It's not Cecelia, is it?"

Mr. Hewitt shook his head. "I just wanted to tell you thank you," he said. He looked directly into Marcus's eyes. His eyes were so much like Cecelia's. Only there was a shadow of pain in the man's eyes. Even now, he looked like he was hurting.

Marcus wasn't at all sure what he was being thanked for.

"Thank you for rescuing Cecelia from me. Thank you for rescuing me from myself." He stuck out a hand to shake. Marcus took it in his, and the man's grip was firm and assuring.

"Thank you for letting me have her for a lifetime," Marcus said. He suddenly had a lump in his throat. "I promise to take care of her."

"I know you will. You'll take better care of her than I ever did."

"That's not true," Marcus protested.

But the man held up a hand. "It is true. I just hope she has forgiven me."

"She has," said a voice from behind them. Marcus turned to find Cecelia standing in the sunlight. She wore his mother's wedding dress, or so he'd been told.

It shone as if there were prisms of crystal sewn into the material. When she moved, the sun reflected off the gown, spilling rainbows of light all around them.

"Goodness," Marcus breathed.

Marcus had never seen anyone more beautiful. Cecelia's dark hair was piled atop her head, with tiny tendrils cascading down her neck. Her ears pointed out through her hair, and she even had her wings displayed. Marcus had almost forgotten how very beautiful they were. She'd been so human in his mind lately that he'd almost forgotten she was fae. That they were fae. That they were part of something so much bigger than themselves.

A blush crept up her cheeks, and her wings pinkened to the same color as her cheeks. He couldn't wait to see her naked, to touch her wings, and to feel her around him, her magic mixing with his in a way that only their magic together could.

"You weren't supposed to hear that," Mr. Hewitt scolded.

She smiled and slid her hand into her father's. "I needed to hear it." She stood up on tiptoe and kissed her father's cheek. Her eyes shone with unshed tears.

"I've made you cry on your wedding day," he said, reaching up to wipe her tear. He heaved a huge sigh. "I had more to say to Mr. Thorne," he said. "But I suppose I can say it with you here."

Cecelia nodded, her gaze curious.

Mr. Hewitt said clearly, "If you ever hurt my daughter, I will hurt you."

Marcus's eyebrows lifted. He choked on his next words. But then he had to remind himself that when he and Cecelia had a daughter, he would feel exactly the same. "If I do, I'll deserve it."

Marcus held his arm out to Cecelia. "Shall we go and get married?" he asked.

But her father knocked his arm out of the way and threaded Cecelia's arm through his. "She's still mine until the vicar pronounces you husband and wife," he said. But he winked at Cecelia, and she beamed under his attention. She needed this. She needed for her father to make amends.

Marcus followed behind the two of them, all the way back to where the family was assembled. Ainsley's hand was in Allen's, and they would be next to get married, Marcus was certain. Allen had already spoken to Ainsley's father, and he almost had the man's blessing.

Ronald and Milly sat in the back row, and Milly had her hand settled within Ronald's. Marcus would never get used to that. He'd always assumed Ronald was a solitary individual. But even Ronald deserved someone to love.

Claire and Lord Phineas, and the Duke of Robinsworth and Sophia, along with the duke's daughter, Lady Anne, took up the second row. The babies were snug in the nursery, thank goodness.

Marcus stepped into place in front of the vicar and held his hand out to Cecelia. She nestled her hand in his, her palms damp and warm. He pulled her close to his side and finally felt like he could take a deep breath. He'd almost missed this. He'd almost given up his chance for a happily-ever-after with this woman.

The vicar's voice rang out loud and clear. "Wilt thou

have this Woman to thy wedded Wife, to live together after God's ordinance in holy estate of Matrimony? Wilt thou love her, comfort her, honor and keep her in sickness and in health; and, forsaking all others, keep thee only unto her, so long as ye both shall live?"

Cecelia squeezed his hand gently, but he needed no prodding. "I will," he said. He would. He would. He would again and again and again.

The vicar asked Cecelia the same question as she looked up at Marcus and said, "I will."

Marcus reached into his pocket and pulled out the ring Mr. Hewitt had given him the day before. He slipped it onto her fourth finger, and she looked up at him, a question in her eyes. It was obvious the moment she realized it was her mother's ring, because tears filled her eyes. Marcus swallowed past the lump in his own throat when Cecelia turned to her father and mouthed the words, "Thank you."

He smiled back, wiping a tear from beneath his eye.

"With this Ring I thee wed, with my body I thee worship, and with all my worldly Goods I thee endow," Marcus said. "I pronounce that they be man and wife together, in the name of the Father, and the Son, and the Holy Ghost. Amen."

And it was done. Cecelia was his. She would be his forever and a day. Nothing would ever separate them, save death, and Marcus would fight that with his last breath. Cecelia looked up at him, her eyes sparkling. He picked up her ring and kissed the purple moonstone in its platinum band. "Mine," he said.

She nodded and stepped up onto her tiptoes to kiss him.

His father coughed into his fist. "Shall we have some cake?" he asked.

Mr. Hewitt chuckled, clapped Marcus on the back with a heavy hand, and said, "I think we should."

Marcus was watching her from across the room. She could feel his gaze on her, and the hair on the back of her neck stood up, as did the fine little hairs on her wings. It wasn't often she wore her wings in public, but His Grace's house was apparently fae friendly. The butler didn't even blink when he walked into the room to find it full of faeries, as Sophia, Claire, Ainsley, and her mother all had their wings on display that day. It was a special day, after all. And they all were safe in the walled garden that was the duke's sanctuary and in the house.

"Your husband looks like he wants to come over here and steal you away," Claire murmured, laughing at her.

"Do you have a painting you can shove us into?" Cecelia asked.

"I doubt that would work right now," Claire admitted, "although I wouldn't be surprised if he were to come and sling you over his shoulder."

It wouldn't be the first time he'd done so. The last time, it was to get her away from her father. To keep her safe. He would keep her safe always, of that she had no doubts. She never had to worry about him harming her or about him allowing anyone else to do so. Marcus loved her. He'd chased the dream of a family for six months, but he'd realized she was his family and the only one who truly mattered, or so he'd told her. His family would be there later. And now, so would she.

"I wouldn't complain if he tossed me over his shoulder," Cecelia admitted.

"Eww," Sophia complained.

"I want to spend some time alone with him before the celebration."

"Are you at all afraid that Mayden is going to show up?" Sophia asked both of them.

"Terribly afraid," Claire admitted. She heaved a sigh. "The man is mad. And he needs to be stopped."

"Perhaps it was a mistake to invite him to such a gathering," Sophia mused. "I'm not certain I want him in this house at all." She shivered uncontrollably, and the hair on Cecelia's arms stood up.

"Finn will have men all over the place. If nothing else, we can get a warning to his wife tonight, if he even comes. He may not show his face. If he has an ax to grind, he'll be here. But he may just want to live a quiet life now that his debts have been paid and he's settled back into society." Claire nibbled absently at a nail. "He threatened to throw me from the turrets last year," she said. "He isn't aware that I can fly." She laughed lightly.

"Not much use tossing one of us off the tower," Cecelia agreed.

"Whatever he does, it will be cowardly," Sophia reminded them.

"Well, this conversation has turned morbid," Claire chirped. "Happy wedding day, Cecelia," she said, taking a glass of champagne from a nearby footman. She handed one to each of the other ladies as well. Claire reached out to squeeze her hand. "You're happy, aren't you?" she asked, her gaze searching Cecelia's.

"Despite Mayden and the threat he proposes, I couldn't be happier," Cecelia said.

Marcus caught her gaze from across the room. He motioned with his eyes toward the staircase.

She shook her head, laughing. They couldn't leave their families just because they wanted to be alone. Could they? Definitely not.

❦

Marcus nodded toward the staircase again, and Cecelia smiled and shook her head. His sisters looked over at him, and Claire shot him a scolding glance. Sophia shook a finger at him. Good God, would he never get the woman alone? He supposed there would be time enough to spend with her, a lifetime in fact, after the celebration.

He nodded toward the staircase again, and she grinned, shaking her head. Her cheeks pinkened. "No," she mouthed.

He walked over to her, his gait slow and unhurried. The part of her bosom that was exposed by her bodice flushed, and Marcus wanted to peel her clothing off to see if she was that flushed everywhere.

"Oh, dear," he heard Claire say. "Your wings are blushing, Cecelia." She laughed. She was right. Cecelia was a delicious shade of pink.

Marcus put his hand at the small of Cecelia's back and began to draw tiny circles. She flushed even more. "Worried about tonight?" he asked.

"Which part of it?" she asked.

He leaned down and spoke, his lips moving against the shell of her ear. "The part where I get to show you your wedding gift."

"Wedding gift?" she asked. "We weren't supposed to purchase wedding gifts."

"We needed a house to move into, didn't we?" he asked.

"You bought a house?" she squeaked.

"Just a small one." He held his fingers a small space apart. "And I didn't buy it. I just rented it. I thought you might want to help me pick the house we'll eventually live in. This one is only temporary."

"Tired of living the bachelor lifestyle?" she asked.

"Ainsley and Allen will live in our old quarters for a time, after their wedding. It's not big enough for all of us, and I'm a little plumper in the pockets than Allen right now, so I volunteered to move out. I think you'll like it." He looked down at her. "And no one will be around to hear you scream when I have my wicked way with you," he said softly.

"I do not scream," she scoffed. But a new blush crept up her cheeks.

"Not yet," he whispered.

Claire made a gagging noise at the back of her throat. "If the two of you are going to carry on like that, I would suggest that you go ahead and leave. Or I'll have no choice but to cast up my accounts."

Marcus looked down at Cecelia. "Do you want to go and see your new home?" he asked.

"What about all the people?" she whispered.

"All the people know what you're going to do,"

Sophia whispered back dramatically. She leaned in to hug Cecelia. "Go. Enjoy the afternoon. You'll be back tonight for the celebration."

"No one will mind?" Cecelia asked.

"No one will care," Sophia said, waving a breezy hand in the air.

And with that, Marcus took her hand and they sprinted for the doorway. As she ran beside him laughing, Marcus's heart jumped into his throat. God, he loved this woman. He couldn't imagine living a day without her. Ever.

They reached the waiting carriage and Marcus handed her inside, just before climbing in himself and settling back against the squabs. He took her face in his hands and kissed her. It was a mix of mouths, and her gentle response nearly undid him. "I have missed you so much," he breathed.

"You've seen me every day," she corrected. "What's to miss?"

"Now that you're my wife, I can kiss you anytime I want. I can hold you anytime I want. I can touch you anytime I want." He touched her shoulder. "When we get home, I want to see you naked with just your wings. I want to touch them."

"They're very sensitive," she whispered.

"I'll be careful," he breathed back.

He spent the next ten minutes kissing her, and she was breathless and he was hard as stone by the time they arrived at their new address. It was a small town house in Grosvenor Square. "It's charming," Cecelia said.

"Not as charming as you are," Marcus said, tweaking

her nose. "It'll do for now." He looked down at her and swooped her into his arms.

"What are you doing, Marcus?" she squealed. "Are you mad?"

He was. "Mad for you, yes," he laughed as he sprinted for the door. It opened, and Cecelia squealed when she saw Mr. Pritchens standing behind the open door.

"Mr. Pritchens," she said, laughing, as Marcus walked by the older man.

"Mrs. Thorne," he said, his haughty nose in the air. Marcus stopped.

"Say that again," he commanded.

"Welcome home, Mrs. Thorne," Pritchens said, grinning at Cecelia.

"What are you doing here, Mr. Pritchens?" Cecelia struggled to get down from Marcus's arms, and Marcus set her on her feet.

"We couldn't have a household without him," Marcus said. Cecelia wouldn't have been happy if she didn't have the old man. "He'll go back and forth with us from one world to the other." She looked up at Marcus, her eyes bright and shiny. "If that's all right with you," he added.

She grinned and smacked his arm. "Of course, it's all right with me," she said. She turned and kissed Marcus quickly. "You make me so happy," she said.

Marcus looked at the older servant. "You, Mr. Pritchens, may take the rest of the day off, if you'll have Cook leave some provisions for us in the kitchen."

"They're already prepared, Mr. Thorne," he said. "You'll find everything you'll need when you're ready for it."

"There's a good man," Marcus said, and he took Cecelia's hand, showing her the house.

"It's lovely, Marcus," she breathed.

It was actually a little too big, but it was all he could find on such short notice. "I thought we might have your father come and stay with us when he's in Town. There's plenty of room."

"He's not coming today, is he?" Cecelia whispered dramatically. Her finger trailed down the front of his coat.

"No one had better show up today," Marcus warned, and then he took Cecelia's hand and tugged her toward the staircase. He raced her to the top, and laughing, they stumbled into the master's chambers.

In the center of the room was a large four-poster bed. An adjoining door led to a dressing room, and a bath was on the other side of that. "It certainly is large," Cecelia breathed.

Marcus had Mr. Pritchens take care of the furnishings, and he'd done an amazing job.

Cecelia's nose wrinkled when she heard splashing from the tub in the other room. "What's that?"

He turned Cecelia toward him. "I had Mr. Pritchens send footmen up with a bath for you."

❧

She nodded. She was slightly overwhelmed. "You make me so happy, Marcus," she said.

He took her hand and laid it flat upon his chest. "You make me complete," he said.

Tears pricked at the backs of her lashes, and she blinked quickly to blink them away.

"The house. And Mr. Pritchens. And chambers for my father."

"On a lower level," he whispered. "Not up here with us."

He spun her so that her back faced him, and he began to unfasten her dress. As he worked at the fastenings, he kissed his way down the center of her back. "If this thing wasn't my mother's, I'd have to rip it off you," he growled. He nibbled on a tiny freckle on her shoulder. How many of those did she have? He would have to count them after he got her naked. He would count them again and again.

He shoved her gown and her dress down over her hips and tapped her leg, saying, "Step," so she would move out of it. He tossed the dress onto a nearby chair.

Cecelia crossed her arms in front of her chest. He pulled the ribbon of her drawers and repeated the motion, the silk sliding along the inside of her thighs like fire, followed by his hand, which slipped up her thigh. She opened her thighs to give him access, but he just chuckled and said, "Not yet," as he untied her garters and rolled her stockings down her legs.

"I'm naked and you're not," she protested.

"I can remedy that quickly," he said, as he began to tear at his own clothing. He was breathless and hard when he stopped, his manhood arching up toward his stomach. Or toward her—she wasn't certain which. "Would you like to avail yourself of that bath?" he asked.

"Only if you'll join me," she taunted.

His brow arched. "A bath? With you? Nothing would please me more." He took her hand and walked with her to the bathing room, his footsteps quiet beside hers. She wasn't even feeling self-conscious. "How should we accomplish this?" he asked.

The claw-foot tub was huge, not one of the simple bathing tubs some houses had. It was large enough for two. "How should I know?" she asked. "I've never bathed with anyone before."

"I saw you, you know," he said as he settled into the tub, his back to the wall. He opened his thighs and motioned for her to get between them. "Come on," he encouraged.

"You saw me do what?" she asked.

"On the night I returned to the land of the fae, I came directly to see you. You were in the bath and you were crying."

She nodded. "I spent a lot of time crying back then."

She laid her head back on his shoulder, and he wrapped around her. The water lapped at her breasts, and his manhood pressed hard and insistent against her bottom. Marcus reached over and picked up a bar of soap from a nearby table. "I have a feeling I'm going to smell like roses by the end of the bath."

She flipped over so that she was on her knees between his, and she took the soap from him. "You're going to smell like me," she warned fiercely.

"I should have come to you immediately and asked why you were crying," he said as she began to soap his chest. He stopped her hand with his, looking into her eyes. "I'm sorry I didn't."

"You couldn't have known, Marcus. But why didn't you come to me when you saw me crying? Why did you leave? I missed you so much."

"I didn't know why you were crying," he admitted. "And you were naked. Totally naked." He reached out and caught her nipple between his thumb and forefinger, pinching it gently. "Much like now. Minus the crying."

Her breath left her quickly, and she forced herself to focus on her task. *Focus on the bath, Cecelia.* "I'm not crying now," she said.

His brown gaze caught hers and held. "I never want you to cry again."

"I can't promise that," she warned. "There will be events like births and marriages and anniversaries that might make me weepy. I'm warning you."

"Those I can tolerate," he admitted. "But I never want you to be sad again. Not like you were then."

Cecelia soaped her hand and ticked his abdomen with it, and the muscles of his stomach rippled beneath her touch. "Enough of that," he warned playfully, grabbing for her slick hands. He drew her to lie on his chest, one of his thighs between hers, and he took the soap from her, running it up and down her spine, and down her arms slowly. If they didn't get out of the tub soon, she would go mad.

"Marcus," Cecelia said. "Do you think we're clean enough?" she asked.

"Clean enough for what?" he asked, flipping her over so that she lay atop him again.

"Clean enough to get out of this tub."

"Not yet," he breathed, taking her earlobe in his teeth and nipping it gently.

His slippery fingers parted her thighs, and he draped one leg over each side of the tub. She still lay atop him, with her head upon his shoulder. "Marcus," she complained.

But then his slick fingers slipped into the tuft of hair at the top of her mound. He tugged it gently, and she stilled. She opened her thighs in invitation. His fingertip raked gently up and down her folds until he found the little nub that had been pounding like mad ever since he'd touched her. He circled it with his finger, as he said very close to her ear, "How badly do you want to come?"

She whimpered, clutching his thighs below her. "Badly," she admitted.

The length of him pressed against her backside. She shifted, letting him slide along the crack of her bottom, until he hissed between his teeth. "Be still," he warned with a laugh.

"I want you inside me," she told him, turning her head so she could kiss the side of his mouth. He took her lips with his, a fierce mix of teeth and tongue, as his fingers continued to play around her nub.

"Put me inside," he taunted, lifting his lips for only a moment.

"Me?" she asked.

"You," he breathed, pressing his manhood against her forcefully.

He reached down and arched his staff away from his belly, and she balanced herself on the edges of the tub, sliding back far enough that he could push at her entrance.

"Take me inside," he whispered, his lips grazing her neck.

"I don't know if I can do it here," she said.

But then Marcus took over and lifted her bottom. She grasped the edges of the tub, hovering over him as he fed his length inside her. "Sink down on me," he said, his voice broken and harsh.

Cecelia impaled herself on his shaft, taking him inch by slow inch. "I've never felt so full," she breathed.

"You should see the view from here," he chuckled. "Amazing." That was when Cecelia realized that he could see his manhood being slowly fed inside her. He pulled her hips lower and she took more of him. And more. And more, until he was inside her fully, and her bottom was pressed against his stomach. "Sit back," he said.

Cecelia leaned her back against his chest, his fullness adjusting to her new position. Marcus let out a hiss between his clenched teeth.

"Don't move anymore," he warned.

"Why not?" she whispered playfully.

"Because you're all warm and snug around me. And I want to stay like this forever." He licked the rim of her ear, and Cecelia felt his manhood jump inside her.

But then his fingers started their slow slide around her nub again, and Cecelia rocked against him. The warm water of the tub lapped against her breasts, and Marcus must have seen it, because he took one breast in his hand and cupped it, pinching her nipple gently between his thumb and forefinger.

"I'm going to come if you can't be still," he warned.

She stilled. But she squeezed him inside her, her walls pulsing madly around his length.

"Don't do that either," he said, and she tightened around him again. "Oh, God," he cried.

He bit down on her shoulder gently, his teeth abrasive and tender at the same time. Heat shot straight to the center of her, and her breath rushed out in tiny pants. "Marcus," she cried.

"You feel like a silken glove on me," he growled next to her ear. "You're tight and wet and hot, and you're squeezing me so tightly."

"I think you're too big for me in this position," she said. "I can't even move on you."

❧

Thank God she couldn't move. If she didn't stop fisting him within her depths, he would come. And he wasn't ready to come yet. He wanted to pleasure her. He wanted to take her in their bed, with their magic surrounding them. He wanted all of her, and he'd yet to have it. He wanted it. Dear God, he wanted it.

But first, he would make her come. He would make her gasp with pleasure. Then he would pull himself from her silken depths and carry her to bed.

His fingers traced a circle around that sensitive little nub, his touch growing less and less gentle as her body responded. Her sheath quivered around him, squeezing him tighter as she moved closer and closer toward the peak.

"Cecelia," he called. "Please come for me," he whispered into her ear. He kissed down the side of her wet neck, and he licked and sucked his way across her shoulder.

With his other hand, he tormented her breast. He tugged on her nipple, elongating it with his fingertips, tugging it none too gently. "Am I hurting you?" he asked.

But his only reward was a loud growl from Cecelia as she thrust his hand away. She pulled her legs inside the tub and sat forward on her knees. Marcus adjusted the angle of his back so he could arch to meet her as she rose and fell on him. Her pace was frantic, and he could tell she was reaching for something she couldn't find.

"Marcus!" she cried.

Marcus lifted her off him. She protested loudly, crying out at their parting. He stepped from the tub, nearly sliding on his arse in the process. But he didn't care. He needed her. He needed her in a bed. He needed to be inside her. God, he needed this woman.

Marcus picked her up and carried her to the bedchamber, where he dried them both quickly. The water he didn't get off her with a cloth he licked from beneath her breasts, from the side of her neck, from the dip where her spine met her bottom.

She was quivering in his arms, and where love had led them, need now took over. "Please," she begged.

Marcus forced himself to slow down, looking into her eyes as he cupped her face in his palm. "I love you," he said.

"I know," she said, her voice shattered. "Don't make me wait any longer."

"Let me see them," he said.

She looked down at her naked body. "What's left to see, Marcus?"

Her nipples were rosy and abraded, and he'd done that. He'd loved her until she was weak and ready.

"Your wings," he said. "I want to see them. I want to touch them. I want to join our magic. Please."

"Oh," she said, her brows drawing together.

Suddenly, there they were, arching behind her, the same flushed color as her skin. They were covered in fine hairs just like her forearms and the rims of her ears. It was a downy softness, and he reached out to touch one. She sucked in a breath.

"Does that hurt?" he asked.

She shook her head. "It feels like when you touch me here," she whispered, and she lifted her breast toward his waiting mouth. "Please," she said.

He closed his mouth gently around the peak, drawing it slowly into his mouth. "Not like that," she said. "Like before." Her eyes were open and needy, and she nearly begged him to roughen his grip on her.

He caught the tip of her other breast between his thumb and forefinger, and drew on it harshly, elongating it, while he took the tip of the other between his teeth and started to gently worry it. Her head fell back, her breath hissing from between her teeth. He had so much to learn about this woman, and a lifetime to learn it.

Marcus pulled her to him and gripped her bottom, tugging her tightly against him. Her wings arched down to her bottom, but he gently lifted her and set her on the bed. "On your belly," he said. She crawled naked across the counterpane, settling on her stomach in front of him. She tossed her hair over her shoulder, and her wings called to him.

"Can I touch them?" he asked.

"You can do anything you want to them," she said,

laughing. She pushed her bottom back toward him. "I wish you'd do it while you're inside me, though."

She didn't have to ask him twice. He straddled her thighs, looking down at the rosy softness between her legs. A drop of moisture seeped from her channel, and he caught it with his finger, lifting it to his lips. "My God," he groaned. She looked back at him over her shoulder.

"Please, Marcus," she said. She arched her bottom toward him. Marcus took his length in his hand, and straddling her bottom, he slid inside her. "Oh!" she cried out as he slid home. He settled deeply inside her.

She felt tighter this way, and he wasn't certain how long he could last like this. So, he pushed her thighs apart with his knee and shoved one leg higher. Then he pushed into her slowly. "I don't think there's much more of me left for you to take," she moaned into the counterpane, right beside where her fingers gripped it tightly.

"I want all of you," he said, as he pushed home. He spread the cheeks of her ass, lifting her leg higher, as he thrust quick and shallow. Her breaths were tiny pants, and her eyes were closed tightly.

"That's hitting some spot inside me, Marcus," she warned.

He slowed down. "Am I hurting you?" he asked.

"Please don't stop," she begged. She arched her back, pushing her bottom toward him.

Marcus dragged a finger along the edge of her wing, and she went crazy beneath him. "They're so beautiful," he breathed, thrusting shallowly within her.

"You can play with them later," she warned. "Finish

this, Marcus," she pleaded. Her voice was husky and she was so wet that her heat wrapped around them both. "Please," she begged.

Marcus picked her up and flipped her over, careful of her wings. He laid her down and slipped one leg between hers, but didn't sink inside her. Not yet. He looked into her face. His arms shook on either side of her head. "Give me all of it," he said.

"You have all of me," she said, her breaths broken as she squeezed her eyes shut.

"Give me your magic," he said. "Please." He wasn't above begging.

"You give me yours," she taunted. But she smiled. God, she could undo him with that smile. She spread her thighs, wrapping her legs around his waist.

He sought her heat in gentle jabs. "Not until you give it to me."

She closed her eyes and shoved his shoulder, rolling him to his back. Then she climbed on top of him, her thighs straddling his. "Stop playing with me, Marcus."

He took her face in his hands and looked into her eyes. "I'm not playing."

She froze on top of him. "Why do you want it?"

"For the same reason I want you," he said.

Cecelia nodded. She sank down on the head of him, taking him slowly inside her.

"Please, Cece," he begged.

"All right," she breathed. She balanced herself on her hands, her palms pressed tightly to his chest. Then she began to rise and fall on him. Her broken little breaths brushed his forehead as he leaned forward to tongue her nipple. His hand sank down to her curls.

"Give me your magic, Marcus," she whispered against his hair. He lay back and looked up at her. She was glorious with her hair hanging about her shoulders, her eyes closed with abandon, rising and falling on his manhood. Liquid heat slid from inside her to coat him and made him slippery. He arched his hips to meet her, urging her to go faster. His hand stroked across the nub that was her center, rubbing quickly in circles, just the way he knew she liked it. She cried out, her mouth open in surprise.

Magic rose from her and mingled with his. "Let me have it all," he whispered. His magic joined with hers, shooting like sparks in the air, swirling around them, taking them higher and higher, until all the magic in the room combusted along with them. It went off like fireworks at Vauxhall Gardens. The air sizzled as her inner walls trembled around him. She stilled when she came, encasing him in quivering, raw heat. He gave all his magic to her, and she took all that he had to give her.

The room quaked around them as she came, and the bed shook as he followed, pouring himself into her. She trembled in his arms, coming apart, and their magic put her back together as she fell to his chest. She cried out, her sheath still milking him, even as she fell limply against his chest.

"Are you all right?" he asked, brushing her sweaty hair from her neck. His hands slid up and down the damp skin of her back.

"Ask me in a few minutes," she said, yawning as she rested on top of him. He stayed inside her until he grew soft, and then he pulled out. She complained. "Don't go," she said weakly.

"We have a lifetime to do that," he said, stroking her cheekbone.

"I'll move in a moment," she said. "I'm too tired right now."

He liked having her wrapped around him. Her wings covered them both, wrapping around his shoulders like her arm might, and he held her there. He didn't ever want to move.

Twenty-Three

"WE'RE LATE," CECELIA SCOLDED AS THEY RUSHED UP the steps of Robinsworth's palatial home.

"If you hadn't thrown me down on the bed and tried to have your way with me again, we wouldn't be late."

She blushed, but she was smiling. "I didn't try to have my way with you. I *did* have my way with you."

He remembered. He remembered it well. She'd rolled from on top of him and then bent her head to place it in his lap. Then it was all over within minutes. They'd only used magic the one time, and then they'd been so exhausted they slept. She'd curled into him as though she was right where she always should have been.

Marcus smacked her bottom as they walked through the front doors. "Good evening, Wilkins," Marcus said to the old butler as the man took Cecelia's wrap. "Where is my family?"

"They are all over the place," the butler said, looking out over the crowd. "Shall I announce you?"

Marcus looked at Cecelia and she arched a brow. "Yes, please," he said.

This was nothing like the last ball he'd attended. He hadn't wanted anyone to know he was there because nothing was right without her in his life. Nothing was as it should have been that day. But everything was right now. His life was the way he wanted it.

"Mr. and Mrs. Marcus Thorne," Wilkins said loudly and clearly. The crowd stopped, turning toward them as they cheered. They clapped hands and clinked their glasses and yelled salutations. Marcus linked his hands with Cecelia and held them high in the air.

The ocean of people parted and Cecelia walked into the throng with Marcus. They accepted well wishes, but then the quartet began to play a waltz.

"Come and dance with me, Mrs. Thorne," he said, tugging her toward the dance floor. The floor cleared until it was just the two of them. He pulled Cecelia into his arms and looked down at her as he swept her around and around. She was beautiful in an emerald green gown, her hair piled high on her head and falling into ringlets to tickle her neck. He could look at her forever. And a day.

Eventually, others filed onto the floor and Marcus had to look up from the pool of her eyes to survey the floor.

"Mayden is here," he warned her.

She looked around without being obvious. "Where is he?"

"To your left with the blonde," Marcus said quietly.

"Will he come to me to give me his salutations?" she asked. Her brow was knit with worry.

"Since the celebration is for us, probably." He jostled her in his arms so she'd look up at him. "Don't worry. I'll be with you the whole time."

She nodded.

"Promise you won't do or say anything dangerous," he said. He couldn't lose her now. He'd just gotten her.

"What could possibly happen that's dangerous?" she asked.

She had no idea what Mayden was capable of. The music stopped and everyone clapped. Marcus led his new wife off the dance floor and walked toward his family. "What did we miss?" he asked of his father.

"He came in as though nothing had ever happened," his father said. "It was odd. And eerie. And not at all what I expected. He bowed over your mother's hand and introduced his wife."

Marcus looked over at him. "The blonde?"

"Yes, the American. A very sweet girl."

"She won't be for long," Marcus warned. Mayden had a way of breaking a woman's spirit.

Lord Phineas looked like he wanted to run across the room and thrash the man to within an inch of his life.

"Did he speak to you? Or to Claire?" Marcus asked.

Lord Phineas shook his head. "Not yet."

"Let's try the direct approach, shall we?" Marcus's father asked.

"Meaning?" Marcus tried.

"I'd like to talk with him. We all would. I'll invite him to my study in ten minutes."

"Do you think he'll go?"

"Only one way to find out," his father said. He adjusted the fit of his coat, shrugged his shoulders, and walked away.

His father walked to the edge of the dance floor and

put his hand on Mayden's shoulder as he moved to walk past him. Mayden looked Marcus's father in the eye, and he smiled. Marcus could read his lips from there. "Of course," the man said. "Ten minutes. I'll see you there."

Then Mayden stepped forward and bowed before Claire. "Mrs. Trimble," he said. "Would it be possible to claim a dance with you?" he asked. His eyes skittered across her face, not landing in any one place.

"I am not feeling very well. I believe I'll have to decline," Claire said. Her hand shook on Lord Phineas's arm. Cecelia wanted to reach out and hug her, because Claire was the one person who knew exactly what the Earl of Mayden was like on the inside.

"I'm sorry to hear that," Mayden said smoothly. "Perhaps later?"

"Perhaps," she said, noncommittally.

He turned to Cecelia. "Mrs. Thorne," he said, his tone jovial and light. "May I claim the next dance?"

⤜⤚

Marcus moved to step forward, but she pushed him back with a glance. "I'd be honored," she said.

Mayden was tall and thin. His hair was dark as night, and his eyes were tiny pinpricks in a sea of nothingness.

He smiled and took her hand into the crook of his arm. A reel began, so she didn't have to waltz about clasped in his arms, at least. She breathed a sigh of relief.

They came together for a moment, and Mayden said, "It was stupid of me to come here."

Cecelia startled. She hadn't expected that. Not at all. "I wouldn't say that," she tried.

He snorted. "Quite bacon-brained of me," he admitted. "I'd hoped to let bygones be bygones. But I see that's not possible."

They stepped apart and then came back together. "You did some terrible things."

"I belonged in Bedlam," he explained. His eyes were troubled.

"Are you still mad?" she asked. She searched his face for the truth but couldn't find any. Perhaps there was none left.

"I am thinking much more clearly now than I have in a long time. A man can become desperate when he's faced with losing everything." He stepped back, and then they switched partners with the people beside them.

She could see that happening. Her father had gone a bit mad when he'd lost her mother. Yet Mayden was speaking of material things. Not a love or a life. Not a soul. He spoke of his wealth. His home. His livelihood, perhaps.

"Your wife is lovely," Cecelia said.

"She's a twit," he snarled.

Cecelia startled. "Beg your pardon."

"She's a treat," he said, correcting himself.

"Oh," Cecelia breathed.

The dance ended and Mayden escorted her back to Marcus, and he went to stand beside his wife on the edge of the room.

After a few minutes, Mayden walked toward the corridor that led to Robinsworth's study. He stepped out of view, and Marcus, his father, Lord Phineas, and the duke all filed out behind him.

Cecelia took a deep breath and walked to stand

beside Claire and Sophia. "I don't have a good feeling about this," Claire said.

"Nor do I," Sophia agreed. She raised a finger to her lips and began to nibble a nail.

"What's the worst that could happen?" Cecelia asked. "Certainly he wouldn't do anything terrible with this many people looking on."

"You don't know him," Claire scolded.

A clatter at the refreshment table drew their attention. Marcus's mother rushed from the dance floor when a table holding three large ice sculptures overturned.

"Oh, dear," Claire said, startled.

"Mother," Sophia said, and both the girls rushed forward to help her.

Everyone in the room was looking in the direction of the clatter. Cecelia noted absently that the American girl who'd married Mayden was in the middle of the throng screaming at the top of her lungs. What the devil?

But just then, an arm snaked around Cecelia's waist and pulled her toward a corridor at the back of the room. "Don't say a word," Mayden hissed in her ear. "If you do, I will have no choice but to shoot blindly into the crowd." Mayden was supposed to be in Robinsworth's study. He must have never gone to meet them after all.

He had a gun. Had he had it all along? It was in his hand, and she heard the click of the lever being pulled back. "I'll go with you," Cecelia said. "You don't have to force me. I wanted to talk with you anyway."

Cecelia worked to adopt the placating tone she'd used with her father when he was drunk.

"Why did you want to talk to me?" Mayden asked as he led her toward a long corridor. He walked quickly down it, his hand at her elbow, gently but forcefully pushing her forward.

"Where are we going?" she asked, rather than answering him.

"Somewhere that we can talk privately," he said. He pushed through a set of doors and then led her up a set of stairs. They circled around and around and around and around, and by the time they got to the top, she was winded.

"Can we slow down just a little?" she asked.

Mayden brushed cobwebs from the entryway of a large stone room. Cecelia walked to the edge and looked through a stone opening. Through the hole, she could see the ground below. "Where are we?" she asked.

"The turrets," he said as he began to pace.

"This is where you killed the first Duchess of Robinsworth," Cecelia said. She struggled to remain calm. But it was difficult.

His mouth fell open, and he stopped pacing to glare at her. "I didn't kill her," he said.

"You didn't?"

"Oh, my God," he breathed. "All this time they thought I killed her?"

Cecelia didn't say a word. She just looked at him. His gaze was clear and steady. Not at all like she'd imagined. He was truly shocked at the revelation.

"I didn't kill her," he said. He laid a hand on his chest and pleaded with her with his eyes. "You must believe me. I didn't kill her. I needed her." He began to pace again.

"Did she love you, too?" Cecelia asked.

He shook his head. "She wanted to make her husband jealous. Nothing more. She was mad."

"And you're not?" Cecelia asked.

"Not right now," he said, laughing.

"Why did you take me? And not one of the others?" Cecelia asked.

"The duchess and her ladyship were rushing forward to help their mother." He looked at Cecelia as though she were the one bound for Bedlam. "You were the only one left. And you are more likely to listen to me."

Cecelia cocked her head to the side as she edged toward the door. "What did you have to say to me?"

"Stop moving," he yelled. He ran a frustrated hand through his hair.

"I'll stay right here," Cecelia said, holding up her hands as though surrendering.

"Tell me what my sins are," the earl said. He made a forward motion with his hands. "Let me hear them. What else do they think I did?"

"They think you killed the late duchess," Cecelia said.

"I didn't. She jumped." He made another forward motion with his hand.

"What happened that day?" Cecelia asked.

"We were up here talking. And she jumped. She just jumped. She said His Grace knew about us and that he was angry. And she couldn't bear her life anymore. I tried to stop her. I tried to stop her."

He didn't look upset by this at all. If anything, he looked irked that he had to stop to explain it.

"Did you love her?"

He waved a breezy hand through the air. "She was a means to an end."

"A means to what end?" Cecelia asked.

He shrugged, pacing again. "I needed funds for my estate. His Grace is good with investments. But she ruined me."

"And she made you angry when she ruined you. So, you shoved her from the turrets. She fell to her death."

"I would never have pushed her." He laughed, but it was a sound with no mirth. "I thought about it many times. But her daughter was with us that day. She walked in looking for her mother. Her mother didn't want her to see me. So, she tried to rush her from the room. But I think the girl could smell her mother's desperation." He laid a hand on his chest. "I would never have shoved her from the tower with the little girl there. I'm not a monster." He looked shocked.

"I didn't know Lady Anne was there," Cecelia said.

"What are my other sins?" He motioned for her to continue.

"You tried to shoot Claire and Lord Phineas."

"Yes, I did do that," he admitted. "But I hadn't slept for days. Do you think they would accept my apology?"

Cecelia bit back a snort. It was difficult, but she did. "We could try. Shall I go and get them?"

He motioned with his gun, jabbing it toward her. She flinched every time he moved it. "No, no. That's no good. I need your help. Tell me what to say to them. Tell me what will fix it."

Cecelia certainly doubted that anything could fix this man. Particularly not while he was alone with her with a gun. Marcus would find her soon. She was sure of it. He would come. He always did.

"I'm not a bad person," the earl said, clasping the sides of his head between the gun and his flattened palm. "She always said I was a bad person. But I'm not."

"Who said you were a bad person?" Cecelia asked. She sat down on the low stone wall that surrounded the turrets.

"She did." Mayden sat down on the other side of the stone room and began to rock slowly back and forth, back and forth.

"Who is 'she'?" Cecelia asked, keeping her voice low and soft, although all she wanted to do was scream and run.

"Her. My mother. The late countess." His rocking became faster and faster. He clutched himself with his arms.

"What did she say to you?"

"I can't repeat it. It's too vile."

Cecelia could help him. She knew she could. "Will you let me help you?" she asked. She leaned toward him. He was leaving her in his mind, she could tell.

"I need for someone to help me," he said. A tear rolled slowly down his cheek.

Cecelia's heart broke for him. "I'm going to reach into my reticule and then I'm going to show something to you," she said slowly. "Will that be all right?"

He looked at her, focusing only slightly, and he nodded.

"I have magic dust, and I'm going to blow it into the air. I want to see the truth. Will you be all right with the truth?"

"The truth about me?" He pressed a hand against his chest. "You can see the truth about me? That's all I've ever wanted anyone to see. I want someone to see the truth."

Cecelia poured some magic dust into her hand and said the words, "See every lie, see every sin, but before we do, let's go back to where it begins." She blew the dust from her hand, and it began to swirl in the air.

A small tornado of magic dust formed in the middle of the space, and the wind spun, waving cobwebs and dirt into her face. But then the dust began to take shape. Rather than the pictures she'd expected to see of scenes from his head or memories, she saw his thoughts. They came out in single words. The word "fear" formed in the cloud, and then it grew teeth like a tiger and chomped its way across the turret.

He'd known fear. Mayden moved his feet from the path of the chomping word. He began to tremble. But he didn't look away.

The word dissolved, and another took shape. "Hopeless" formed in the dust, and it wafted about like a kite caught in a storm. It had no direction, and it had no place to land. It just floundered about, with nothing to anchor it. "Rage" formed next, and it beat itself about in the dirt, bouncing off the walls and against the floor.

This was what was in the man's head. And it was there in the most elemental of ways. It was almost as though he'd never grown past a certain point in his life.

Suddenly, lifelike people made of magic dust shimmered in the middle of the room. A couple dancing. Their kisses were loving, their laughter real. He gasped. "My mother," he said. "And my father." He reached a hand into the mist, and they vanished. He cried out. "Come back." He rubbed the heels of his hands into his eyes. "That was before he died. Before she became sad."

The next image was that of a woman in bed and a little lad running to her side, only to be told to leave. He needed his mother, and she'd shooed him from the room. She threw things at him until Cecelia could even feel the lad's pain.

"Your mother changed after your father died," Cecelia said calmly.

He nodded, continuing to watch. Two men formed in the dust. They looked alike. "My brother," he said.

"What happened to him?" Cecelia asked.

Then image changed to that of a duel, and she saw the man fall to the ground in a pool of blood. "He died," Mayden said simply.

She saw the image of three caskets being lowered into the ground. They couldn't all have died at the same time, but this was in his mind, after all. "My mother," he said. "My brother. And my father." He took a deep shattered breath. "They all left me."

"They all died."

He turned to her and snarled, "They all left me!"

She nodded, finding it easier to agree.

"When did you break?" Cecelia asked softly.

The image changed, and the vision of a little lad being smacked by an older woman, probably his mother, came into view. "I changed then." The scene changed to a different one of violence. "And then." Still the same woman, another scene. "And then."

The little lad grew up to be a man. But the man was broken. She could see it in his eyes. And he could as well.

"This is what I am," he said.

"Our memories can make us, or they can take us," Cecelia said. "It looks like yours took you."

"They took me," he repeated, but his tone was flat.

"It's not your fault," she said.

He looked up at her as though he looked for salvation.

"My sins, show them to me."

Cecelia turned to face the wall. She couldn't watch any more.

He grunted as each scene changed. She could hear that much. He began to fidget. And he scrambled to get away from the images until he was pressed against the low stone window, and he sat inside its frame.

"Don't fall," Cecelia said.

"I have done too many bad things."

"It's all right. I can take your memories and put them in a box. I can fix you."

"No one can fix me." He let the gun fall to the ground, and it went off with a resounding boom and a flash of light. Cecelia covered her ears and waited for the pain to hit her.

❧

Marcus searched the ballroom calling Cecelia's name over and over. "Why did you let her walk away from you?" Marcus shouted.

"We thought Mayden went with you," Claire explained. She buried her face in Lord Phineas's chest.

"Where would he have taken her?" his father asked.

Marcus jerked his compass from his pocket and flipped it open. It would show him where home was. Cecelia was home. "West," he said. And he began to run in that direction. Mayden probably hadn't taken her from the house, that much Marcus was sure of. He had a reason for being there. Now Marcus just had to figure out what it was. He ran through the corridors of the castle, with his entire family and Cecelia's father running behind him. When he reached the lowest level of the turret, the compass began to spin. "Where now?" he asked himself.

But then a shot split the quiet of the open space. "Cecelia!" he cried. He couldn't lose her. He simply couldn't. He would die without her. He ran as fast as he could up the winding staircase.

He stopped in the doorway of the open room, and his heart jumped from his chest when he saw her standing there. Cecelia was safe. She was well. She looked out the window, rather than at the scene behind her. She held her palm flat, urging him to stop. How could he?

Mayden sat in the open stone window, a look of revulsion on his face.

"Are you all right?" he asked. Mayden was too engrossed in the changing scenes before him to even look at Marcus.

"He dropped the gun and it fired. But I'm fine."

"I've never been so scared," Marcus said. He turned to hold his family back. "Stay," he said to them.

"I will trade my life for hers," Cecelia's father said. "Let me up there. I don't care what happens." Marcus refused to let him pass.

Cecelia finally turned and looked at Mayden. "I can help you." The dust settled at their feet, all the life gone from it.

"I hurt too many people," Mayden said. His eyes brimmed with unshed tears.

Marcus agreed. But Cecelia said, "I can help you, if you'll let me. I'll take your memories and lock them away in a box. You can start anew."

"It's too late."

Mayden rocked in the open window. And Marcus could almost feel his pain. "He's broken, Marcus," Cecelia said. "But we can fix him."

"I'm not certain there's any fixing him. He's not redeemable."

"There's hope," Cecelia said.

"The hope died inside me a long time ago." Mayden pointed toward where the dust had fallen. "The things I've done. I wasn't even aware of all of them."

"Did you show him everything?" Marcus asked.

Cecelia shook her head. "Only some of it."

"There's more?" Mayden asked.

Cecelia nodded.

Mayden smiled. But he looked directly into Cecelia's eyes and said, "Thank you." Then he leaned backward and fell from the window.

Cecelia ran to him, but Marcus thrust her out of the way. He reached for Mayden, but the man slipped through his fingers. He leaned over the side and caught the sleeve of the man's coat. He grunted, holding tightly to Mayden's arm.

"You can't save me. No one can," Mayden grunted, trying to shake loose of Marcus's grip.

"I can if you'll let me," Marcus ground out. He reached to catch Mayden's jacket with his other hand. But the material tore, and Mayden wiggled. "Hold still. I'll pull you up."

"Let me go," Mayden said clearly.

"I can't. My wife won't like it." His grip was slipping.

"She'll have to be angry at you, because I won't let you save me." He jerked his shoulder, until he began to slide from the sleeve of the coat. "Thank you for trying," Mayden said. And then he slipped free of the coat entirely. Marcus reached, trying to catch him as he slid free. But he moved too fast. And then he was gone.

Marcus ducked back inside the turret, refusing to watch when Mayden hit the ground. A soft thud met his ears, and Cecelia rushed into his arms. Marcus pressed his eyes closed tightly, trying to forget the memory of the way the man looked into his eyes, right before he shook loose of his grip.

"I always thought he was a coward and so weak," Marcus breathed.

"Oh, Marcus," she said. "He was in so much pain."

"I saw some of it," he said. "Are you all right?" he kissed her forehead. Cecelia sobbed into his shirt.

"How could he survive after all those years of abuse?"

"He didn't," Marcus said. "Something died within him a long time ago." He looked at his father. "Will you go and check to be sure he's not in pain?"

Claire covered her face with her hands and cried. Then she wiped her eyes and said, "Who would have thought I'd be crying about the Earl of Mayden's demise?" She laughed, a watery chuckle. "Marcus, you have to be certain he has a funeral. And treat him with respect from here going forward."

"I promise we'll take care of him." He kissed Cecelia's forehead again.

"He wanted absolution," Cecelia said to the room. "He wanted forgiveness."

"Well, he has it," Lord Phineas and the duke said at the same time. They were the two people he'd wronged the most. And they'd just forgiven him.

"Can we go home?" Cecelia whispered to Marcus. She kissed his neck softly. "Please. I need you."

He needed her, too. More than anything.

Epilogue

MARCUS HELD HIS BABY GIRL, A CLOTH BETWEEN HIM and her because she really liked to cast up her accounts, usually on his shoulder. He looked over at Cecelia and winked. "I think she's getting hungry again," he warned. His daughter wiggled in his arms, and he adjusted his grip on her so that he could look into her face.

"Just because she made a noise doesn't mean she's hungry," Cecelia declared. "If you want to look at my breast, you just have to ask nicely." She leaned across the picnic blanket and kissed him softly.

"Haven't you two figured out that's where those things come from?" Allen asked, looking toward Marcus's new daughter. Allen's eyes shone brightly and he appeared more relaxed than Marcus had ever seen him.

"There's more to it than kissing, little brother," Marcus teased. "Do you need for me to educate you?"

"Yes, please!" Ainsley cried, from where she lay with her head upon Allen's knee. His hand rested on her swollen belly. "Because we have no idea where babes come from."

Ainsley and Allen had married almost nine months ago to the day. And she was heavily pregnant with their first child. Allen couldn't be happier. And Ainsley was glowing. Though she was a bit uncomfortable at this point.

"At least ours will not be a miracle birth after only seven months," Allen scolded.

His mother called out from where she raced down the stream with Lady Anne, Sophia, and Claire's older children toddling behind them. "Seven-month babes are the thing now. In fact, Marcus was so brilliant that he had to be born after a mere seven months himself."

"Oh God," Marcus groaned. "Can we change the subject?"

"Yes, please," Cecelia said as she took the baby from his arms. He wrapped his arms around them both. There was nothing better than having his daughter and his wife in his arms at the same time. He'd thought Cecelia made him complete, but it just got better as time went by.

Claire and Phineas helped to keep the small children from the river. Sophia and Robinsworth had left to walk alone down the river some time ago. Marcus's youngest sisters, Hannah and Rose, sat on a blanket, both taking turns holding the newest additions to the family. Both Sophia and Claire had new babies.

"I love it when we're all together," Marcus's mother said as she ran past them, chasing one of the toddling babes.

"It exhausts me when we're all together," Lord Phineas said. He scooped one of the children into his arms, making him squeal. Marcus couldn't tell them all apart. Not when there were so bloody many of them.

Marcus's father lay in the grass, making a chain of daisies. He leaned over and placed it on Marcus's daughter's head. She looked up at him, blinking her blue eyes at her grandfather.

They spent a lot of time in the land of the fae. Marcus and Allen took turns handling their father's lands in the other world, and they split their time in the land of the fae as well. They made time, however, for days like this when they could all be together.

Cecelia's father sat down on the blanket beside Marcus and Cecelia and held out his hands. "Let me hold her. You two can go take a walk or something."

Cecelia wiggled her brows so only Marcus could see it. He grinned and pulled her to her feet.

"Wait," Lord Phineas said. "We were supposed to be next."

"Too late," Marcus teased. "We have someone to watch our one child." He pointed to where Mr. Hewitt held his daughter. "The joy of having only one child, Finn. Too bad you'll never experience that feeling again." He chuckled loudly.

"I'm going to call it," Allen called toward their retreating backs. "Another babe nine months from today!"

Marcus certainly hoped so.

Cecelia walked over to the sign that stood by the riverbank and dragged her fingers along the raised letters.

Unpardonable Errors

1. Never let a human adult see you in faerie form, unless that human is your spouse.
2. Never let your dust fall into the hands of the untrained.
3. Never share the existence of the fae with anyone who might betray the fae world.
4. Never use your magic to cause harm.
5. Never be afraid to fall in love with a human.

The unpardonable errors had changed only subtly, but they had changed, and for the better. Marcus and Cecelia had worked hard in their positions as two of the Trusted Few, and change had overcome the land.

Beneath the sign were written the words:

Love deeply.
Live passionately.
Magic abounds.

Marcus slid his hand into Cecelia's and she squeezed it gently. They looked back at the group gathered on the hillside. The magic between them was stronger than ever, and it would last well past their lifetimes.

**Read on to discover more
magical Regency stories by Tammy Falkner:**

A Lady and Her Magic

The Magic of "I Do"

Available now from Sourcebooks Casablanca

From *A Lady and Her Magic*

August 1817

IF THE DUKE OF ROBINSWORTH HAD KNOWN IT WOULD be so difficult to raise a daughter alone, he never would have killed his wife. He would have coddled her, wrapped her in lace and taffeta, and put her on a shelf so the whole world could view her beauty.

Even though he'd never admitted it, everyone knew he'd killed her. And though he refused to share the details, they were all correct.

His daughter broke him from his reverie when she stomped her foot and demanded that he purchase not one, but two, sweets from the vendor.

Ashley was quite used to the antics of his daughter, and although they were annoying, they never bothered him overmuch. When she became too unruly, he simply left her with a nurse. If it happened at home, he left the manor. He'd even left the country once. But she was always there when he returned, always just as petulant as she had been the day he left. He'd resigned himself to the fact that she would never change.

Anne was a perfect re-creation of his late wife. Her long blond curls danced around her face. Her porcelain skin and blue eyes reminded him of a doll he'd seen once in a shop window. The only difference: the doll didn't have a temper like Anne. Yes, she had inherited that from her mother, too.

When Anne was younger, she would drop to the ground and kick and scream when she didn't get her way, flopping about like a fish out of water. Now she simply scrunched up her pert little nose and screeched.

Ashley winced as she shrieked out the words, "I want it!"

He took a step toward the child, fully prepared to throw her over his shoulder and drag her back to her nurse, who waited on a park bench nearby, when a woman stepped forward. His breath caught in his throat as she entered his line of sight. She was the opposite of his late wife, who'd been blond and thin and fragile.

His gaze traveled over the woman's rounded hips to her ample breasts, nearly hidden among the frills and folds of her light-blue gown. He lingered there, imagining how she would look in a gown that didn't have quite so many trimmings hiding her curves. When his eyes finally rose to meet hers, her flashing hazel orbs held censure. Ashley coughed into his hand in a horrible attempt to hide the smile that wanted to erupt. It had been years since he'd been so well scolded. And she'd yet to even speak to him.

Before he could say a word to her, the auburn-haired nymph looked down her nose at his daughter and said, "Ladies do not shriek."

His own little termagant rolled her eyes in a horrid display of social ineptitude.

The woman raised her eyebrows at Anne and said, her voice a bit crisper, "Ladies do not roll their eyes."

"But I want another," Anne snarled, stomping her foot.

The beautiful woman smiled at his daughter, a dimple appearing in her left cheek. People very rarely smiled at Anne because she was so obnoxious that most gentlewomen turned from her in disgust.

"May I tell you a secret?" she asked of Anne. Then she looked at Ashley, who nearly fell over trying to avoid leaning toward her so he could hear her soft voice as she spoke to Anne. "Do you mind?" she asked, smiling as she asked him for permission to speak to the girl.

"No," Ashley said, waving his hand negligently. "You may disclose all the secrets you wish." He wanted to add that she could whisper a few in his ear as well, but he assumed she'd take that as an insult.

She knelt down to Anne's level and whispered in her ear. Anne's nose turned down slightly until she suddenly smiled. She covered her mouth with her fingertips and giggled.

"Go on." She nudged Anne forward. "Try it." She shot Ashley a quick look that encouraged him to play along.

Anne tugged gently on his sleeve. "Yes, Anne?" he said quickly, finding it painful to tear his gaze away from the stranger long enough to look down at his own daughter. But when he did, he was surprised to see the pleasant smile that curled her lips.

"Papa, may I please have another treat? I regret to inform you that they are pitifully small."

Ashley glanced up at the lady, who smiled at what must have been his perplexed look. He stared at her for a moment, unable to draw his eyes away, until Anne tugged at his sleeve and whispered, "I should like to grow up to be as sweet as the lady someday."

Ashley turned to the street vendor and asked for two more treats. He promptly gave one to his daughter, who was delighted by her newfound ability to win her father's favor. Then he looked over at the lady who'd transformed his daughter and winked.

∽

Sophia felt certain she turned ten shades of red when the man turned and winked at her. It was such a masculine gesture, and not one that was commonly tossed in her direction. Of course, considering that he was the Duke of Robinsworth, Ashley Trimble, to be more exact, it was completely fitting.

It did gratify Sophia a bit to see that the child took her advice and approached her father in a gracious and respectful way. She smiled softly when he placed the treat in the girl's hands and bent to kiss her forehead.

Sophia turned to walk away but heard quick footsteps behind her. "Miss?" The child called for her. Sophia looked down at her smiling face. She held up a second treat and said, "My papa said this one is for you."

Sophia hesitated for a moment before she took the wrapped square from the child. "Thank you very much."

"Wait." When the girl's father's voice reached her, it hit her like a runaway horse, making the hair on her neck stand up and her belly drop toward her toes. His quick footsteps hurried across the cobblestone walk toward her. He stopped, his blue eyes darting to and fro in the nearly empty park. "If your chaperone sees me speak to you, I fear she'll steal you away almost as quickly as you appeared." He let the last trail off as he waited for her to fill the empty space.

Quite the opposite. Her grandmother had contrived the scheme so they could meet in the first place. "I appreciate the flattery, but I have not required a chaperone for a number of years. We do things differently where I'm from, you see."

"And where might that be?" His blue eyes danced at her.

Unpardonable Error Number Three: Never share the existence of the fae. "I'm certain you've never heard of it."

His eyes narrowed almost imperceptibly. Should she extend her hand to him? Try as she might, she was unable to remember all the social proprieties this world was based upon. Her grandmother had repeatedly tried to drill them into her throughout the years. And failed. "My name is Sophia Thorne, Your Grace," she finally provided.

His gaze grew shuttered at the words "Your Grace," almost as though a heavy curtain dropped between them that was difficult to see through. She wished she could bite the words back as soon as they left her lips.

"My reputation must precede me," he said as he looked away. Sadness suddenly overwhelmed his features. "I'll let you be on your way." He bowed slightly and turned from her.

"Your Grace?" Sophia called. He stopped and looked back over his shoulder, no hint of the playfulness she'd seen earlier present in his gaze.

"I've never rested much faith upon the opinions of others, Your Grace," she said slowly. "I prefer to draw my own conclusions."

A sardonic smile broke across his face. "You could very well ruin *your* reputation by being seen in my company, Miss Thorne."

She shrugged. "One must have a reputation in order to ruin it, Your Grace. And to be more succinct, one must care."

A smile that might be genuine slowly lifted the corners of his lips. "I thank you for the help with my daughter. How did you do it?"

She shrugged again. She'd simply treated the child with respect and firmness, both of which the girl was surely lacking. But that was neither here nor there. "Most women learn to manage men at an early age," she laughed. "It appears as though your daughter has not."

"Not until today."

"I was happy to help." Sophia held up the wrapped square of candy. "And these are my favorite," she admitted, unable to keep from smiling at him.

The little girl tugged at her father's sleeve. "Can we go home now, Papa?"

The duke pulled his watch fob from his pocket and flipped it open. "Actually, I do have some things to attend to," he said apologetically as he touched the top of his daughter's head. "Tell Miss Thorne good-bye and thank you," he instructed her.

Instead of dropping into a curtsy, the girl locked her arms around Sophia's waist and squeezed. Sophia was almost too surprised to return the embrace.

"Perhaps I'll see you again another day," she said to the little blonde.

"I can only hope," the duke said quietly, his gaze meeting hers only briefly before he turned away, took his daughter's hand, and started down the lane that led to the entrance of the park.

Sophia took a moment to catch her breath. It wouldn't do for her to swoon in the middle of the park. Not at a mere suggestion from the dangerous Duke of Robinsworth. The man was a walking scandal. A walking scandal that made her pulse pound so loudly she could hear it.

"Well, that went better than I expected, dear," her grandmother said as she stepped into her line of sight.

"Better than I thought," Sophia lamented.

"I wasn't sure if you'd be able to feign the mannerisms of the British *ton*. But you did fairly well."

She certainly still had a lot to learn about this world. The land of the fae might look similar, but none of its magic was present in this world. Here, people wore full clothing, and not a single one of them had wings or pointy ears the way she did. Just willing her own wings away was difficult and not something she usually had to concentrate so hard to do.

"He seemed discontent about my lack of a chaperone," Sophia said. "Do you think I need one, to look like one of them?"

"Perhaps we should have Margaret shadow you a little more," her grandmother suggested.

Sophia moaned. The idea of Margaret watching everything she did made her nervous. The house faerie didn't like this world or anything about it, including its people. The maid wouldn't say why, but she had a feeling it had something to do with Sophia's mother. "I need to learn to walk like them."

"Stiffly and unyielding?" her grandmother said with a laugh. In their world, comfort reigned. Clothing was serviceable. There were no layers worn simply for show. In order to fit through keyholes and slide under doors, one must be appropriately attired.

"Maybe I should have saved this mission for Claire after all." Indecision rose within her. No. She could do this. She could help the Duke of Robinsworth's daughter.

"You must learn to use your senses, your mind, and your heart more than your magic. You can do it, Sophia. I wouldn't have allowed you to come if I didn't believe it."

"Oh, come now," Sophia cajoled. "You wanted an opportunity to come through the portal, to see the fish."

"I'd love to know their crimes. Knowing they were once fae scares me a little." Her grandmother shivered lightly.

"They seemed amiable enough."

"Only because you had something they wanted to trade for passage. Otherwise, we'd still be at home waiting for the night of the full moon."

The fish that guarded the portal were granted a reprieve on the night of the moonful, the night the midnight wind swirled, carrying passengers from the fae world to this one. Any other night, wary travelers must trade something of value to get past the fish and away from the land of the fae.

"This mission is very unlike my others," Sophia said, more to herself than to her grandmother.

"Most missions don't include a handsome duke." She grinned. "A duke who makes one's heart go pitter-patter." For some reason, her grandmother's mild, cherubic smile sent fear skittering up Sophia's spine, making her wonder what devious plot was hiding behind her grandmother's innocent facade.

~

Ashley stepped through the front door of his home to find his butler, Wilkins, standing at attention in the entryway. The regal, spry old servant rushed forward to take his hat and coat.

"Any news for me, Wilkins?" Ashley asked absently as he shrugged out of his jacket, took the correspondence the butler placed in his hands, and sorted through the stack of notes quickly.

"Your brother awaits you in your study," the butler said.

A smile broke across Ashley's face. "I imagine he's sampling my best whiskey?"

Wilkins smiled, then added glibly, "Not since I removed all the decanters upon his arrival, Your Grace. You should be aware that he partook of more than his share of spirits before he arrived."

His brother had never been one for taking spirits in moderation. Ashley chuckled. "That bad, is he?"

"Worse, Your Grace," Wilkins said, nodding his head slightly.

"Oh," Ashley said as he turned and held up a finger. "Did you have any luck finding a suitable governess for Anne?"

The man sighed. "Unfortunately, no. The agency refuses to send another of their applicants. Not after what happened the last time."

Ashley tried to remember. "Remind me of what happened last time."

"Lady Anne set the governess's hair on fire. On purpose."

"Oh, yes. I remember. There was a stench for days." Wilkins's lip curled as he obviously remembered the same smell. "Are there other agencies you can try?"

"I'll keep looking."

"Thank you." Ashley smiled as he walked down the corridor and turned the corner to enter his study. There, seated in a deep leather chair, was his younger brother, Lord Phineas, or Finn, as his friends called him. "I heard a rumor that you were in my study and that evasive maneuvers had to be taken to keep you out of my stock," Ashley said, extending his hand.

Finn rose to his feet unsteadily, grasping for the arm of his chair as he lost his balance. The man looked positively miserable, his eyes rimmed with red, his face blotchy and pale. "Ah, yes. But he forgot the bottle you keep in your private stash," Finn said as he held up a glass, lisping a little on the last word.

Of course, his brother would feel free to invade his private space at will. Never one to mince words, Ashley said, "You look like hell."

"I feel like hell," Finn grumbled back.

"Dare I ask what the matter is? It's a bit early in the

day to be so deep in your cups." He urged his brother to sit before he toppled over. He was nearly as big as Ashley, so it would take at least two footmen to bring him back upright.

"Oh, I had a bit more enjoyment than I'd planned," Finn groaned as he adjusted himself in the chair.

Ashley sat behind his desk and steepled his hands in front of him, waiting for the man to tell him what the matter was. It didn't take as long as he thought for his brother to unburden himself.

"Do you remember the chit I set up in Mayfair?"

"Vaguely." If Ashley remembered correctly, there was nothing truly remarkable about the girl.

"She's up and left me."

"And?" Certainly, worse things could happen to a man. Like being shunned for killing one's wife.

"And she started a bit of a rumor."

"About?"

"My lack of physical attributes and attention to her needs," Finn mumbled.

Ashley tried to hide his chuckle behind a cough into his closed fist.

"It's not amusing," Finn pointed out.

"Certainly, it is," Ashley said, laughing a bit louder.

"How do you deal with it? The whispers behind your back? The constant judgment from your peers?"

Ashley shrugged. "One becomes accustomed to it with time." He'd had seven years to learn to accept his lot in life. The only time it rankled was when he met a lady like Miss Thorne. Then he wished he was anyone but himself.

Finn reached for the whiskey bottle again. Ashley

intercepted it and moved it out of his brother's reach. "Drinking any more will be a waste, because you'll not remember the taste of it when you wake up."

Ashley stood and called for Wilkins. The man appeared within moments. "Let's find a room for Lord Phineas and help him to it, shall we?" he asked of the butler.

Wilkins nodded his head and called for footmen to assist. "If I may be so bold, Your Grace, the rest of London should know what a good man you can be," Wilkins said.

"I prefer to let them think the worst." Ashley sighed. "They've no expectations of me that way."

Ashley returned to his study and began to open his correspondence. Despite his sordid past, he was a bit too well connected to be ousted completely from society. For the first two or three years following his wife's death, he'd been avoided as though he had a communicable disease, as though the propensity to murder was contagious.

Then the few friends he had, namely his brother Finn, Matthew Lanford, and Jonathon Roberts, whom he'd met at Eton many years before, had rallied around him and forced him to resume his place in the House of Lords and step back into society. They all believed him innocent of any wrongdoing. It was unfortunate that they were all incorrect.

The clip of quickly moving slippers in the corridor made him groan and hang his head. Within seconds, the Duchess of Robinsworth flung open his door and burst inside his sanctuary, without even the good graces to knock.

"Mother," was his only response as he looked down at the note before him. "What brings you to my home?"

"You really should replace that butler," she scolded.

"And why should I do that?" he asked as he closed his ledger. She obviously had a purpose for visiting. And would most likely get to it as soon as she got over whatever slight Wilkins had given her. He would curse the man, but the butler seemed to be one of the only people who could keep his mother in line.

"He's impertinent. And rude."

Said the pot about the kettle.

"He blocked my entrance to the old library. The one in the west wing. He stood right there in the doorway and refused to let me pass. Of all the nerve." She harrumphed and dropped into a chair.

That wing of the old house had been closed for longer than Ashley could remember. Since before his father had died when he was a boy. "And what purpose did you have for visiting the west wing, Mother?" he asked as he poured himself a liberal dose of the whiskey Finn had left behind.

"It's awfully early to be drinking, dear," she scolded.

"It's awfully early for you to be visiting, Mother," he returned. His mother never rose from bed before the luncheon hour. "Shouldn't you be sleeping off the excesses of the night's activities?"

"I wouldn't call them excesses," she mumbled.

He fished a note from the pile of correspondence Wilkins had given him. "You do not find one thousand pounds to be an excess?" he questioned.

"Give me that." She held out her hand and leveled

him with a stare that would have made him quake in his boots when he was younger. With her icy glare and pinched brows, she could freeze him in his tracks when he was a boy, but no longer.

"I think not," he returned. Then he took a deep breath and dove directly into the issue at hand. "I believe it's time for you to move back to the Hall, Mother." He would hate having her underfoot, but he couldn't keep an eye on her if she wasn't at hand.

She pulled back and turned up her nose. "I'll do no such thing. My town house is perfectly acceptable."

"You mean *my* town house," he clarified.

"It's mine in theory," she huffed as she sank primly onto a chair across from him.

"The amount of money you're losing at the gaming tables is tremendous," he said as he withdrew more notes from his drawer. They arrived nearly every day. From people his mother had gambled with and lost. They all knew she wasn't good for the debts. Yet they played with her anyway because the Duke of Robinsworth never left a debt unpaid. His presence in their drawing rooms might not be valued. But his purse certainly was.

"I'll take those," she said again.

"Why, Mother? You cannot begin to pay them."

Her face fell. "I do not know why you feel you have to be so cruel," she said as her eyes welled up with tears.

"I do not understand why you gamble with money you don't have." He tapped the cards on the table. Then he made a clucking sound with his tongue. "But I'm prepared to pay them in full."

"As you must, Robin," she said quietly, using his childhood nickname.

"On one condition," he amended.

Her face contorted slightly. "Which is?" she said from between gritted teeth.

"I'm closing the town house effective immediately. You'll be moving back to the Hall."

She jumped to her feet. "I will do no such thing," she gasped.

He continued as though she hadn't spoken. "I will reconcile your debts. Every last one of them. Then you will cease gambling with money you do not have. You may use your pin money any way you see fit."

"But there's not enough," she protested.

Still, he continued. "You will spend nothing more than your pin money. You will move back to the Hall. You will assist me with my daughter."

"Anne hates me."

Anne hated everyone. "You will assist me with your granddaughter. She could use a feminine presence. You will behave respectably and set a good example for her."

"You need a wife," she snapped. "It's unfortunate that no one of respectable breeding will have you."

Oh, his mother knew how to throw the barbs that would hurt the most. "Then I am free from the wife search, it seems, since no respectable woman would pay me her favors." He leveled her with a glare. Though Miss Thorne had graced him with a smile and no fear in her eyes.

"It took years for me to get over your past deeds. To find my way back into society. You have no idea how arduous the task was." He couldn't gather sympathy for her, despite the look of anguish in her eyes. "If I move back to the Hall, I will once again be cast beneath your dark cloud of suspicion."

"Do you think I killed my wife, Mother?" he clipped out.

"Of course not," she rushed on.

"Then I would assume a mother who finds no fault with her son will be quite content to return to the family estate."

"My friends won't know what to think."

"Quite frankly, Mother, I don't give a damn what they think," he drawled. "I'll have Wilkins begin the preparations to move your household."

"And just when do you think this will take place?"

"As soon as I bellow down the hallway," Ashley replied. Wilkins would take great pride in ruffling the duchess's feathers.

"That man hates me," she grunted. "When I'm in residence, I'll expect him to treat me as befits my station."

"He'll treat you as well as you treat him, Mother."

"I'd prefer being dropped into a vat of hot oil over being nice to that man." She jumped to her feet and headed for the door.

"I'm certain that can be arranged," Ashley called to her retreating back.

From *The Magic of "I Do"*

Autumn 1817

A FAERIE WITHOUT MAGIC WAS ABOUT AS USELESS AS A carriage without a horse. If Claire Thorne had known that this would be her reward for trying to save her sister from the dangerous Duke of Robinsworth, she never would have gotten involved in her sister's mission. She would have stayed at home. The land of the fae was so much more comfortable than the land where others resided.

Claire refused to look at her abductor. She refused to acknowledge his presence, although he did have her magic dust. It was in his pocket at that very moment. Despite the fact that she'd warned him it could explode in untrained hands, he'd taken it with no hint of hesitation. And now he refused to give it back. Claire lifted her chin and stared out the coach window. If anyone had told her a sennight ago that Lord Phineas would take her hostage, she would have laughed in his face. Yet here she was, at his mercy.

"Oh, blissful silence," he said. He must have said

it to himself, because he certainly couldn't be talking to her.

"You really should return my dust to me before it does you harm." She didn't look at him as she talked. She continued to stare at the changing landscape. They'd left behind the bustle of Mayfair and were headed toward... nowhere, it appeared.

"And just what kind of harm might a little bottle of shimmer do to me?" He looked much too composed.

"It could explode and blow off an arm." She finally turned to look toward him and found him grinning at her unrepentantly. That man had a smile that could stop a lady's heart. Though it had no effect on hers. Well, almost no effect. His sparkling blue eyes made him look impertinent enough to annoy her to no end.

He held out his hand and appraised his arm with a critical eye. "I can live without an arm." Lord Phineas swiped a lock of hair from his forehead and lowered his arm back to his side. He arched a golden brow at her as though taunting her to continue her threats. He hadn't seen threats yet. Just wait until she turned him into a toad. Or a pig so that his outside could reflect his inside.

Claire let her gaze roam up and down his body slowly. "It might blow off something you use on occasion." Her eyes stopped at his lap. He fidgeted in his seat. "It's really quite volatile in the hands of the untrained."

That wasn't true. Not in the least little bit. But he didn't need to know that. In his hands, the dust was useless. Just shimmery flecks of shiny things he didn't understand. In her hands, however, it was quite useful.

If she wasn't afraid to commit one of the Unpardonable Errors—never use your magic to do harm—she would take a chance and wrest it from his possession. But if she had the dust in her hands right at that moment, she would use it to harm him. In a most satisfying way.

She forced herself into a casual shrug. "Take a chance. Blow off an appendage. Perhaps you'll be lucky and it'll be the smallest one. One you probably don't get to use much."

His smile vanished. "I can assure you there's nothing small about my appendage."

She grinned. "That's not what *she* said…" She left the taunt dangling in the air. His face flushed. She must have touched a sore spot. But since he was holding her hostage, he deserved to be just as uncomfortable as she was.

How the devil could a faerie be aware of his problems with his mistress? Katherine had only left him a few weeks before. It wasn't his fault that she'd spread a bit of a rumor about his prowess in the bedroom. One that was *completely* unfounded upon reality. He narrowed his eyes at Miss Thorne. "Are your people omniscient?"

She didn't answer. She simply turned to look out the window again. Blast and damn. The woman was already driving him toward Bedlam and he'd only had her in his possession for a few hours. His brother, Robin, would owe him dearly for this. Very dearly.

The carriage hit a rut in the road and she bounced in her seat. She uttered a most unladylike oath as her head bumped the roof of the carriage. "Beg your pardon?" he asked. He cupped a hand around his ear. "I didn't quite hear that."

"If I'd meant for you to hear it, you would have heard it." She adjusted her skirts, settling back more heavily against the squabs. The bounce had left her looking a bit disheveled, with a strawberry blond curl hanging across her forehead. She blew the lock of hair with an upturned breath.

She really was quite pretty if one could get over the shrewish behavior. Her body was tall and willowy, her limbs long and graceful. Her heart-shaped face would probably be beautiful if she ever graced it with a smile.

"Just where are we going?" she asked. She still didn't look at him. She gazed out the window with the countenance of someone who had the weight of the world upon her shoulders.

"My house in Bedfordshire."

Her shoulders stiffened and then she exhaled deeply.

"And just what recommends such a place?"

"It has bars on the windows and heavy locks on the doors." It didn't. But she didn't have to know that.

"It will take more than bars and windows to keep a faerie under lock and key." She sniffed and raised her nose in the air.

"Then thank God there are ropes aplenty. I will tie you to my side if I must. I did promise Robin I'd take care of you." That was a bit of a long and sordid tale, and he still didn't understand the half of it. "Pray tell me how you people came to exist."

She arched a delicate brow at him. "The same way you did." Her face flushed scarlet. "Do you really need me to tell you about reproduction?"

Damn her hide. He didn't need her to explain anything about reproduction. This lady knew how to jab him where it hurt, though. He would have to take great care with her. He grinned slowly and leaned forward. "Please do. If you're lacking anything in the telling of how babes are made, I'll fill in the blanks for you. Certainly, you have questions about it."

"Should any pressing questions arise, I'll be sure to let you know." She looked back out the window. Damn, he hoped that Robin finished up his business soon so he could free the harpy.

"How long do you plan to keep me there?"

"As long as it takes for Robin to finish his business." The sooner, the better.

"I'm certain he's done by now. So we can turn around and go back to the city." She looked quite pleased by that idea. A smile tipped her lips and the beauty of it nearly took Finn's breath away.

"He'll send word when he's done. I'll set you free not a moment before."

She laughed lightly, and the sound raked over his skin like silky fingertips in the night. "Only an idiot would think he can keep a faerie confined." She snorted lightly. It was a most unladylike noise, but he found himself biting back a grin at the sound.

Finn leaned over and looked out the window at the cloud-filled sky. If he couldn't keep her confined, the inclement weather would. Unless he was mistaken, the snow would begin to fall before they reached their destination. Then she would be as confined by the elements as she was by him. Perhaps he wouldn't have to tie her to him. He'd have to wait and see.

⚓

Robin had sent a messenger to the house to ready it for company before he'd left for… wherever it was he'd gone. But that didn't help Finn at the moment. Evidently, they'd arrived before the messenger did. None of the staff greeted them at the door. Where the devil were they? Mr. Ross should at least be nearby. He never left his post. And Mrs. Ross, the cook-housekeeper, should have been there to greet them as well. Blast and damn. Finn moved to pull off his gloves but changed his mind. It was damn cold in the house. And dark. And empty.

"Hullo," he called. His voice echoed around the empty foyer.

"Looks like no one is home. Let's head back to London," Miss Thorne chirped. She started back toward the door.

"Something is wrong," Finn murmured to himself. "Wait here," he muttered as he started toward the kitchen. Certainly someone would be in the kitchen. But that room was empty as well. "Where the devil is everyone?"

"It appears as though your house isn't quite ready for company," Miss Thorne said, a satisfied smile on her face. "I believe we should make the trip back before the weather gets any worse."

Just then, the back door opened and a tall man stepped through it. He had an apple clenched between his teeth and bit into it viciously. He stopped short when he saw Finn and Miss Thorne standing there. "Beg your pardon," he said around the mouthful of apple. He held up one finger as he chewed and swallowed so hard that Finn could hear the gulp across the room. "My lord," he finally croaked out. He bent at the waist, and that was when Finn finally recognized him.

"Benny?" Finn asked. That man with shoulders as broad as the doorway couldn't possibly be Benny Ross, the son of Mr. and Mrs. Ross. The last time he'd seen Benny... He couldn't remember the last time.

"Yes, my lord," the young man said. "It's a brisk day, isn't it?"

If brisk meant cold enough to freeze a man in his tracks, yes, it was. "Where are your parents?" Finn asked. "Did you receive the notice that I would be arriving?"

"Yes, my lord. We received it. That's why I'm here. Papa took a fall down a flight of stairs a few days ago." He held up a hand when Finn began to protest. "Don't worry. He's going to recover. Just got a nasty bump on the head and a sprained ankle. He'll be right as rain in no time."

"And Mrs. Ross?" Finn asked. Certainly she was on the premises.

"She has refused to leave Papa's side."

This wasn't good. Not good at all. He had a house with no servants. An offended faerie and a house with no servants.

"That settles it," Miss Thorne chirped. "We'll be going back to London." She waved at Benny and said, "It was nice meeting you."

Benny looked to Finn for confirmation. "You'll be leaving, then?"

Benny looked much too happy about that. "No," Finn sighed. "We'll be staying."

"I was about to say, you don't want to get caught in

this storm." Benny parted the kitchen curtains to look out. "It looks to be a nice one."

"Is there anyone else who can come and take care of the house? One of your sisters, perhaps?" If Finn wasn't mistaken, Benny had five sisters, all of whom were older than he was.

Benny flushed. "Oh no, my lord. Papa suggested that, and Mama said it wasn't a good idea. What with you being a bachelor and all."

Mrs. Ross thought he would defile one of their daughters? He shrugged. One of them was quite attractive.

"But I'll be here for you. Mama sent a cold lunch. And I'll go back and get the evening meal before the storm sets in fully." He looked quite pleased with himself. He pointed toward the front door. "Shall I go and take care of the horses?"

"Build a fire, first, will you?" It was growing colder by the second. Even the kitchen, which was always hot as blazes, was cold enough to make his face numb. "In the sitting room, the library, and the bedchamber."

Benny's brow rose. "One bedchamber, my lord?"

Finn nodded. "Yes, just one."

❧

One bedchamber? Was the man daft? There was no possible way Claire was going to share a bedchamber with him. "Have you lost your senses?" she hissed as Benny stalked out of the kitchen toward the front of the house. "I will not share a bedchamber with you."

"I'm afraid you don't have a choice, Miss Thorne," Lord Phineas drawled. "Trust me, the idea of it doesn't settle well with me, either."

He didn't like the idea of sharing a bedchamber? She highly doubted that. A small part of her was momentarily offended by his comment. She'd been told she had striking features. "Why don't you want to share a bedchamber with me?" she asked impulsively. She wanted to bite the words back as soon as they left her mouth.

"I tend to favor a warm bed partner, Miss Thorne. Not a cold one." He stalked past her and into the corridor.

Her offense at his lack of interest was absolutely absurd. But it niggled at her more than a little. She shoved the thought aside and forced her attention back to the facts at hand. "I think we should go elsewhere. At least an inn would have staff."

"They have staff where you come from, Miss Thorne?" He continued down the corridor toward… Where was he going? "In your land, Miss Thorne?" he prompted.

Of course. Her land was structured much like his, except hers was prettier. And in hers, things tended to be a little more fanciful. "My grandfather is one of the Trusted Few, my lord. Do not doubt my origins."

"Trusted Few?" he parroted, his brow quirked at her. A grin tugged at his lips. Why was that amusing?

"The governing body in our world. Much like your aristocracy. The House of Lords."

"Only you have a house with a trusted few?" He chuckled. "Certainly, you do." He finally came to a grand room lined with books, which must have been his library. Claire gazed at the overstuffed shelves. One of her favorite pastimes was reading, and she nearly salivated at the thought of looking through all the books. She forced her attention back to him. "When will we be leaving?"

"When Robin sends words that his business is concluded." He dropped into a chair behind his desk and began to sort through a stack of correspondence. "Is Ramsdale really your father?"

"No." She didn't say more than that. Just the single word.

"Robin says differently."

"We were raised by our grandparents." She turned and pretended to peruse the shelves. Talking of her parents still hurt a little. She had never met them. She'd been raised with the fae, along with her brother Marcus and her sister Sophia. There were never any parents in their lives until Sophia stumbled across the Ramsdales. They'd lived in London all her life, right where she could have found them, if she'd only known they existed. Claire still hadn't met them. Nor did she plan to. Nor did she plan to meet her human brother and sisters. The children her parents had kept.

"Would you prefer that I call you Miss Thorne? Or shall we throw out all social constraints and call one another by our first names, Claire?" he asked, a crooked grin lifting the corners of his lips.

"Miss Thorne will do nicely." she corrected.

"You may call me, Finn, *Claire*." He was taunting her. She was well aware of it. And he was enjoying it.

Benny bustled into the room with an armful of wood. "My lord?" he asked quickly. Lord Phineas motioned with an impatient hand toward the hearth.

Benny began to stack wood in the grate and lit it with a quick flick of his flint.

"There," he said, dusting his hands together. "I'll take care of the bedchamber next." Lord Phineas nodded, obviously distracted by the contents of his correspondence.

"Thank you, Benny," Claire said. The boy flushed at her praise.

"I put your things in his lordship's bedchamber."

"That will be all, Benny," Lord Phineas barked.

Benny bowed to her quickly and fled the room.

"You need to clear up the boy's misconception."

"What misconception would that be?" He looked up at her, his blue eyes flashing.

"The lad is under the impression we'll share a bedchamber."

Lord Phineas stood up slowly. He crossed the room to stand in front of her and bent down by her ear, where he said softly, "My darling, we *are* going to share a bedchamber."

Discover a new LOVE

Are You In Love With Love Stories?

Here's an online romance readers

club that's just for YOU!

Where you can:
- **Meet** great *authors*
- **Party** with new *friends*
- **Get** new *books* before everyone else
- **Discover** great new reads

All at incredibly BIG savings!

**Join the Party at
DiscoveraNewLove.com!**

Everlasting Enchantment

by Kathryne Kennedy

Powerful magic is afoot

Millicent Pantere has lived her entire life in the notorious London Underground. She cares nothing for the problems of the crown or the intrigues of society. But the ladies of the realm are acting strangely, and Millicent is coerced into tracking down the rumors of a mysterious man—a magic man who comes in the night and disappears at dawn.

And so the hunt begins

Millicent's search leads her to one of Merlin's legendary relics and the seductive knight whose fate is bound up with it. Centuries ago, Sir Gareth Solimere made the mistake of seducing the wrong woman, and he has been trapped ever since by a diabolical curse. He's looking for the one who can break the enchantment—but in this world, there is no love without betrayal…

Praise for the Relics of Merlin series:

"Kennedy will sweep you away and into a world of magic, mayhem, and fractured love."—*Night Owl Romance*

"Enchanting! This series is amazing, and I am completely hooked."—*The Long and Short of It Reviews*

For more Kathryne Kennedy, visit:

www.sourcebooks.com

Double Enchantment

by Kathryne Kennedy

Too much of a very good thing…

High society enjoys their powers based on their rank, but Lady Jasmina Karlyle's magic causes nothing but trouble. Her simple spell has gone horribly wrong, and now she has a twin running around the London social scene wreaking havoc on her reputation. When both she and her twin get intimately involved with gorgeous shape-shifting stallion Sir Sterling Thorn, Jasmina finds herself in the impossible position of being jealous of herself…

Still isn't enough…

Sterling is irresistibly drawn to Jasmina. She seems to have two completely different sides to her personality though, and the confusion is driving him mad. Is love just the other side of lust…or is what he has with Jasmina much, much more than that?

"A hugely imaginative story with terrific characters, a complex plot, and a heartwarming love story." —*Star-Crossed Romance*

For more Kathryne Kennedy, visit:

www.sourcebooks.com

Enchanting the Lady

by Kathryne Kennedy

Their magic lives within each one of them...

In a Victorian England with a rigid hierarchy of magic, lion shape-shifter Sir Terence Blackwell is at the bottom rung of society. Only Lady Felicity Seymour, who has no magic, no inheritance, and no prospects, may be willing to judge the man strictly on his own merits...

However deeply it may be hidden...

When family pressures push Lady Felicity into a terrible fate, she has only Sir Terence to turn to. As the two outcasts are propelled by circumstances beyond their control, they are forced to explore the unseen depths beneath society's facade. And what they discover about each other is more real and more beautiful than they ever could have imagined...

"Kennedy has totally enchanted us with this book. It's like reading an adult version of *Beauty and the Beast* with a bit more spunk." —*Yankee Romance Reviewers*

"Casts a magic spell on the audience from the moment the heroine expects to fail her test and never lets go until the final magical revelation." —*Midwest Book Review*

For more Kathryne Kennedy, visit:

www.sourcebooks.com

About the Author

As half of the Lydia Dare writing team, Tammy Falkner has cowritten ten books, including *In the Heat of the Bite*, *A Certain Wolfish Charm*, and *Wolfishly Yours*, which was named by *Publishers Weekly* one of the Top 10 Best Fall Romance Books of 2012. She is a huge fan of Regency England, and her latest series explores the theory that the fae can walk between the glittering world of the *ton* and their own land. The first two books in the series, *A Lady and Her Magic* and *The Magic of "I Do,"* garnered glowing reviews—*RT Book Reviews* said, "Funny, sexy, and enchanting romance… 4.5 Stars."

Tammy lives on a farm in rural North Carolina with her husband and a house full of boys, a few dogs, and a cat or two. Visit her website: www.tammyfalkner.com.